She may survive the war . . . but only if a mysterious enemy doesn't kill her at home.

With the Civil War threatening the citizens of Macon, Georgia, young Caroline Hannah is forced to leave her studies at Wesleyan Female College. When she arrives at Looking Glass Plantation to live with her mother's cousins, she instantly senses peculiar tensions in the family. Cousin Sophronia is welcoming, but Cousin Penelope clearly doesn't want Caroline there. Why? Is Penelope capable of channeling her disapproval into threats, violence, even murder? After the terrifying incident at the mill, Caroline sank wearily into bed. Night fell, and still her strength had not returned. Letting go, she slept. And dreamed.

Screaming and struggling and beating her fists against the pillow, Caroline fought death in a cotton-lined coffin. A streak of light came toward her. Chaddy was bending low.

"Hush, child," she said. Setting the candle beside the bed, she grabbed for a basin as Caroline bent to vomit.

The nightmare and the retching reoccurred throughout the night. When daylight finally came, she breathed a thankful prayer that she had been spared and joyfully watched the sunrise. Gingerly, she moved sore muscles. Pain stabbed, wakened her fully and drove the fuzz from her brain. Now recalling the frightening episode with more clarity, she clapped her hands over her mouth in horror. She had not stumbled and fallen into the press. *She had been pushed.*

Trembling violently, Caroline relived that instant. She had discounted all of the things that had happened since she came to Looking Glass Plantation.

But there was no discounting those hands. Someone was determined to kill her.

Other Civil War Novels By Jacquelyn Cook

Sunrise

The Gates of Trevalyn

The Greenwood Legacy

The River Between Series:

The River Between

The Wind Along The River

River of Fire

Beyond the Searching River

Rivers Rushing To The Sea

Image in the Looking Glass

by

Jacquelyn Cook

Bell Bridge Books

This is a work of fiction. Names, characters, places and incidents are either the products of the author's imagination or are used fictitiously. Any resemblance to actual persons (living or dead), events or locations is entirely coincidental.

Bell Bridge Books
PO BOX 300921
Memphis, TN 38130
Print ISBN: 978-1-61194-128-9

Bell Bridge Books is an Imprint of BelleBooks, Inc.

Copyright © 1986 by Jacquelyn Cook

Printed and bound in the United States of America.

All rights reserved. No part of this book may be reproduced in any form or by any electronic or mechanical means, including information storage and retrieval systems, without permission in writing from the publisher, except by a reviewer, who may quote brief passages in a review.

A mass market edition of this book was published
by Zondervan in 1986.

We at BelleBooks enjoy hearing from readers.
Visit our websites—www.BelleBooks.com and
www.BellBridgeBooks.com.

10 9 8 7 6 5 4 3 2 1

Cover design: Debra Dixon
Interior design: Hank Smith
Photo credits:
Frame (manipulated) © Rainbowchaser | Dreamstime.com
House (manipulated) © Aviahuismanphotography | Dreamstime.com

:Llig:01:

Dedication

To Lynne and Baby Dog, who inspired it, and to
John Grover Cleveland Pace, whose experience
gave it life

Jacquelyn Cook

Chapter 1

Purple trumpets shattered against Caroline's wildly rocking hoop skirt as she ran heedlessly along the garden path past spikes of foxgloves. Crushing the letter against her mouth to stifle her cries, she plunged through the arch of the shuttered-and-latticed gazebo and sank to the cool marble floor. She had no direction, no one to care for her. Leaning her head against the bench she shook with sobs.

Fighting for control, Caroline clapped her hands against round cheeks rosy with embarrassment. She had left Cousin Penelope standing, mouth agape. Even before the tall, plain woman handed Caroline the letter upon her arrival, Penelope's expression had belied her cordial invitation to take refuge on Looking Glass Plantation.

Papa's instructions had been to leave Wesleyan Female College and come to southwestern Georgia for safety, but even here the signs of war threatened normal life. When Caroline had alighted from the train in the village, clusters of soldiers were waiting.

Tension had quivered on the sultry air as the buggy bumped along the red dirt road that snaked its way through an impenetrable pine forest. Caroline wondered why the strapping farmhand, Will, who had come to meet her, had scanned the woods with the eyes of a bird about to take flight.

Surely we are far from the battle lines, she thought.

Now as she smoothed the crumpled letter and tried to read Papa's loving words, she reflected, *Nothing is as it seems*. She noted the date, April 1, 1864, one month ago, but once again her eyes riveted to the strange handwriting that added contradictory words to the page. Both her father and her fiancé, Samuel, had been killed in this war that was tearing apart the states and everyone's lives.

A short-legged black dog skidded by the doorway, yipping. It trotted back to her and licked her face.

"Oh, Shadow . . ." She scooped the dog into her arms and buried her golden curls into the fluffy fur. "You're the only one left in the world to love me."

Loneliness overwhelmed her. There was no one anywhere to write a loving letter to her, to share her small triumphs and joys, to turn to with her insurmountable problems. Her cousins would not want a dog in this perfectly manicured home. Remembering the way Penelope had drawn away in surprise when they had met just now, she felt *she* was not wanted either. Even if her tuition had been paid, she lacked train fare back to her friends at school.

Stroking Shadow's silky ears, she smiled sadly and tried to remember the warm feeling of her school chums pressing around her like cheeping biddies around a mother hen. Isolated from dilemmas, they had been happy at school in spite of the fact that this silly war had been going on for three years. Enjoying the challenge of the rigorous courses, Caroline had helped her friends and encouraged everyone to study together as they worked diligently toward college degrees. With all of their sweethearts and brothers away at war, they missed having young men call upon them. Searching for fun, the vivacious girl had led in singing happy songs after vespers. Long after "lights out," the roommates whispered together of their dreams. Caroline's goal was to get an education, have her fill of fun, and then marry Samuel.

Dead! Dead! The throbbing thought numbed her. The world seemed upside down. Past and future died with Papa and Samuel.

Shadow squeaked as the trembling girl squeezed too hard. Murmuring an apology, Caroline patted the dog's long ears and set her down on the marble floor of the gazebo. Throwing off her blue bonnet and running her fingers through her long blond hair, she stared up at the peaked, shingled roof and wondered how she could go on living with all of her security ripped away and no one to love her. A breeze, filtering through the latticed sides of the summerhouse, cooled her cheeks. Opening the drawstring of her reticule, Caroline fished out her handkerchief, dabbed at the tear streaks, and stood shakily. She did not know which way to turn. She sighed. The first step must be to apologize to Cousin Penelope for her rude behavior. She drew in a determined breath.

The bitter fragrance of surrounding boxwoods suddenly mingled with a whiff of lavender. Rustling taffeta alerted her that someone was approaching along the garden path. She shrank from the open doorway behind one set of the green wooden shutters that screened four walls of the octagonal gazebo.

"Find her and send her away!" A voice echoed sharply in the stillness. "You should not have . . ." She gulped a rattling breath. ". . . told Rufus you'd let her visit. It is useless to—umh—open old wounds."

Behind the sheltering shutter, Caroline compressed the steel hoops in her crinoline to keep her voluminous blue worsted skirt from being seen through the doorway. She could not face them yet.

"You know I can't send her back, Sophronia," answered Penelope in a nasal whine. "Rufus fears Wesleyan might be forced to close its doors as so many other institutions have done since the war. He's too far away to look after her. You know there's no other family!" Her tone changed to smug satisfaction. "I was delighted to write him that we'd keep her 'til he could come. When times get better, he will find the money to send her back to school."

Caroline dropped her head in her hands, thankful that she had sensed Papa lacked funds to pay tuition and had suppressed a pout when he told her to leave the Macon, Georgia, college for safety below the battle lines. As her mother's cousins, Sophronia Bearden and Penelope Greene, strolled toward her, she swallowed the bitter taste of panic. Trembling with fear of discovery, she wondered how she could leave here with only a few coins in her reticule?

The nasal voice continued hesitantly. "She must have run into the kitchen garden. Rufus intended to come for her soon, but I'm very much afraid that letter contained bad news . . . The way she bolted—perhaps her fiancé . . ."

"The idea of having her here is foolhardy! You know," she said, panting, "no good will come of this!" The older woman's voice was breathy and tremulous, but it commanded attention.

"Now, Sophronia, you must understand that their home is north of the battle zone. Right now it's totally inaccessible. Besides that, Berry will want to stay here with a pretty girl his age, and Rufus will come, and we'll have parties—"

"You're letting your emotions get the better of your good sense, Penelope. There's no telling what—umh—might happen if she stays, and . . ."

Their voices drifted down the path. Caroline remained drawn back stiffly. Shadow cowered under the safety of her skirt. Afraid of strangers, the tiny dog shivered silently. Caroline waited until she was certain they had left the garden. Resetting the tortoiseshell combs that held back her tumbling curls, she straightened her rumpled clothing, put on her bonnet, and composed her dainty features. She must try to piece her life together. The first step was to face her cousins. She started resolutely down the path.

Confused by the intricate geometrical design, she was unsure which curve or angle of the path to take. Shadow followed tail down, her small body drooping.

"It's all right, Shadow," Caroline whispered to steady her own nerves as they advanced along cleanly swept walks bordered by clipped boxwoods. Perennial flowers filled the beds in a gay profusion. This was a sunny place of well-ordered beauty; yet, Caroline shivered with the contagion of Shadow's fear. Evidently, Papa was wrong about this place being safe. From the moment she had reached the nearby town she had sensed a tension in the atmosphere. Somehow, it was not the sleepy village it seemed.

Trying to relax, she bent over the circular rosebed and took deep breaths of the sweet fragrance of La France and Marechal

Neil. Touching the dainty buds of Devoniensis, she wondered if Mama had smelled the roses when she came for extended visits. According to Papa, she had especially loved the motherly Sophronia. Although she and Penelope were nearer the same age, they were never close. Papa met Mama while she was visiting here. They married after an engagement of only a few months, a shockingly short time twenty-five years ago.

Smiling at the remembrance that their love had flowered in this garden, Caroline chided herself for her silly fear. Reaching the place where she had run into the brick-walled, formal area, she examined the foxgloves with chagrin. The tall spikes were as high as the petite girl's head. With a worried frown, she picked up some of the trumpet-shaped purple blossoms knocked off in her haste. Only the lower blooms had been disturbed. The fresh ones at the top of the spikes still gleamed, and their little, spotted throats looked as if they were spilling tiny drops of dew.

"We must be more careful, Shadow, if we are to be welcome here."

At the entrance, marked by two large hydrangeas, she stepped through the wrought iron gates into the wide avenue bordered by tremendous boxwoods. She looked around warily but did not see the sisters.

On the left was a neat building with a clean-lined efficiency that suggested a plantation office. No one was stirring among the outbuildings behind the main house. Beyond the cookhouse, she wandered through the kitchen garden where culinary and medicinal herb beds were bordered by tilted bricks. Fragrance drifted from freshly watered mint. Its clean scent was so strong that she could not smell the garlic, although she identified the tall, straight stems topped with round lavender globules.

Farther down a narrow road, stood a smokehouse, a "necessary house," a barn, cribs, and further still a row of cabins. Seeing no one, she staunchly returned toward the front door determined to behave like a proper guest.

Circling right, she approached the entrance of the shining white Greek Revival mansion. She felt dwarfed to insignificance by the huge round columns that rose thirty feet from ground level to the second story.

Gathering her courage, she crossed the wide front porch, tapped at the double doors over which a wrought iron balcony hung suspended, and held her breath as moments stretched nervewrackingly before a large woman pulled back both doors. Her round face puckered in dismay as if she were about to cry, and she twisted her long white apron which fell nearly to the floor with only the hem of her blue and white cotton skirt peeping out.

"I . . . ," Caroline stammered. She had expected Penelope to open the door again. "I . . . I'm Caroline Hannah."

"Lord 'a' mercy, chile," she said, puffing. "I know you be Miss Mary Lillian's girl. Look just like her." She clucked her cheek and a smile spread over her broad face. Then she shook her head until the gold hoops at her ears trembled and the white kerchief tied around her hair threatened to come askew. "You be too young and pretty. You shouldn't of come to this here plan'ation." She clucked again. "Bad clouds here. Bad clouds. Go back where you come from!"

"Nonsense!" snapped Penelope, startling them. "Stop frightening the girl, Chaddy." She motioned Caroline into the wide entrance hall that extended completely through the middle of the house with rooms off to either side.

"I apologize for my shameful behavior earlier, Cousin Penelope. I was brought up much better than that, but the letter you gave me contained terrible news." Tears flooded to the surface, choking her. She thrust the letter toward Penelope unable to say more.

"I was afraid you had bad news, but young girls are so emotional. Surely it's not as terrible . . ." Her eyes found the notation at the bottom, and her plain features crumpled with grief. Caroline noticed that she had great difficulty controlling herself. From the folds of her full-skirted black dress, she produced a handkerchief whose tatted edge matched her collar and blew her large, hooked nose.

They stood in uncomfortable silence. Was Penelope so upset about her father's death or about having an unwelcome guest?

Blowing her nose again, Penelope said, "Chaddy will show you to your room. When you've had time to freshen up, come down to the parlor, and we'll have tea." She gestured to the room at her left. "This news does change your status, but a cup of tea always helps one to bear the worst situation. Later we will see what to do with you." She turned away.

"Please, Cousin Penelope . . ." Caroline's voice squeaked with misery. "May I take Shadow to my room just for now? She's very well-behaved, I promise you. She's much too frightened to leave me until she gets used to the strange place." Her last words came as a near wail as she moved aside to show Shadow cringing behind. With her legs tucked under and her soft, appealing eyes concealed by a fall of hair, the Spaniel part of her showed only in her long, silky ears.

Penelope looked with disgust at the dejected lump of black fur. Then she said with a snort, "I don't like animals in my house, but she certainly is a pitiful specimen. Take her with you for tonight. But see to her."

"Oh, thank you, ma'am." She scooped Shadow up with one arm and her carpet satchel with the other and followed Chaddy as she puffed her way up the spiral staircase with Caroline's larger bag.

Having enough problems without the old servant foretelling doom, Caroline was determined not to be affected by her superstitions. Meekly mounting the stairs, she wondered how to befriend her. She followed silently as Chaddy opened a door on the right side of the hall.

"Oh, it's lovely!" Caroline stepped into the serenity of warm cream walls. The beautiful bed of white iron and gleaming brass looked inviting. The canopy above it was whipped cream dotted swiss topped by a brass crown that skimmed the ceiling. The dotted swiss draperies tied around the bedposts and the dust ruffle brushed the floor in deep scallops.

Caroline relaxed. She scuffed her feet slightly before she stepped onto the goldenrod of the needlepoint rug. "It's lovely. Thank you, Chaddy."

Taking off the hot coat of her worsted traveling costume, she went to the marble-topped washstand, poured water from the porcelain pitcher into the bowl, and splashed it on her face. Greatly refreshed after removing the soot from the train ride, she peeped around the linen towel.

Dark face clouded with a scowl, hands on ample hips, the old woman watched with eyes darting and lips muttering.

"I promise we won't be any trouble, Chaddy." Caroline flashed her sunniest smile. "And we don't eat very much." She included Shadow who had immediately hidden herself underneath the bed.

"Humph. Us got food in the storehouse. Feed all the no 'count folks in this here county." She smoothed her wrinkled apron. "Feed a scrap of a girl and a rag of a dog. But you cain't stay here. You got to go tomorrow."

"I wish I could, but I don't have the money for train fare or for tuition if I did get back to school." She struggled to make her shaky voice pleasant. "Why don't you like me?"

Chaddy shook her head in a motion that set her earrings jingling. "I loved Miss Mary Lillian. I dreamed last night that pretty thing come here again—and she died. That must be you. Sumpin bad'll happen if you stay."

Startled by her words, and seeing by her dourly drooping cheeks that she believed them, Caroline forced herself to laugh. "Get along with you now, Chaddy. I'll be fine. I must get ready for tea. Cousin Penelope will be waiting for me." She turned her back.

Brushing the cinders out of the golden curls that fell halfway to her waist, she wondered why Chaddy was determined to prophesy doom. Her reflection did resemble Mama. Staring in the looking glass, she could hear again Papa's loving voice: "You grow more like dear Mary Lillian every day, Caroline . . . the way your hair escapes its fastenings into golden ringlets around your face. It's apparent that you're going to remain just as tiny as she."

For a moment she was warmed as she remembered his approving smile and eyes full of love. Rather than arguing with his assessment, she had reconciled herself that she would always be too short and treated like a child. She had not wasted time being dissatisfied with her looks.

The wan face looking out of the mirror was tearful as she recalled how her father had lavished love on her without resentment even though Mary Lillian had died giving birth to her after only a few happy years of marriage. He never stopped loving Mary Lillian. He enjoyed retelling experiences that they had had together and sharing her excitement over the small joys of living.

Trying to take courage from the memory of their love, Caroline squared her shoulders and hurried to present herself to Cousin Penelope and Cousin Sophronia.

When Caroline stepped into the parlor, Cousin Penelope was already seated before a blue and white porcelain tea service. The room was beautifully appointed with the warmth typical of aristocratic Southern homes; however, Caroline shivered with a chill of nervousness as she sat beside Penelope on the heavy, square-shaped Empire sofa.

Looking around the room, which preserved the pure form of the Greek Revival with simple elegance of architectural detail in woodwork, moldings, and fireplaces, Caroline felt that her smile was stiff. "It's a perfect background for your Empire furnishings with their use of Greek curves and metal ornaments." She cleared her throat, trying to gain the proper register for polite, tea-time conversation. "Oh, I love the rich, bright colors of that picture! Is it silk embroidered on silk?"

"Yes," Penelope agreed curtly. Her black hair was parted in the middle and pulled back severely into a knot at the back of her neck. "Sister is not feeling well. She's taking tea in her own room." She passed a plate of tiny, flaky biscuits.

Caroline ladled on soft butter and sticky fig preserves. Suddenly she realized she was eating more than was considered ladylike.

"We still have enough of what we raise here," said Penelope looking down her hooked nose, "but other things are in short supply or selling for outrageous prices. Salt is five dollars a sack, and flour is seven to nine dollars a barrel. Of course, we are glad to share with you—until you can make other arrangements."

"Yes, ma'am." Caroline swallowed a large mouthful. "I appreciate your letting me visit. Surely I'll be able to find out soon if there's enough from my father's estate for me to finish my education. With a degree, a suitable position should become available."

"A degree?"

"Yes, ma'am, I finished the usual academy for young ladies." Blistering her lip with a scalding sip of tea, she chattered nervously. "I learned how to sew and play the piano, how to enter and leave a drawing room correctly, and how to paint a daisy in watercolors, but, oh, I wanted to learn more. I finally persuaded Papa to let me enter Wesleyan Female College." Her voice shrilled and words tumbled out unbidden. "Did you know it's the first college in the entire world to grant honors, degrees, and licenses to women the same as the ones conferred to men in colleges and universities? When Catherine Brewer received her diploma in 1840, it was the very first ever awarded from a women's college."

"It's time girls were allowed more than a butterfly education." Penelope nodded with a smile of approval.

"Yes, but even though Wesleyan's charter was granted way back in 1836, many men still oppose it and hold the position that women are incapable of learning." She laughed and shrugged her narrow shoulders. "My Samuel was one of them. He thought we should be married instead of my wasting time in school. The only reason Samuel agreed to an extended engagement was that the states started seceding and he . . . and Papa joined the army. The best solution was for them to leave me in college—" A sob jerked forth, unbidden. "Some parents have become frightened by the war and sent for their daughters, but the college is steadfastly continuing classes. If only I could go back . . ."

"Now, now don't you worry." Suddenly Penelope was all smiles and friendliness. "We will be delighted to have a pretty, young thing like you for a visit. Go to your room now and rest. Berry won't be here tonight, but change that dirty frock before you come down to supper and meet Sophronia."

Returning to her room, Caroline tried not to dwell on the fact that Penelope's apparently friendly invitation to take temporary refuge here had emphasized the words *pretty* and *young*—the words Chaddy kept muttering.

Emotionally drained, she stepped out of her grimy traveling attire and the steel hoops and petticoats Paris fashion decreed. Wearily she crept beneath the linen coverlet. Tears slid down her cheeks. Even though she had not seen Papa and Samuel for two years, she had been secure in the knowledge of the love they lavished, asking little in return. Surrounded by friends in similar circumstances, waiting for the war to be over, Caroline had filled days, from morning until late at night. Now the only thing to fill the aching void was the scent of Shadow, hiding under the bed, reassuring her that one warm, friendly being loved her. Sleep came in drifts. The dread of meeting Cousin Sophronia still awaited her. The plantation was a place of sunshine, flowers, and beauty; yet strange contradictions made Caroline shiver. She felt like hiding under the bed with Shadow.

Chapter 2

Gathering darkness alarmed Caroline when she awoke. Fearing she had slept past suppertime and further affronted Cousin Sophronia, she fumbled to light a candle. Having been too upset to unpack, she resigned herself to a mass of wrinkled clothing. To her delight she discovered that someone had folded her petticoats and everyday cottons into dresser drawers and hung the best clothes in the large wardrobe.

Quickly she selected her Sunday best, a yellow silk with five flounces beginning with a narrow tier below the waist and ending with a deep ruffle at the hem. The loose borders spread and fluttered as she brushed her hair in a head-hugging style. With her hair falling loose, she looked like a little girl. Wrinkling her nose at her reflection, she added a flat, double bow of velvet ribbon to the crown of her head to add height, give courage.

Hurrying down the stairs into the ladies' parlor where they had taken tea, she stopped to look in the petticoat mirror on the console below the keepsake-covered shelves of the étagère to make sure that no crinoline was showing. Anxiously, she moved beyond the Corinthian columns that framed sliding doors opening into the gentlemen's parlor. This room was also empty. The twin parlors were separated from the dining room by another pair of sliding doors of beautifully etched ruby glass.

Smiling in relief, she stepped into the dining room, brilliantly lit with candles glowing in sconces around the walls and in a chandelier hanging low over the table. Each branch of the crystal chandelier swooped down in a graceful curve and back up to lift a lighted candle. Refracted light twinkled from the lustrous woods of the furniture and the gleaming silver.

A slender young girl entered with platters of food.

"Good evening," said Caroline sweetly.

The girl's face contorted. Opening her mouth soundlessly, she set a platter of fried chicken down with a whack.

"I'm sorry I startled you. I'm Caroline Hannah," she said in a soothing tone. "I'll be visiting here for a while."

The frightened girl made no reply.

"What's your name?"

"Ret," she whispered shyly.

Cousin Penelope bustled into the room. "Ah, my dear Caroline, you look greatly refreshed. A little more food and rest and things will look much better to you tomorrow."

"I don't know what I should do without you, Cousin Penelope. Thank you so much for your kind hospitality."

"Think nothing of it." The tall woman waved both hands to dismiss her appreciation. "Come, sit down. Sister is too ill to join us tonight." She passed a bowl of dried field peas. "We'll have better fare as soon as the garden comes in."

Gnawing a drumstick ravenously, Caroline took a second piece of cornbread and assured her, "It seems a banquet to me!" The piercing black eyes slowed her down. Eating more politely, she struggled for something to say. "You mentioned that Berry would not be here this evening. I think I've heard the name, but I don't remember who he is."

Penelope beamed. "Berry Bearden. My nephew. A fine young man. I'm very proud of him." Her sharp features softened with tenderness. "Sophronia's son, you know. He is in business and does a great deal of traveling. He visits here every chance he gets. The dear boy is so attentive to his elders."

Sophronia's son must be well past middle age, especially since he was not in the army, Caroline thought. She dismissed him with a bite into a crisp watermelon rind pickle. "Is that all of the family? It seems that I recall hearing of another sister named—Adeline?"

"Adeline died—quite young," she replied. "Sophronia is a widow, so that leaves just us three."

At that moment Chaddy entered with dessert.

Penelope brightened with the air of a pleased hostess. "I know you'll like this sweet potato pudding. It was our mother's favorite recipe. Tell me, how were you allowed to take your dog to school?"

Hating to put down a spoonful of the fluffy cinnamon cloud dessert, the girl laughed easily for the first time since her arrival. "I didn't take her there; I found her there. Shadow was a stray. One day between classes I was sitting out on the veranda. Along came some boys chasing a pitiful little dog. Throwing rocks. Whooping like Indians. I just had to run out and stop them."

"You're just as softhearted as Rufus was," Penelope said, smiling.

Pleased that Penelope had thought well of her father, Caroline beamed at a newfound friend. She resumed the story in a heartier voice. "I discovered the dog had been alone for quite some time. The boys had taken to making sport of her daily. She was pitifully afraid. I thought she was a puppy—she was just a tiny rag of dirty hair and bone. I just hid her in the flowing sleeves of my dress and slipped her to my room."

"Isn't she a puppy?"

"No. When my roommates and I fattened her up, we realized she's an old dog. She was well-trained by someone, but I never could find out who. She became my shadow. It was hard to keep her hidden at school." She took another bite of crusty pudding. "I just couldn't leave her there. Shadow's been so mistreated that kindness can't seem to overcome her fears." Caroline's blue eyes met Penelope's. "I promise to watch her and not to let her cause any trouble."

"See that you do. Sophronia would be distraught if she dug up any flowers." She gestured with her spoonful of pudding. "You must be careful not to upset Sophronia."

"I'm sorry Cousin Sophronia is not feeling well and I could not meet her." Caroline winced slightly at the untruth; she was thankful the meeting had been postponed. "Is she seriously ill?"

"Her health is bad. She will do well for a time and then have another . . ." Penelope pursed her lips wryly. ". . . spell."

Penelope arose brusquely and led the way into the music room, where she suggested that Caroline play the piano for her.

Caroline lifted her skirt daintily around the stool and sat with hands poised nervously over the mother-of-pearl keys while Penelope showed her the front panel, inlaid with mother-of-pearl and softly colored lacquered flowers. Caroline knew that her simple Chopin étude, performed dutifully, did not do the piano justice. Pleading weariness, she excused herself, took Shadow for a short walk, and then tumbled into bed.

Awakened next morning by a fresh, cool breeze, Caroline responded with youthful resiliency to the beautiful spring day. Penelope was right, she nodded. She did feel a great deal more courage to face the sudden turn of her life. Dressing hurriedly, she descended the curving staircase, noting that, although it was early for her city ways, this household had been stirring for some time. Dew-freshened roses were on a hall table that shined without a speck of dust. She looked about uncertainly, then followed the hallway to the back of the house. She stood for a moment on another columned porch. At the left corner the dogtrot, a covered walkway with a raised wooden floor, connected with the cookhouse.

The drifting aroma of frying ham drew her into the semidarkness of the brick-walled kitchen. Sniffing the clean smell of wood burning in the fireplace and the spicy scent of herbs hung from the mantel to dry, she squinted to adjust her eyes.

"So, you woke up, lazy bones." Chaddy laughed before pulling a dour face. "You best hurry if you're goan to get to Anderson to catch yo' train."

"I'm not going to catch a train today, Chaddy." Caroline dimpled. "I'll get up earlier tomorrow, but I'd be obliged if you'd give me some breakfast now. That ham smells so-o-o good!"

"That's fo' dinner." Chaddy frowned. Her broad face was too used to smiling to remain foreboding, and she began to beam happily as she bent over a huge iron pot hanging on an arm over the open fire. She dipped a stuffed sausage out of the boiling grease.

Caroline settled on the bench in front of a simple table of native pine and waited. Chaddy brushed hot coals from the top of a black iron Dutch oven sitting on short legs over more coals on the hearth and took out large, brown biscuits. She poured coffee from a blue enameled coffeepot sitting on the hearth. Caroline's house in town had one of the new iron cookstoves, but food had never tasted as good as this meal cooked entirely on the open fireplace. Savoring the biscuits, soft inside, crusty outside, she licked her greasy fingertips.

Ret slipped into the room with a pail of foamy milk in each hand. Without a word, she strained the liquid through a clean, white cloth, poured a glassful of the warm milk, and set it by Caroline's plate with a shy smile. Chaddy chided Ret for finishing the milking so late. Both cast sidelong glances at Caroline as she ate.

Afraid to ask for food for Shadow, Caroline made herself stop eating and fed the little dog her leftovers. Then she wandered through the lower floor looking for Cousin Penelope. Unable to find her, she returned to her room, took a book from her carpet satchel, and went to the front porch to read.

Choosing a rocking chair in a sunny corner, she retreated from her problems by immersing herself in the romantic poetry of Lord Byron. Shadow fidgeted at her feet. Turning, twisting, shaking her thick black fur, she finally let out a disgusted snort, sidled off the porch, and burrowed under the shade of a boxwood at the edge of the porch. Caroline smiled at her sleeping pet and curled around her book.

"Screee! Screee! Screee!"

The book clattered to the floor as Caroline jumped to her feet and looked around wild-eyed. Where was that shrieking coming from? A lean, but powerfully built man swung down from his horse and limped toward her. Clinging to a column, she looked down into the flower bed waiting for Shadow to bark. Startled, she saw that it was the dog who was emitting the frightened screams.

"Hush, Shadow, hush," she soothed. "He won't hurt you." Her voice shook.

The tall man in a trim-fitting uniform of Confederate gray swept his hat from neatly cut brown hair and bowed gallantly. His mustache quivered as he said something unintelligible above the din. Dropping his eyes, he stood waiting patiently.

Cheeks blazing, Caroline scrambled down and squatted in an unladylike fashion to stroke and coo to Shadow. She sensed this man was an officer even before she stole a look at his gold collar and cuffs.

"I'm so *sorry* that I frightened you," he said in a deep, quiet voice. "I'm Jeremy Medlock, at your service, ma'am." He bowed again and clicked his heels together. "I should have made myself known." A sadness welling in his eyes and lining his tanned face lifted suddenly with a warm smile. "But I hadn't heard that a lovely young lady had come to Looking Glass Plantation."

"I'm sorry that we acted so silly." Caroline giggled nervously. "With all of the gentlemen away at war, we're only used to seeing a few old men." Her words caught in her throat as she looked up into the first young and handsome face she had seen in many months. "And, and small boys," she finished lamely. Recovering her composure, she flashed a dimpled smile. "Shadow has had a very bad experience with boys."

"Boys can be troublesome." He laughed, tilting his head sideways in a boyish grin that lifted the corners of his drooping mustache, spread across his clean-shaven cheeks, and sparkled from his eyes.

Tongue-tied, Caroline pressed her hands to her chest as the frightened pounding changed to a tremulous sensation she had never felt for Samuel. With innocent blue eyes, she stared at the officer.

"I would not have come upon you unannounced but I have business with Miss Penelope."

The tall woman emerged from the hallway as if on cue. Undoubtedly she had been summoned by Shadow's screams. Penelope frowned at the book on the floor.

With down-cast eyes, Caroline fervently wished they had caught her reading something more edifying than the writings of a scandalous man like Lord Byron.

"Good morning, Lieutenant Medlock. You are looking for me, I believe." Her dismissing tone clearly indicated that their business was private, and she did not intend to conduct it in front of an outsider.

At least she saved me from chattering on foolishly, Caroline reflected as she strolled across the yard carrying Shadow. Straining to hear the man's deep voice drifting after her, she caught the mention of money and realized they were negotiating. Heading toward the formal garden with as much dignity as possible, she forbade herself to look back. She would not forget his face, nor the way his sorrowing eyes met hers and warmed with delight.

From behind a sheltering screen of crape myrtle bushes, she watched as he strode to his horse. She pondered why the lieutenant was so far from his troops and the battlefield. Shadow had judged him an enemy, yet, something in the proud and uncomplaining way he tried to hide his limp caught at her heart.

Lest he catch her watching and think her a silly schoolgirl, Caroline hurried away toward the kitchen area. In a pen behind the milking shed, two prancing calves, their faces foamy from nuzzling their mothers' warm bags after Ret had milked enough for the family, waited for their mothers' return for the evening milking. The milch cows had not yet moved very far down the lane. They turned to stare at Caroline with curious brown eyes. She smiled at their interest in a stranger. They were evidently docile because they were allowed to run loose and forage for themselves. The garden was enclosed with vertical boards, and the cornfield was encircled by a split rail fence.

Barking in rapid spurts as if to assert herself after her embarrassing encounter with the lieutenant, Shadow ran suddenly toward the cows. The raw-boned cattle started in surprise and retreated from the yapping dog in a side-stepping fashion.

"Shadow, come back! Shadow!" Caroline pleaded anxiously.

"Stop that dog immediately," a voice commanded. "Don't let her—umh—upset the cows."

Whirling, Caroline saw a large, soft-fleshed woman at the kitchen door. Her ears pricked to the same breathy voice that had said, "Send her away." It was Cousin Sophronia!

Chapter 3

The yapping ceased. Turning back, Caroline saw Shadow running frantically toward her with the cows pounding close behind. Shadow stumbled and rolled on her head just as one cow's long face loomed near.

"Shadow, come here!" Caroline screamed, fearful that she was about to lose a dog and her new home. Cows crashed toward them from one direction while Cousin Sophronia advanced angrily from the other.

The split rail fence offered the only protection, but it looked so precariously stacked that it would surely collapse if the cows butted against it. Dropping Shadow over it, Caroline grasped a rough end at a zig-zag, forced her toe in a crack, and scrambled over. She found it surprisingly strong, held firmly by its own weight. The cows stopped at the fence with their horns lowered threateningly.

Cousin Sophronia approached the trembling group. Flapping her taffeta skirt at them, she shouted, "Hoo-eee, Hoo-eee, get on now." The cows clattered down the road. The large woman turned toward Caroline. "You must not let your dog upset the cows," she admonished, her puffy, sagging cheeks and the folds about her throat shaking. "We cannot risk drying up the milk."

"Yes, ma'am, I promise to keep her away from them. I'm sorry." She climbed back over the fence as decorously as possible.

Adjusting her steel-rimmed spectacles as Caroline came closer, Sophronia lifted her crinkled cheeks in a surprised smile. "My, my, you certainly are Mary Lillian's daughter." She pushed back strands of white hair clinging damply to her forehead, and her forbidding look softened into pleasant wrinkles about her eyes and mouth. "I loved your mother like my own child; I'm so sorry to hear the sad news about your father. We are your family now," she said, puffing. "You are welcome to stay here until we can make arrangements to get you back in school."

Surprised at her swift change of attitude, Caroline stared openmouthed, not knowing what to say. "I—we will try not to be any more trouble," she stammered. "I know it's an imposition with the war shortages and all, but—"

"Nonsense, my dear. Looking Glass has always been open to houseguests." She paused. Pushing up her spectacles, she assessed the girl for a long moment. "It's just that this is a dangerous place for a young girl right now. We are so near to . . ." She shook her head. "But I guess you will be safe enough if you stay in the house—umh—and garden. Don't go beyond calling distance. Penelope was not thinking properly when she invited you here. However . . ." She put her arm about Caroline's shoulders and directed her toward the house. "We will manage somehow."

Caroline pondered her words. The battle zone was far from here. She could not be referring to the war. With a puzzled frown, she deposited Shadow in a spot near the kitchen and followed Cousin Sophronia into the house.

Sophronia insisted upon taking Caroline on a tour of her home. As they moved from room to room, she dropped heavily into the most convenient chair and gasped for breath as she pointed out lovely pieces of Chippendale and Hepplewhite, which blended beautifully with other furniture made by her own plantation workers.

Chatting pleasantly and making Caroline feel that she was indeed welcome, Sophronia showed off her favorite pieces, a walnut bed brought with the family when they moved down from South Carolina to settle in Georgia and a fine Argand lamp. She explained that it had burned sperm oil. When that became unavailable because of the war, they had switched to camphene only to have that supply exhausted also. Now there were only homemade candles for light.

The morning passed quickly and Penelope called them to dinner. The noon meal was a large one with hot vegetables and fried ham made delightful with plum sauce and other condiments and lots of butter for the little fried patties of cornbread.

Conversation with the two cousins was flowing comfortably when a sudden commotion at the front entrance made everyone stop midword. As the plantation was far from the village of Anderson, it was unlikely that callers would simply drop in. Caroline saw that both her cousins were patting their hair into place and straightening their frocks.

A young man came striding into the room. Brushing a kiss on each wrinkled cheek and seating himself at the table seemingly in one continuous movement, he said, "You didn't tell me we had a beautiful guest." He gazed frankly at Caroline with an expectant smile on his round, boyish face.

Wishing she had imitated her cousins' hair-straightening, Caroline felt flustered. She knew from her mother's picture that, although she had some of her features, she lacked her beauty. *These people are seeing her, not me*, she thought. Yet, somehow the close attention he was paying made her feel pretty.

"This is Caroline Hannah, Rufus and Mary Lillian's daughter." Penelope smiled broadly at him. "You've heard us speak of Berry, of course."

"Oh, you're the smart young lady who attends Wesleyan Female College. Have they had to shut down because of the war?" he asked absently between helpings of food that Chaddy was showering upon him.

"No, no, they're still open. I . . . I hope to go back."

She wished that she could think of something intelligent to say instead of worrying about her faded cotton print and the frayed ribbons of its border swirls. She had bought almost nothing new since Papa had gone to war. Sitting back, slightly removed from their family chatter, she noticed that the white organdy collar and cuffs on Cousin Sophronia's plum colored taffeta were slightly shabby with age also. By contrast, Berry's doe-colored waistcoat and dark trousers were the latest fashion, and his bright cravat looked expensive. Since he was not in uniform, Caroline decided he must do something important. He looked very young and carefree compared to the war-weary Lieutenant Medlock.

While he entertained his mother and aunt with anecdotes of his train trip, Caroline adjusted to his unexpected appearance. Samuel had been away for such a long time. She felt silly that she lacked expertise in handling the flattering attentions of a gentleman. She laughed to herself as she realized the sisters were reacting to him like schoolgirls also.

The simple meal had become an occasion. They sat around the table for a long time after eating, savoring the pleasure of good conversation. At long last they moved into the parlor.

Cousin Sophronia seated herself in a rosette-carved, cherry rocker and began to knit. Berry settled attentively on a sumptuous Federal stool at her feet and idly played with her yarn. They seemed enclosed in a small circle of love.

Longing for Papa, Caroline glanced at Penelope. She, too, felt shut out. Bitter loneliness soured her features. Understanding how it felt to have no one to love her, Caroline sighed. Determined to shake off self-pity, she pushed her cheeks upward in an effort to erase a Penelope expression from her face.

Moving across the room, she picked up a picture enclosed in a leather box about six inches long. Bright copper scrolls decorated the edges of the glass. The woman seated in the center of the photograph had red hair and wore a black dress that appeared to be watered silk. The young boy beside her wore a shirt of the same red. Standing behind them was a small man with a long white beard wearing a black suit.

Caroline looked across the room with a sidewise glance. Although Sophronia's hair had turned white and her face had become puffy and sagging, this certainly must be she. The boy had black curls, large teeth, and a too-large hooked nose. Could this be Berry? She had thought him debonair, even handsome, when he first came into the dining room. Out of the corner of her eye, she saw that since the rest of his features had grown to fit his teeth and nose, he was indeed nice looking. The teeth had become an expansive smile, and the nose only served to keep him from being too pretty in his dandified clothes.

Realizing she was staring at him, he turned and smiled.

In red-faced confusion that she had been mooning over his looks, Caroline blurted the first words that popped into her mind. "You look more like your Aunt Penelope than you do your mother and father."

Sophronia scowled, obviously offended.

Searching for words to cover the insult, Caroline lied. "I've never seen this artistic form of photography before." At least she had never thoroughly examined an ambrotype, she consoled herself.

Berry crossed to Caroline and took the leather box from her hands and lifted out the glass to show how the red velvet lining gave color to part of the picture while a piece of black silk colored the other areas.

"The silk is from my trousseau," said Sophronia pleasantly, with no lingering trace of offense.

"The ambrotype is a photographic process that came into prominence at the end of the French daguerreotype era," said Berry with an air of importance. "An English sculptor, Frederick Archer, made public his wet-plate or collodion process in 1851, but it was an American, James Ambrose Cutting, who patented the ambrotype in 1854. He used a glass plate coated with collodion as a base for the silver salt. He took the title for the collodion negative from his middle name."

Pleased that he was treating her as an educated female, she replied, "I'm familiar with the more modern tintype patented by Hamilton Smith in 1856."

"Yes, that is more commonly seen today," agreed Berry. "It is actually an ambrotype made directly on black japanned metal."

"The ambrotype is more artistic and allows the use of colors," said Sophronia. "I believe that new-fangled tintype will rust and fade. I'm glad this photograph of my dear departed Josiah will last forever. A traveling photographer came around in the summer of 1855, just before my husband died. Berry was twelve at the time . . ." The rest of her story was lost in a spell of coughing.

Quick mental arithmetic told Caroline that Berry was slightly younger than she.

As they put the little memory box back together and replaced it on the table, Caroline could see Penelope over Berry's shoulder. She sat working diligently over some rough material. Feeling a kinship with her in aloneness, Caroline vowed to be more friendly toward her.

Short, choking coughs suddenly racked Cousin Sophronia. They all turned toward her and stood helpless to ease the tortuous coughing.

"Do you need your medicine?" Penelope was at her side. "But, no, I gave it to you right after dinner," she answered herself.

"I took it myself just before dinner." Sophronia coughed again. "Hand me a handkerchief, Josiah, dear."

Caroline thought that she was misaddressing Berry. With a start, she realized that she was speaking to a tall fire screen behind her. She flung her fist to her mouth and gnawed her finger in horror as Sophronia carried on a conversation with the thing. Sophronia turned to Caroline with glassy eyes that looked but did not see.

"Oh, Mary Lillian, my dear. How lovely you look in that yellow silk."

In dismay Caroline grasped handfuls of her faded cotton print.

"Your face looks yellow, too. Are you ill?"

Her dinner in her throat, Caroline felt ill indeed with the shock of her cousin's hallucinations.

"She should be in bed," Penelope murmured. She grasped her by the elbow and helped her from her rocker.

Shaking, Caroline sank weak-kneed into a chair.

At the door Sophronia turned and looked at her. "My dear Mary Lillian, it's a shame you died so young."

Chapter 4

Too weak to move, Caroline sat quivering. Slowly she lifted shaking fingers to her cheeks. "Do I really look yellow?"

"No." Berry laughed. "Of course not. Don't let Mama upset you. She has . . . spells, but she'll be fine again when she rests." He shrugged.

"But, but I don't understand what they all mean about my mother. Why does it matter that I look like her?" Caroline's strained voice echoed in her ears. "I've always been told that she died in—that she died when I was born. Papa wouldn't have lied to me."

"I'm sure he wouldn't. Don't worry your pretty head."

Agitated, she persisted, "Chaddy keeps mumbling about 'bad clouds' and telling me to leave because something bad happens to anyone young and pret—a girl. What . . . became of . . . Adeline?"

"I don't know. Weak heart, I think. Chaddy's a superstitious old woman. Every time she has a dream, she asks each one of us what it means and spends a whole day muttering about some evil prophecy." He grinned. "What you need is a pleasant outing away from old folks. Get your hat and I'll hitch the horse to the runabout."

Relieved at getting out of the house, Caroline jumped up with renewed energy, then hesitated. "Cousin Sophronia warned me not to go farther than the garden." She looked down at her hands and added demurely, "Cousin Penelope would think it improper if we were unchaperoned."

"Well, *Cousin*," he said, laughing, his inflection of the word indicating that he thought their kinship close enough to insure the proprieties but distant enough to allow a pleasant relationship. "You will be safe enough with me, and it's proper that I show you the plantation." He started out the door and poked his head back to add, "Times are changing, you know."

Laughing, Caroline hurried to get her things. When Berry brought around the buggy, she saw him note her tulle bonnet with its curtain of lace covering the back of her golden hair. His pleased expression clearly indicated he liked her company. She settled happily into the red leather seat and prepared to enjoy the ride.

The beautiful spring afternoon exhilarated her. They clopped along a road with red clay banks. The bright red seemed to intensify the greenness of the lush May foliage that overflowed every spot that had not been constantly cultivated. Caroline's tenseness dissolved as they passed through orderly rows of young corn springing to life.

Chatting pleasantly, Berry pointed out each object with childlike joy as if he were seeing it all for the first time, too. He explained that Penelope had taken over the management of the large plantation after Josiah's death when Berry was just a boy.

"She's carried on the work without a man since the war began, and she's done a fine job. She runs everything and looks after us all. Working so hard makes her a bit gruff, but that's just her way. You'll get used to it." As he talked, he looked into her face in a way that was flatteringly attentive.

"What do you do?" Something in the way he constantly brushed off each speck of dirt told Caroline he never took the responsibility of supervising the plantation.

Berry laughed. "I look after some of Mama's business, which furnishes me with an excuse to ride the trains without drawing attention to myself." He grinned with the air of a small boy revealing a secret. "It gives me a chance to bring quinine and other medical supplies through the blockade to the hospital." He gestured as if he were pointing out something nearby.

"What hospital?"

"The one at the prison."

"The prison?"

"You don't know about it?"

"No, they kept hinting that something around here makes it unsafe for me to be here, but they didn't explain."

"Oh, I think you'll be safe enough. The Yankees rarely escape."

"Yankees?"

Berry laughed at the force of her exclamation. "Do you hate the Yankee invaders as much as Aunt Penelope does? She speaks bitterly of the War of Northern Aggression."

Avoiding his question, she replied, "Cousin Penelope was doing some business with a Lt. Jeremy Medlock. I wondered about him . . ." She felt a blush rising as she spoke the name. "I mean, I wondered why he was here—away from the battle zone."

"He's stationed here under Captain Wirz. He buys grain and produce from our plantation and others in the area."

"She hates the Yankees, yet she feeds them?"

"She deals with Medlock as long as he has money."

Leaving the cultivated fields behind, they rode through dense woods. Pines, oaks, and magnolias towered above a thick undergrowth of palmettos, bamboo cane, and hanging vines. Suddenly they emerged from the cool darkness of the forest. On the brow of a hill, Berry tethered the horse.

"This is Camp Sumter," he explained. "The prison was placed here because it's remote from the theater of war, and there's a good water supply." He helped her down from the buggy with a flourish. Solicitously careful that her skirt was not caught, he then grasped her elbow a shade more tightly than was necessary to guide her over the rough ground.

Twirling her parasol, Caroline smiled prettily up at him. She glanced across the hillsides as he pointed.

"On the other side you can see the hamlet of Anderson. It's a station near the end of the Southwestern Railroad." He laughed offhandedly. "At least the locals still call it after John W. Anderson. Since 1856, the Post Office Department has called it Andersonville."

He squeezed her arm, smiled lingeringly, then moved on beyond a swordlike screen of palmettos. From this high vantage point, they looked down into the prison. She gasped in amazement, horror.

"You can see it's secure." He pointed to the wall of pine logs trimmed to close-fitting squares. "Twenty-four-foot trees are buried five feet deep. That inner wall is about the same. The prison covers about twenty-six acres."

"There must be hundreds of men crowded like ... rats ... in that little pen!" Blue eyes wide, face pale, Caroline let her parasol fall limply to her side. "Where did they all come from?"

"Thousands," he said. "Well, when General Lee fought Grant in Virginia, thousands of prisoners were taken by both sides. The first ones brought here, in February of 1864, were those captured at Manassas—what the Yankees called Bull Run—why, the place was completely full before the construction was even finished."

"It still doesn't look finished. There are no buildings!"

"Only the huts they make themselves out of logs and blankets or overcoats. They call them 'shebangs'."

"They're terrible!" She clapped her hand over her mouth. Human beings crawling in and out of lean-tos fashioned of limbs, bushes, and clay, roofed with any available cloth for shade, made her stomach turn. Many of the poor wretches were hatless, even shirtless, and their bony ribs seemed to shine in the sunlight.

"The prison was planned for 6,000." He lifted his shoulders in an expressive shrug. "But more prisoners have poured in all spring."

"Then one of them might have ... shot Papa." She recoiled. "Or ... or put a bayonet through ... Samuel." She shuddered and turned away, sickened by her first sight of the enemy.

As they climbed back into the buggy and continued their ride, Berry resumed amusing chatter, but Caroline's dark mood remained. She closed her eyes but kept seeing the awful place.

The image of Lieutenant Medlock, who was one of those in charge, swam before her, too. Sinking down in the buggy seat, she now understood the despair in his eyes.

When the buggy rolled back into the yard, Shadow greeted Caroline in her strange, circling habit. With her head and feet reversing in place and moving in an arc, the little dog circled endlessly, unable to get where she wanted to go. Caroline scooped her up and hugged her.

"Such a pretty little dog," said Berry casually.

"She's too scruffy to be pretty," Caroline said, laughing, "but she's awfully sweet."

The next few days whirled by as Berry entertained Caroline with rides and games. His mother was soon herself again, and everyone acted as though nothing had happened. She joined them for poetry reading. They had such fun that they quite forgot about the war, or the "unpleasantness," as Cousin Sophronia referred to it.

They were in the midst of pulling syrup candy when Cousin Penelope came in to say that the sheep needed shearing. She asked Berry to attend to it.

"Oh, I'm sorry, Aunt Nel, I can't." He pulled the warm, brown candy into a long strand and reversed ends of the loop he and Caroline held together with buttery fingers before he turned to her with his sunny smile. "I'm sorry to say I need to be on my way again."

With Berry's sudden departure, the days settled into a routine. Penelope superintended the sheep-shearing herself. Caroline was constantly amazed at the way she handled the workers. Although Lincoln had freed the slaves a year before, most of them remained on the place. She spoke to them in a much more quiet and gentle tone than she used with Sophronia or Caroline. Under her watchfulness the crops of corn, peas, cotton, vegetables, and fruit progressed.

Caroline would have enjoyed riding about the farm with her more had Penelope not vented her frustrations by snapping at the girl. Berry had said she would get used to Penelope's ways; however, Caroline spent her days much more pleasantly helping the motherly Sophronia.

Although they had not been reared for rough work any more than Penelope had, they picked seed out of cotton, spun, knit, and sewed for the war effort.

One especially busy day, Cousin Sophronia pushed back strands of white hair and said in her quavery voice, "We are becoming drones because of the 'unpleasantness.' I believe I will speak to Chaddy about food for a dinner party."

Caroline snapped to attention as Sophronia turned at the door and spoke breathlessly.

"We will—umh—invite the officers from Camp Sumter."

Caroline's fingers flew over the rest of her work. That day she molded two dozen candles of beeswax and tallow, lapped thread with her own hands for three yards of cloth, hanked seven broaches of cotton, and commenced to knit a soldier's sock. She had earned her night's repose, but before she went to bed she happily wrote in her journal, "I will see *him* again."

The house buzzed with the excitement of party plans. When Penelope grumbled and complained that she could not spare salt from their meager supply, Sophronia replied adamantly that they would have a barbecue. Caroline listened in surprise to their exchanges. Penelope bossed everyone, but when Sophronia asserted her authority, she had the final say. It was only then that Caroline noticed that everything on the place was monogrammed with the letter B. The plantation belonged to the Beardens not the Greenes! Thus Sophronia Bearden, not Penelope Greene would have her way.

Caroline scampered about the yard watching excitedly as a thirty-five-pound pig was selected by Will, the farmhand who had met her at the train station. He dressed the pig, removed the head and feet, and sawed it in half lengthwise so that it would lie flat. Amused by Caroline's curiosity, Will kept up a constant stream of banter as he pierced the meat with sharp iron rods. Laughing uproariously at his own jokes, Will filled the sixteen-inch-deep pit with small green oak wood. Placing the meat carefully on the spit over the coals, he basted it with a strong salt solution containing a little cayenne pepper. Then he sat back with his hat over his eyes, waiting to baste and turn the meat all night over the aromatically smoldering fire.

Caroline wandered into the cookhouse to watch Chaddy. She had boiled down the head, feet, and ears of the pig into a jelly to be served cold. Caroline's stomach turned. She had eaten soused meat before, but after having seen it made, she vowed never to eat it again.

Ret was sent out to gather wild maypops from the roadsides to make preserves. Shyly she showed Caroline how to add twig legs to the little green ovals to make toy pigs.

Chaddy brought a jar of wild spring berries from a hidden supply and made strawberry soup for the first course. She boiled fresh onions in four successive waters, cooked fresh okra, and prepared butter beans which had been dried last season and stored in wooden boxes. She directed a young boy in the proper skinning of rabbits caught in the woods. Seeing that she dropped them into the same cauldron with the frying spring chicken, Caroline resolved to be careful selecting her piece.

Surveying the preparations with pleasure, Sophronia said jauntily, "Who cares about the blockade? We make all our necessities, but England and the United States will soon learn they cannot do without our cotton."

Penelope shook her head grimly over the plantation's diminished salt and sugar supplies. And since the fall of New Orleans, they would receive no more Texas beef, leather, or horses.

Ushering Sophronia from the hot kitchen, Penelope said, "Now, Sister, don't overtire yourself and have one of your spells while company's here. Go rest 'til the party."

Remembering the frightening attack, Caroline waited upon Sophronia solicitously until time to dress.

Putting on her favorite yellow silk, Caroline fashioned her hair into clusters of long curls on each side of her face, then presented herself for Cousin Sophronia's approval.

"Oh, my dear, that won't do at all!" she exclaimed in dismay. "I've said nothing about your wearing your old clothes around the house as we have no way to buy anything new right now, but it would not be seemly—umh—to wear yellow with your father and your fiancé so recently deceased." She shook her sagging cheeks reprovingly. "A proper young lady must not be seen in public unless she's wearing mourning."

"I have nothing dark," Caroline said. "Except my worsted traveling outfit, and it would be hot and inappropriate."

"No, that won't do. Come." She hurried down the hall. "We'll find something suitable in the plunder room."

"The plunder room?" Caroline trailed her anxiously.

At the doorway Sophronia reached up and slid back a heavy bolt. "We still keep it locked from habit, although there are no children here who might be tempted to hide in the trunks." She led the way into a room with unfinished walls. Moving through a clutter of trunks and wooden quilt chests, Sophronia opened a large armoire. "We should find something that will do nicely. When Adeline died, she was in mourning for her intended, who was killed in an accident." She thumbed through the hanging frocks. "I should have thought of this sooner. You are just Adeline's size."

Gloom descended with the whispering taffeta over Caroline's head. She shuddered, feeling eerie in Adeline's mourning clothes.

Papa and Samuel belonged to another person, a sheltered child who is gone forever, she thought. *And now Lieutenant Medlock will see me in this depressing black.*

Seeing Caroline's crestfallen face, Sophronia relented slightly. "Since you're so young and pretty, I will allow one hint of decoration. I have just the thing!"

She led the way to her room and took out a beautiful locket made with a twisted gold thread around a beveled glass. "This has been handed down in Josiah's family, and I want to give it to you."

Caroline would have been more pleased with the brooch if she had not wondered if the woven hair within the shadow frame had come from Adeline's golden head.

Cousin Sophronia pronounced her toilet acceptable at the precise moment they heard carriage wheels. Arm in arm they went down to greet the guests.

As a distinguished-looking gentleman alighted from his horse, Cousin Sophronia introduced Lt. Col. Alexander W. Persons, the commander of Andersonville Prison. Large brass buttons on his uniform added to his authoritative air.

Colonel Persons presented them to the Wirz family who had arrived in Andersonville only a few weeks before. Tall and slim, Captain Henry Wirz wore a red sash diagonally across the breast of his Confederate uniform. Behind his wife came three little girls, Susie, Cornelia, and Cora. The youngest, Cora, was about eight.

A lanky, sixteen-year-old boy hovered in the background, but Caroline looked away without catching his name, for at that moment Lt. Jeremy Medlock stepped forward to be formally introduced.

As he bent over her hand, Caroline breathed the clean scent about him and fervently hoped her toilet water was stronger than the mustiness of her borrowed gown. His worn uniform was carefully cleaned and pressed, and his brown hair and mustache evidently had just been trimmed. Caroline nodded as he lifted his head, her eyes smiling her welcome. Suddenly the old black dress did not matter. Jeremy Medlock took no notice of it. His full attention was directed at her face.

"It's a pleasure to see you again, Miss Caroline." He smiled his boyish grin. "I apologize once more for frightening you." His blue eyes crinkled at the corners, and his whole face had a look of hope for forgiveness.

Assuring him that there was nothing to forgive, Caroline followed Cousin Sophronia into the parlor. As the lieutenant remained at her side and continued to chat pleasantly, she felt happier than ever before.

After her first flush of pleasure, Caroline realized that, although he seemed attentive, he was somehow reserved. Wanting to appear more than an empty-headed girl, she ventured, "Have you seen the May thirteenth copy of the *Sumter*

Republican? I thought President Jefferson Davis's message to the Senate and House of Representatives of the Confederate States of America quite eloquent."

"Yes, ma'am, I read it," Jeremy Medlock answered, with no surprise at her change from frivolous chatter. "I especially agreed when he spoke of the 'unjust war commenced against us in violation of the rights of the States.'"

Proud of her education, Caroline launched a discussion of the view in the North that the Federal government should have expanded powers and the view in the South that the United States Constitution left all undefined powers to the individual states.

Hearing her, Colonel Persons joined in expounding on the issue of opening the public lands in the West with Federal government improvements. Suddenly the room buzzed with a debate as heated as if the bloody conflict had only begun instead of dragging drearily on the last three years.

Caroline knew that Lieutenant Medlock was a plantation owner instead of a professional soldier when he spoke of the South's need for a low tariff to trade its cotton for cheap foreign goods instead of the high tariff that had been imposed to protect the Northern manufacturers.

"And they cannot understand that it takes an army of workers to produce the cotton," interposed Penelope. "They waited a whole year after the Southern states seceded to add the issue of slavery as an excuse for invading and destroying our homes!"

"Let's stop this gloomy talk of politics and ruin." Sophronia interrupted the angry words that were adding nothing new to the old problems that had caused the War Between the States. "If we are to die, let it be but once—not daily!"

She turned to Captain Wirz, who had remained quiet. "I understand—umh—that before your practice of medicine in Louisiana, you came from Switzerland. Tell us about that lovely country."

Cousin Sophronia did not look at Caroline, but her cheeks burned with reproval for her having opened the conversation.

Her shoulders drooped as attention turned to Captain Wirz, a nice-looking man with an aquiline nose and regular features. His black hair, beard, and mustache were well trimmed. He answered Sophronia's questions with accented but fluent English; and it was evident that he was highly educated.

Polite conversation flowed easily until the arrival of the other guests, Dr. and Mrs. B.J. Head, who had made the nine-mile trip from Americus. Cousin Sophronia requested that Caroline take Mrs. Head to a guest room where she might rest and freshen up after the long carriage ride. Mounting the spiral staircase, she turned to look back. Jeremy Medlock was smiling at her.

Caroline could hardly wait to rejoin the group. Everyone had assembled in the side yard where the bare dirt had been swept perfectly clean with brush brooms and a long table laden with food was set up under old pecan trees large enough to shade them all.

Jeremy threaded his way to her side, and they carried their plates to a bench slightly apart from the group. Companionably, they laughed about Shadow and chatted pleasantly as they ate the spicy barbecue and buttery vegetables. The sincere interest in his eyes spoke to Caroline's yearning for a friend. She found herself pouring out the anguished story of her coming from Wesleyan and learning of Papa's death. Suddenly realizing she was blurting out far too much personal distress to a new acquaintance, she brushed a tear from her eye and turned the conversation. "Tell me about your plantation, Lieutenant Medlock."

Pain spread over his lean cheeks. With bitterness edging his deep voice, he answered, "I have no plantation. The Yankees destroyed everything! Their cavalry was advancing through North Carolina in pursuit of our men. People were evacuating the plantations, but my . . ." A muscle twitched beside his sorrow-filled eyes. ". . . my mother refused to leave our home. On November 9, 1862, the Yankees swashed into Willow Springs like devils. Mother's Negro servant drew a knife and took his station by her, telling them he would kill the first man who laid a finger on her . . ." His voice broke.

Caroline grasped his arm without thinking of propriety. "Did they . . . ," she gasped.

"They did not kill her directly." He sighed. "The soldiers sacked the house. Threw out everything. Broke, chopped the furniture to pieces. Built a fire of it." He pushed back his brown hair with the heel of his hand. "They cut up the corn crop, killed the hogs, sheep, cows. Threw them all into the fire."

Horrified, Caroline knew now that the terrible rumors she had been hearing about Yankee destruction were true. "I'm sorry. How awful! Oh, I'm sorry."

"Mother died soon after it happened. When my father returned home from his command and found his life ruined, he died of a heart attack."

Watching the tall man sink in despair, she realized he must hate the Yankees a great deal. "Oh, Jeremy," she whispered. The depth of his grief was so much greater than her own. Tears slipped down her cheeks.

At long last he smiled sadly and said, "I apologize for burdening you. One so young and lovely should not hear such a tale."

"No, no. I'm glad you shared it." Caroline swallowed hard, knowing Cousin Sophronia would have reproved her again if she had heard the conversation. Once more she had been the cause of raw wounds being opened. The old lady was right that this should be a time of relaxation and party talk, but it was difficult to behave normally in such terrible times. Caroline bit her lip and resolved to refrain from saying things that pierced directly to the nerve. Making an effort to murmur words of consolation, she suggested a walk in the formal garden.

They strolled along flower-bordered paths in shared silence. Breathing the wafting fragrance seemed to relax their tenseness. When they had gotten away from the group, Shadow slipped out of hiding and bounced to Caroline's side.

"I'm sorry I frightened you, little one," said Jeremy, reaching down to pat her.

A low growl rumbled in Shadow's throat as she cowed down and groveled on the ground in fear. Suddenly she screamed, "Scree! Scree! Yip, yip, yip!"

"Shadow! Be ashamed! Lieutenant Medlock wouldn't hurt you," Caroline scolded. The terrified dog continued to screech. Caroline scooped up the lump of fur and cuddled and cooed. She shook her head at the dog's reaction. Surely this man was gentle and kind.

"Who is this unusual man—your commanding officer?" Caroline was searching for a noncontroversial topic of conversation. "Why is a physician in charge of the inner prison? Are there so many sick among the prisoners?"

"Well, no, he's not here as a doctor," he answered slowly. "Henry Wirz joined the army to resist President Lincoln's unconstitutional coercion act. His right arm was badly shattered in the Battle of Seven Pines, and he was promoted for bravery." His voice showed respect for his superior officer. "Since he was no longer fit for active service, he was detailed to take charge of the Military Prison at Richmond and subsequently was sent to Andersonville."

"I'd wondered why he keeps his right arm fastened to his breast buttons. He seems a nice man, but the prisoners are kept like animals in a pen . . ."

Fortunately, a sudden commotion interrupted the conversation, for Caroline realized she had brought up another sensitive subject. They hurried back to find everyone gathered around Sophronia.

"She must've had another spell." Caroline clutched her throat in dismay.

Dr. Head bent over her, examined her swollen arm, and took her pulse. "Her heartbeat is quite irregular. We must get her to bed. Lieutenant, please assist me."

The two men tried to help her walk, but she sagged. Swiftly Jeremy caught her in his strong arms and lifted her. Trailing behind as he carried Sophronia up the stairs, Caroline saw Jeremy wince. Although Sophronia's weight was driving pain to his injured leg, he tried to hide his distress.

As Jeremy laid Sophronia's semiconscious form on the bed, Caroline covered her with an afghan. Sophronia looked up through fluttering eyelids. Suddenly stiffening, she cried with amazing force, "What are you doing with my brooch? You stole Josiah's family heirloom!"

Chapter 5

Fist to her mouth, eyes wide, Caroline backed away.

Sophronia repeated the accusation. "You stole my brooch!"

Ret materialized from nowhere. Dr. Head waved his arm, signaling Jeremy and Caroline to leave the room.

Caroline looked up at Jeremy with her eyes pleading for understanding as they stood outside the door. "She gave it to me! She suggested I wear it." Breathing a shuddering sigh, she plunged on with her words tumbling over each other. "You see, she has these strange spells. The last time she thought I looked yellow . . ." The ridiculous words echoed in the empty hallway.

Shaking his head sadly, Jeremy took her elbow and ushered her back downstairs. The party atmosphere had evaporated. Penelope tried valiantly to assume the role of hostess, but the guests said polite good-bys. The Wirz family climbed into their unusual double-seated, open buggy, and the officers mounted their horses.

Trembling with disappointment, Caroline watched Jeremy Medlock ride away. A wisp of suspicion had kept them stiffly erect as he bowed over her hand in a correct farewell. Chafed that he could possibly believe she had stolen the brooch, she realized her own distrust of him had ignited from Shadow's assessment.

Hugging the dog, she wondered if Jeremy could have hurt her. Shadow's violent reaction must have a cause, yet she could not believe him cruel. She did not want to believe it. As his horse rounded the drive and he slipped from sight, she buried her face in Shadow's black fur. She must sweep Jeremy Medlock from her thoughts. Lonely, longing for someone to care about her, Caroline realized she had been hoping for something unobtainable.

Image in the Looking Glass

"He doesn't love me, Shadow," she whispered against the fuzzy ear. "I must not let myself love him."

Dr. and Mrs. Head remained as overnight guests. The lovely lady's sweet smile and attentive ear offered friendship, but Caroline's thoughts kept straying to Jeremy Medlock.

By the next afternoon, Dr. Head decided that Cousin Sophronia's heartbeat had stabilized and that he must return to his practice in Americus. Caroline missed the reassurance of his balding head nodding instructions and Mrs. Head's pleasant chatter. It was lonely with only Penelope for company.

When Cousin Sophronia was feeling stronger, Caroline sat beside her bed reading the *Sumter Republican*. The local weekly paper devoted most space to notices from the office of the Ordinary, which administered estates, but she found accounts of a few marriages. With an eye to her patient's pallor, the nervous girl omitted the obituaries. Sophronia listened quietly to an editorial on what to expect if Lincoln were re-elected. Caroline skimmed dispatches from different battlefields, searching for lighter news.

"Here's an amusing story on the front page." She laughed. "A most remarkable and romantic courtship occurred in the city of Petersburg last week, the parties to which were both ladies of respectability—the one a blooming widow, the other lovely damsel yet in her teens. The latter acted the part of the gay Lothario . . ." Caroline glanced at Cousin Sophronia, wondering if she should continue. Her watery eyes had livened with interest.

"'The whole affair was intended as a jest,'" she continued. "'A bevy of girls, mischievous, wild, and fond of excitement, having heard the widow had avowed her intentions not to enter the matrimonial state again, determined to test the sincerity of her vow.'" Caroline and Sophronia laughed companionably as she read the detailed story of how the girls procured a handsome uniform in which they dressed one of the most beautiful girls. "Oh, listen to this: 'To give her a manly appearance, a mustache and imperial were obtained.'"

Caroline read on how the girls engineered the introduction and courtship. The article included the correspondence in which marriage was proposed and accepted. The deception was discovered only at the point when the 'soldier' returned from battle for the wedding ceremony, complete with mock minister.

"Shameful!" pronounced Cousin Sophronia, laughing heartily.

"The writer doesn't name the participants, but he states they were well-known society ladies." Caroline grinned. "The last sentence says, 'The whole affair points a moral . . . ,' but the print is blurred. I can't imagine what the moral could be."

Cousin Sophronia sat up against her pillows when Caroline read an advertisement from B.W. Smith and Company that a fresh supply of genuine Landreth's garden seeds had run the blockade and had been received for sale at the drug store.

"Ret," she called. The silent girl appeared immediately. "Fetch Penelope."

Caroline had noticed that the girl slept in Cousin Sophronia's room and always remained close by her side. While she was gone, the old woman told how Ret's mother had called Sophronia to her deathbed and had given the child to her. Her sweet smile as she related the story explained why the two seemed devoted.

While Sophronia instructed Penelope to make a trip to buy some of the coveted seed, Caroline went to her room to get the brooch, thinking that with Cousin Sophronia back to her normal self, she would return it with thanks for being allowed to borrow it.

"She's probably forgotten the whole affair," Caroline told herself.

The brooch was not on the marble-topped dresser. Deciding Ret had put it away while dusting, she searched drawers with growing frustration. Turning up camisoles and petticoats and peering into every corner, she could not find the brooch.

"Ret," Caroline called softly into the hallway.

The reed-slim girl appeared swiftly, silently.

Caroline jumped and stammered, "I . . . I can't find Cousin Sophronia's brooch. Have you put it away?"

Ret shook her head.

"Did you give it back to her?" Exasperation sharpened her voice.

"N'am." Her eyes were fearful. "Ain't seen it."

Certain that Cousin Sophronia was too weak to have walked down the hallway to get it, Caroline said more kindly, "Please help me look for it."

A thorough search turned up nothing.

Penelope stepped into the room and looked down her nose at the disarray. With a sniff for comment, she added, "You two assist Sophronia to her sitting room. She's sent for her solicitor, and I see his carriage coming up the drive."

Sophronia's sitting room was set apart from her bedroom by beautiful Corinthian columns that echoed the pair separating the twin parlors below. Caroline and Ret settled her in a rocking chair with a silk quilt over her knees just as Chaddy puffed up the stairs to announce Robert Abernathy.

Eager to escape, Caroline paid little attention to the elderly gentleman. Anxious about the brooch, she hurried to catch up with Chaddy.

"Chaddy," she said, frowning, "I've looked everywhere for Cousin Sophronia's brooch. Did you get it off my dresser and give it back to her?"

Chaddy's gold earrings danced as she shook her head negatively. She clutched Ret by the collarbone and hustled her down the stairs. "You no 'count girl. Did you take the pretty?"

Grasping the banister uncertainly, Caroline wondered if she should explain that she was not accusing Ret. She decided not to follow because the girl was always afraid to talk in her presence. Perhaps Chaddy could get to the bottom of the mystery. Drooping wearily, she passed the open doorway to the sitting room and heard her name. Turning back to see if Cousin Sophronia was calling, she realized her fate was under discussion.

"Caroline's father's estate has been completely destroyed because of this 'unpleasantness,'" Sophronia said firmly. "He was unable—umh—to cover her last tuition. I want you to arrange funds," she said coughing, "for her to return to school."

Robert Abernathy cleared his throat. "Well, Miss Sophronia, your son, Berry, required all of your liquid assets for his last . . . excursion. This school term is nearly over. Ahem. Perhaps in the fall . . ."

"Very well." Her voice was crisp with annoyance. "That will have to do. But see to it that Berry—umh—does not deplete my assets again. We must send her this fall. Now, to another matter. I want you to rewrite my will."

Again his manner was delaying. "My dear Miss Sophronia, you have been ill, but you are greatly improved. Let's not rush into changing your will."

"My mind is made up. You know that Looking Glass Plantation belonged to Josiah's family. It should pass to Bearden blood." She sighed deeply and her voice trembled wearily when she continued. "There is also the question of accepting responsibility."

"Legal matters take time, you know."

Not wanting to eavesdrop on their business, Caroline tiptoed down the hall to her room. She hugged herself happily at the promise of returning to college. Cousin Sophronia was such a sweet, generous person. Suddenly her hands crept upward over her mouth, stifling an exclamation. When Sophronia had not known Caroline was listening, she had sharply commanded that the girl be sent away. Was the talk of tuition to help her or to get rid of her? Falling across the bed with her head buried, she could not be sure. Nothing here was ever what it seemed.

Caroline decided she must have a talk with Chaddy. She slipped out of the house that afternoon while the sisters napped. Finding the kitchen empty, she threw a shawl over her head against a cool rain and walked down the lane to the quarters. At the first cabin, a dog ran out barking furiously at her and Shadow.

Image in the Looking Glass

Chaddy came to the door and shouted harshly, "Get on ole hound, hush, hush yo mouth." Then she grinned a welcome. "Come in from the rain, chile."

Blinking her eyes to adjust to the dimness of the light, Caroline saw a bent old woman huddled near a flickering fire, craning her grizzled head over the quilt square she was piercing.

"This be Patience." Chaddy gestured toward the woman.

"Good evening." Caroline nodded. "Chaddy," she began briskly. "I'm upset about Cousin Sophronia's brooch. I must return it. She gave it to me, but she forgot about it when she had her sick spell, and..." She sighed, suddenly deflated. "She thought I took it. I simply must find it, but I was not accusing Ret—" Something moved. Blinking again, she saw Ret shrinking sullenly in a dark corner. She finished lamely, "of... of stealing it."

"I've whupped the girl. She won't say. Miss Frony raised her too soft. Too much petting, not enough whupping."

"Oh, I'm sorry, Ret!" Caroline apologized quickly. "Cousin Sophronia may have come to my room to get it. Would you—could you please look for it in her room to set my mind at ease?"

"No," said Chaddy, jiggling her earrings. "Old Miss been off her feed three-four days before this spell. She ain't et enough fo' strength to walk. Just like Miss Adeline."

"What?" Caroline's attention snapped from Ret to Chaddy. "What about Adeline?"

"She had these same ole spells and weakness 'fore she died." Chaddy shrugged. "'Cepting she was young and pretty." She poked out her lips and frowned dourly.

"How sad," Caroline murmured and cast about for a way to change the subject. She leaned toward the mantel and fingered the newspaper that had been folded and cut to form a lacy pattern. "What a smart way to fix a pretty scarf."

Chaddy beamed. "Sit down, girl. We'll have some good eating." She selected some slender sweet potatoes, placed them in the fireplace, and banked the ashes around and over them. Then she took apples and looped a knot of string on the stems.

Caroline watched in fascination as she fastened the long strings to nails protruding under the mantel. She twisted the strings tightly and then sat down with satisfaction. Slowly the apples turned around and around and baked on all sides.

Settling heavily in her chair, Chaddy began to sing and chant. Patience put down her quilting and clapped her hands and tapped her feet on the floor. Caroline followed her lead.

"Honey, ball the Jack," Patience sang out, "ball the Jack."

Ret obediently came from her corner and began to dance to the rhythm. Caroline watched for a while as she went down the floor and back up, down and up, then she tried to follow the motions. Clumsily at first, but laughing and trying, she danced faster and faster. At last the two girls fell back on the braided rug laughing, panting, completely out of breath. Ret smiled at her shyly. Apparently, all was forgiven.

The curtaining rain closed the cabin's inhabitants into a warm circle around the fire. Chaddy brushed the ashes from the potatoes and squeezed them to test their softness. The skins slipped back from tangy orange meat.

While chatting pleasantly, Caroline laughed when juice from her apple dripped down her chin. "Chaddy," she said, "this was a more delicious meal than the fine French cooking we had before the war."

Stretching lazily, hating to leave, Caroline forgot that she had not received the information she sought. She had enjoyed an enchanting afternoon, but the elderly ladies would be waking up with jobs for all of them. Caroline hurried to inquire of Sophronia first because she was in no mood to face Penelope's sharp tongue.

Caroline escaped her for that day, but the next morning she encountered Penelope in the garden cutting leaves from the foxgloves. Glowering, the austere woman cut the dead bloom stalks with an angry snip.

"It looks as if Sophronia could at least stay well enough to tend to the flower garden," she snapped. "The fading blooms will trigger the death of the plant." Putting down her basket, she said, "I heard you talking sharply to Charity. You should address her as '*Aunt* Chaddy' and say 'Yes, *ma'am*' to her. The elderly Negroes deserve respect."

"Yes, ma'am," Caroline replied meekly. "I had not realized that I was treating Chaddy rudely. I've had little experience with servants at school—"

"What is this about Josiah's locket pin?" Penelope interrupted, tolerating no excuse. "I saw you wearing it at the barbecue."

"Yes'm, but Cousin Sophronia *gave* it to me. She told me to wear it."

"You're just like your mother," Penelope accused. The older woman's face contorted angrily. "You come here pretending to love Sophronia and get her to give you everything. You're a taker. Just like Mary Lillian."

"But . . . but, I didn't ask . . ."

"I'm the one who provides your food, but you don't even pretend to love me!"

Backing away, feeling as if she had been slapped, Caroline stepped on Shadow hidden under her skirt and fell sprawling.

Penelope looked at Shadow scrambling from under the hoop. "That silly dog!" She spat the words, turned abruptly, and walked away.

Stroking Shadow, Caroline sat in the middle of the path. Not physically hurt, but feeling bruised, she shook her head sadly as she mused about Penelope. She could not love her, yet she could sympathize. Penelope longed for people to love her and think highly of her, but she was determined not to be the first to show love. Caroline supposed she either feared rejection or she did not want to waste affection on someone who would not return it.

"I can't like her," Caroline whispered to Shadow. "She's unpleasant to be around." She sighed, remembering that when anyone failed to respond to her directives exactly as she thought they should, Penelope had only harsh words to say about them thereafter. "But, I should understand," Caroline nodded. "I have no one to love me." Shadow licked her face, and she laughed. "I have you, and I must be more thoughtful of Penelope."

As busy days passed, Caroline tried harder and began to get along better with Penelope. She realized that if she had heard her talking to Chaddy, she had also overheard Sophronia instructing the solicitor about the money. Probably because she knew that Caroline would be returning to school, she had become more pleasant. Yet, whenever Caroline failed to give her the full attention she felt she deserved, Penelope refrained from speaking to her, except for the barest words of necessity, for long periods of time.

Relief from the daily grind came without notice. Berry came bearing gifts of sugar and tea. He warned this would probably be the last because the South's stores of food were depleted and even the supplies he had been slipping through the blockade had been cut off. He brought no salt at all. Now Caroline understood why Penelope had been upset by Sophronia's insistence on having a barbecue. Hearing Berry's tales about people throughout the South starving, Caroline looked at the beautiful furniture and silver and knew that even Berry could not convert these things to food.

Chaddy did her best to provide festive meals for Berry; however, without salt, the vegetables from the garden were flat and tasteless and everything that had been preserved was gone.

Berry left shortly, and Caroline wondered why he took such little responsibility for the Bearden land, which would someday be his.

With everyone depressed after Berry's departure, Penelope declared that since they were down to their last tea and sugar, they should really enjoy it. Although the oven, which was built into the brick wall, was normally used only one day a week, she had it fired. The next day when it had heated, she shooed a loudly muttering Chaddy aside, saying that she would bake with the precious sugar herself. She emerged from the cookhouse with her cheeks rosy.

As excited as a child, Sophronia decreed this to be a party. They put on their best afternoon frocks and sat in the parlor.

Chaddy brought in an elaborate silver tea service. Ret followed with a tray of golden cookies delicately browned around the crisp edges and glistening with sugar on top.

With a small brass key, Cousin Sophronia unlocked a life-sized wooden pear. From the silver foil lining of this lovely tea caddy, she took the last of that valuable commodity and brewed it. Passing the sugar cookies, she laughingly said, "This is one time you may lick your fingers, child."

Caroline smiled lovingly at her. She enjoyed Cousin Sophronia's company. Although her body was frail and her wits slipped occasionally, her mind was kept agile by a lively interest in other people. For once, Cousin Penelope joined in the conversation, and the three were giggling like schoolgirls when Chaddy came to the door and announced Lieutenant Medlock.

"Good afternoon, ladies." He bowed politely. "I'm sorry to interrupt your festivities." His eyes lighted at the sight of Caroline in fluffy yellow organdy, and he brushed a spot on the sleeve of his worn gray uniform. "I would not bother you with business but I have an urgent need to buy whatever foodstuffs you can spare."

"Sit down, Lieutenant. Join us for tea and cookies. We are celebrating the last of our sugar." Sophronia laughed ruefully.

"I know we should've saved it to preserve our fruit," interposed Penelope quickly, "but Sister did so need a treat."

Jeremy laughed a deep, pleasant rumble as he folded himself onto a small chair. "Can you imagine what my fellow officers would say if they could see me enjoying a tea party while they . . ." His voice trailed away as he spread a lace-trimmed napkin on his knee.

"Caroline," Sophronia chirped, as sprightly as if Jeremy were her beau, "now it's a real occasion, and we forgot mint for the tea. Quickly . . ." She clapped her hands. ". . . run to the kitchen garden and pinch a few sprigs."

Speechless from the tingle Jeremy's presence gave her, Caroline ran to do Sophronia's bidding. She was chagrined that he had caught them squandering their last supplies when people across the South were starving, but, oh how glad she was that, for once, she looked her best. Snatching up the dark green leaves, she hurried back to the parlor, face aglow.

"Mint, Lieutenant Medlock?" Caroline poised a shaking hand over his cup.

"Yes, thank you, Miss Caroline." His eyes locked with hers for a brief moment as her fingers crushed the aromatic mint into the thin china cup perched precariously on his knee.

"It's been a long time since you last favored us with your company, Lieutenant Medlock." Sophronia smoothed the crocheted collar of her lavender silk.

Watching him hesitate over the cookie tray, Caroline realized that she had been eating greedily while Cousin Penelope only drank tea. *She is more unselfish than I had thought,* Caroline mused.

"Where are you from, Lieutenant Medlock?" Sophronia inquired. "Tell us about your home."

Caroline winced.

Masking the pain he had revealed to her, Jeremy answered smoothly, "I'm from North Carolina, ma'am. My family's plantation is . . ." He swallowed and resumed quickly. "You remind me of my mother." He brushed sugar from his mustache. "This puts me in mind of the time Mama made her famous biscuit pudding. It was her specialty, you see. I can still see the funny expressions that went 'round that table as each one dug in." He chuckled at the remembrance. "With all of the good puddings she always made, we never forgot that one." He spread his hands expressively. "She forgot to put in the sugar."

They all laughed.

"My dear departed Josiah's family came here from South Carolina," Sophronia mused.

"My ancestors moved down from the Carolinas too," broke in Caroline. "I s'pose that's why I'm named—"

"Yes, it is." Sophronia nodded.

"I've heard you received another shipment of prisoners recently," interrupted Penelope. "Wherever will you put them?"

"Yes, ma'am, they continue to arrive, and the prison is badly overcrowded. But the weather is pleasant. I don't worry as much about lack of shelter," he said, a lock of brown hair falling over his forehead, "as I do lack of food." Slowly savoring one crisp cookie, he looked at Caroline as if he were trying to drink in her beauty to sustain himself.

"Prisoners of war should not expect to be mollycoddled," snapped Penelope, drawing him back.

"They must be fed," he replied in a quiet even voice.

"I have field peas to sell, and that is all."

"Perhaps Chaddy can spare some eggs," added Sophronia. "And a little butter—umh—although our butter is pale as we have no cotton seed meal to feed the cows and make it rich and yellow."

"Our butter would not be a drop in the bucket toward feeding so many," Penelope said.

"I must buy everything I can get."

"If you have finished your tea then, Lieutenant, we will see to loading the peas." Penelope rose. Her businesslike manner clearly terminated the social visit.

Jeremy stood immediately. Disappointed, Caroline gulped her last swallow and said quickly, "You have a terrible burden with so many of the enemy on your hands." She arose in a flutter of yellow ruffles, thinking of following them outside. She must speak to him alone, try again to explain about the brooch. Cousin Penelope stopped her with a reproving glare.

Jeremy Medlock looked deep into her eyes and answered slowly, "Yes, Miss Caroline, a terrible burden indeed." He bent over her trembling hand and brushed it lightly with his mustache. He turned, kissed Sophronia's hand, clicked his heels, and bowed gallantly. "Thank you for sharing your treat."

He was gone. Hoping for another glimpse of him, Caroline hurried to the window. His kiss had been so polite that it meant nothing, but she touched her lips to the back of her hand and felt warm again as she held it against her cheek. Watching until she saw him ride away, knowing Cousin Sophronia would understand, she turned back only when Jeremy disappeared from view.

"You should not be toying with someone else's beau," Sophronia scolded, shaking cheeks that now drooped with fatigue.

Uncomprehending, Caroline stammered, "What—who do you mean?"

"You know very well who I mean, and you are just . . . causing trouble all-umh-over again. You'll be the death of us all, Adeline." She started to rise and fell back in her chair. Slipping into a faint, she gasped, "You're turning yellow again!"

"Chaddy!" Caroline called, mystified, terrified by the mental lapse. "Aunt Chaddy!" She ran from the room, screaming.

Chapter 6

Caroline felt yellow. After Chaddy and Ret had taken Cousin Sophronia to bed, the trembling girl stared into the looking glass to see if she were yellow. The face that stared back looked wild-eyed, pale. Suddenly nausea overwhelmed her. Retching violently until she sagged weakly, she climbed into her bed and collapsed against the pillows. Her thumping heart seemed to bounce against the feathers. She clutched her chest as her heartbeat and breathing pounded with syncopated rhythm.

What is happening? Unable to stay on the bed, she paced frantically about the room, wondering if she were dying. Was she going crazy? Was this the strange malady that caused her cousin to suddenly lose her mind? Was madness what Chaddy muttered about?

Forcing herself to lie on the bed, trying to relax, she reminded herself that Cousin Sophronia was an old woman. She sat bolt upright. Adeline was—had been—young.

The walls of the room seemed to draw closer. She staggered into the hall. Chaddy and Ret peered at her with big, round eyes. She ran down the stairs.

In the yard, Caroline took a deep breath, fighting agitation. Shadow bounced toward her. Clutching the warm body for reassurance, she could be certain of her affection. Only of hers. Panic returned. There was no Papa, no Samuel to turn to. That security was gone. *The love they lavished made me trust my heart too easily.*

Yellow spots made her blink her eyes and stumble to a bench. Gray nebulous suspicions swirled in her mind. Sophronia's charming manners had fooled her into thinking she loved her. True feelings emerged when her mind slipped. Penelope thought well of Papa and let her stay—but she was an unwanted mouth to feed. Shaking her head, trying to clear it, she knew Chaddy and Ret did not want her here. They seemed friendly and forgiving when she visited them, but servants were trained to do and say what was expected. Had they smilingly poisoned her? That thought was impossible. Pressing her hands to her temples, tearing her hair, she wondered, *Am I going crazy?*

Jumping up, Caroline walked briskly around the garden paths and gradually regained control. Alternately walking and resting on shaded benches, she began to breathe more normally. Her heart eased its hurtful beating, but it was a long time before it slipped into unheeded regularity. She was afraid to tell anyone. She trusted no one.

Caroline barely touched her supper. The next morning she continued to be ill. She could feel eyes upon her back. Everyone watched. When she went into the kitchen at midmorning, Chaddy and Penelope had been discussing her and continued to talk over her as if she were a child.

"She needs a dose of calomel," said Chaddy firmly.

"Perhaps," agreed Penelope. "I'd give her quinine if I had some. Maybe Berry can get a little through the blockade."

They agreed upon calomel for now. Chaddy dispensed a dose from the nearly depleted supply. Caroline felt a great deal worse.

The next afternoon Penelope went to Caroline's room and told her to get up and follow her. She walked briskly along the road through the quarters. Weak and faint, Caroline was staggering by the time they reached an area of pine woods.

Noting her exhaustion, Penelope said, "It's not much farther. I was out here checking the turpentine boxes when I noticed something." She led the way through tall pines gashed with inverted "V's" until she came to one with neither gash nor turpentine collection box. "Look."

Caroline looked, but did not see what she was indicating. Penelope touched a large peg of green wood that had been driven into the rough bark of the tree. Caroline stared uncomprehendingly.

"This is the work of a witch."

"A witch? I don't believe in witches. My college professors would . . ." She laughed. Looking at Penelope's stern face, she faltered. "And Papa says the Bible forbids witchcraft, says to put all such away if one would walk with God!"

"That may well be." Penelope eyed her through narrowed slits. "Nevertheless, these rural people believe. Someone wanted to get rid of you so they consulted a witch," she said matter-of-factly. "Each day when I ring the dinner bell, whoever bored the hole in this tree comes by and gives the peg a tap. With every tap you get sicker. They believe when they drive it up completely, you will die!"

Caroline's legs gave way. Too weak and sick to argue about religion and education, she clutched her head, which was spinning so that she could hardly think. Sinking to the ground, she spread her fingers over her scalp to keep her brain from flying away.

From the moment she had arrived, she had known she was not wanted, but she had tried to make herself useful. She had begun to feel at home. Tears slipped down her cheeks. Someone must hate her terribly to play this sickening trick. A bitter taste of panic rose in her throat. She lifted her beseeching eyes to Penelope.

"Someone must be watching you. We must do what they would think would reverse the spell," Penelope said quite seriously, "to protect you."

"What?" Caroline asked.

"You must pull out the peg, clean out the hole, put it all in this croaker sack, and throw it in the river." She held out a stiff jute bag.

"No," said Caroline firmly. "I'm frightened that *somebody* means me harm, but no superstitious spell can hurt me." She squared her shoulders and looked Penelope in the eye. "I won't have any part of it!"

"Humph, you said yourself there are witches in the Bible."

"Yes." Caroline laughed and stood her ground. "Papa used to read the Bible to me each night before he put me to bed. I'll never forget the story of the evil Jezebel. Witchcraft was one of her sins. But God's people are to have nothing to do with it or those who consult the dead or diviners or idol worshipers or . . . I appreciate your warning me, Cousin Penelope, but just leave it." She nodded. "I'll have no part of it."

"Humph!" Penelope snorted again and threw down the gunnysack. "You've got more gumption than I'd 'a' thought!"

After Penelope brought her back to the house, Caroline sat for a while on the porch. She thought a ride would clear her aching head, but knew she would not be allowed to go without a chaperone. Looking around, she saw no one watching. Slipping quickly to the stable, she hitched old Joe to the runabout. Climbing into the red leather seat, she decided to go in the opposite direction from the village in hopes of locating a nearer neighbor. Surely there was someone who would aid her if a need arose.

Feeling terribly alone, Caroline wished for Berry. It had been fun when they rode along here together. The thick undergrowth that closed in along the clay banks of the road made it excitingly secluded and romantic. Now, the flickering shadows suggested an eeriness that unnerved her, made her resolve to oblige whoever wanted her to leave Looking Glass.

The slow clop, clop of Joe's hooves matched the beat of Caroline's throbbing head. As soon as Berry came again, she would get him to take her away. She flicked Joe's reins. At this rate it would take forever to get anywhere. A good horse could cover ten miles in an hour, but Joe was old and his feed had been cut so drastically that even this light buggy was almost too much. She could not hurry him. Sighing, she tried to concentrate on Berry's taking her away.

But where can I go? She had no way of knowing if her friends' homes had been evacuated because of the war. She could think of no welcoming place. She only knew that she wanted to be far, far from here.

The fresh air was beginning to clear her head, and as she rode past the cotton fields where the hands were singing at their work, Caroline felt more secure. None of these people had reason to hate her. Because they knew who she was, they would take care of her. As her dizziness lessened, she tried to laugh at her fears.

The sound of singing died away as the road left the fields and plunged into pine woods that closed darkly on each side.

Slapping the reins, she startled Joe, and the buggy lurched forward as he began to run.

The squeaking buggy careened around sharp curves, and she held on tightly for a quarter mile before they came to a steep hill. Again Joe proceeded with a slow clop, clop. Caroline held her breath as they crept up the hill. She could not see beyond the crest. She peeped fearfully behind. *Was someone following?* The rear view was blocked by gnarled oaks that reached for each other across the narrow road with crooked, bony fingers.

The hill dropped off suddenly. The buggy plummeted, leaving her stomach behind as Joe was forced to run between steep red banks. Up hill and down the awful process was repeated for a mile as Caroline wondered what lay beyond each crest, around each curve.

A dead end loomed. Joe stopped. The crossroad stretched east and west. One way led to the prison, but she had been laughing and talking when Berry had turned. Which was which? Either way, she knew that the enemy was near.

Caroline sat at the crossroad afraid to go on.

Few Yankees escaped, but they continually tried. The prisoners were allowed to dig wells because the overcrowding had polluted the pure water of Sweetwater Creek on which the prison was built. Berry had told her that wells often became escape tunnels.

A shiver tickled its way up her spine, and she hastily decided to turn east. Anything was better than sitting still. This added fear was much worse than the first. The witch's spell might only be intended to frighten. She dared not think of the terror that might lie at the hands of a desperate escapee.

Joe moved slowly in spite of her frantic urging. The rampant undergrowth clambered to the road's edge. Thick vines writhed and twisted between the trees. As the dappled sunlight flickered over them, she seemed to see gaunt-faced men behind each one, ready to reach out and grab the slow-moving horse.

"Come on, Joe, you can make it," she encouraged him. The sound of her own voice made her feel less alone. "Surely there's a house somewhere. Let's try just a little farther."

Joe broke into a trot. It was not her words but the smell of water that made him run. They could go no farther; before them was a red muddy river. Exhaling thankfully that she had not gone toward the prison, she let Joe drink his fill at the wide river.

She felt better. She had made a fruitless trip, but she would show whoever might be watching that they could not frighten her. Letting Joe rest and eat grass, she walked about trying not to appear nervous. The sun was sinking. She dared not stay longer, but Joe was not ready to go. Repeating "giddyap," she slapped the reins several times before he consented to move at an infuriatingly slow pace.

About halfway home, Joe pulled to the side of the road unmindful of the tugging of the reins.

"Please, Joe, please. You can't eat now," she wailed, looking about at the dark woods. She slapped the reins harder, but he only flicked a brown ear and kept munching.

At last she climbed down from the buggy, took hold of his harness close to the bit, and pulled him up the hill. The baying of hounds sent fresh terror through her. She jumped back into the runabout as it began to roll downward and willed Joe to keep running. Could it be hideous Cuban hounds after an escaped prisoner? Joe cared nothing for Yankees. At the bottom of the next rise, he stopped. He refused to carry her.

Pulling and pleading and promising oats, she plodded the rest of the way home, cajoling him along. After what seemed an eternity, they sighted the house. He snatched the bit from her hand and left her standing openmouthed as he ran with the rattling buggy to the barn.

The house shone white and beautiful in the evening sun. Caroline felt weak with relief at seeing it, even though someone there wanted to be rid of her.

From that moment on, the house was at once a refuge and a prison from which she must escape. Illness vanished but nervousness remained. She pondered who might be her enemy and how she was to get away. Watching Ret and Chaddy and even poor Cousin Sophronia, she tried to decipher which one had consulted the witch. Patience could feel she had wronged Chaddy and Ret and hate her. That old woman might think herself a witch!

Early one morning Cousin Penelope said that she had to run an errand in Anderson, and Caroline begged to go along. Penelope fed Joe extra oats, and he trotted willingly for her. The heavy perfume of magnolias and gardenias filled the soft June day as they started down the drive. It was such a lovely day that she scarcely minded the fact that Sophronia had made her wear the ugly mourning outfit. A light fragrance drifted from the honeysuckle that looked like a delicate bridal veil tossed over bushes and fence rails. Caroline breathed with pure pleasure. She would not worry about escaped prisoners today. Even a Yankee was no match for a strong-willed woman like Penelope.

As they came into the red dust of the tiny village, her joy was complete. Coming out of a rough wooden building marked "Commandant of the Interior Prison" was Jeremy Medlock.

Lifting the veil from her black mourning hat, she dimpled an engaging smile at him. Cousin Penelope sniffed loudly at her forwardness and stalked into Benjamin Dykes' General Store.

Jeremy hurried down the hill and greeted Caroline with obvious pleasure. She trembled at his touch as he grasped her elbow to help her cross the street. Realizing he was escorting her past the tavern on the opposite side, she averted her eyes from the stairway up the front of the building to the two doors on the second story. A lady was not supposed to know about such a place, but she had heard whispers. They chatted warmly as they passed the Quartermaster Commissary Storehouse and crossed the railroad track to sit on a bench outside the depot. Caroline hoped that Cousin Penelope would take a very long time with her errands.

"I've had a strange, unsettling experience," she began hesitantly, shivering, wishing she could feel the safety of his arms.

"What happened?" He grinned at her with that warm boyish smile and his blue eyes searched hers candidly.

She leaned toward him and whispered, "Someone got a witch to cast a spell on me!"

He laughed a shocked snort. "You don't believe in witches!"

"No, but I'm frightened that someone on the plantation wants to be rid of me."

"Surely you're mistaken." He smiled as if she were an adorable child. "Everyone there seems to love you." His voice was calm, reassuring.

"On the surface, yes, but one of them must hate me. I must leave there!" Her hand fluttered toward him. Catching herself, she jerked it back. "Remember someone tried to make it look as though I was a thief, but this is worse. Right after you left our tea party, Cousin Sophronia had another of her spells. She thought I was Adeline and scolded me. Again, she said I looked yellow." Caroline bent her head over her twisting hands. "This may sound foolish," she said in a very small voice, "but this time I felt yellow."

Tweaking his mustache, Jeremy tried to hide amusement. Her story was spilling over with more than she meant to say. She did not want to tell him that she was afraid for her sanity. Slowing down, choosing words more carefully, she related how her first sense of being unwelcome had grown into a real fear that someone would go to any length to frighten her away.

". . . And then I became quite ill for several days. Cousin Penelope discovered that someone had placed a witch's curse on me. She took me into the woods and showed me what they had done." She told him the details of the frightening experience.

His blue eyes became grave. "If they went to that much trouble, they might try to do you real harm." He bent toward her with concern. "When a person's mind goes wrong, they're not responsible for what they do...."

"Oh, I can't believe dear Cousin Sophronia was behind it. She's so gentle, so kind. Perhaps one of the servants—I'm afraid I haven't handled them well. Being at school, I've become unused to instructing servants..." Her voice trailed off weakly.

Jeremy's lean face clouded doubtfully. "One way or the other, I think it's time to terminate your visit. Much as I'd miss the brightness you bring, you'd best go home."

"I have no home." Tears filled her blue eyes. "My father's whole estate has been lost because of the war. I have no other relatives, no way to get to my friends. Cousin Sophronia has said that she will send me back to college in the fall. With a degree, I can find suitable work, a place to live." She hiccupped breath. "But I can't be certain she will remember." She could hold them back no longer. Tears flooded down her cheeks.

Stiffening, Jeremy ducked his head. "My mother would have liked you so much," he said huskily. "She would have enjoyed having you come to her . . ." His deep voice broke. For a long moment they sat in silence. "I can think of no way to help you. I have no home, no parents, nothing. Thanks to the—Yankees." He spat on the ground, and rubbed his mustache with the back of his hand as if to rid his mouth of the bitter taste of the word.

The roar of a locomotive, the hissing of steam and the screeching of brakes filled the air. Not wanting to look at him, she was glad that the train had suddenly intruded and they could say no more. Afraid he thought that she was throwing herself at him, asking him to marry her and care for her, she was mortified that she had let her longing show.

Jeremy stood wearily as the train stopped. "Duty demands my attention. There is nothing I can do but call myself a fool and leave you where you may be in danger." Starting toward a detachment of guards, he stopped to hide the fact that his leg gave way and turned to look back. Very softly he said, "Be careful."

Caroline watched as he joined the guards and began to give orders. She could not hear above the din as the locomotive took on water and wood, but she watched with discouragement the Third Regiment of Georgia Reserves, a ramshackle group of slick-faced boys and bent-backed old men. The so-called soldiers were dressed in whatever their wives or mothers could make. The South had run out of gray dye, and the material was dyed with boiled hickory nuts. Some pieces of the clothing were a dark butternut brown—as the trousers Jeremy was wearing today—while other coats or pants had come out a light caramel color. A few men had caps, but most wore old, floppy brimmed hats.

These men had been quickly mustered on May 11, and had reached Andersonville on May 20, to replace the seasoned troops. They were a rag-tag group, replacing the 26th Alabama who had left to rebuff General Sherman's army advancing upon Atlanta.

Noting Jeremy's painful limp as he moved about setting his men to unloading the train of its cargo of human cattle in blue uniforms, Caroline wondered if he were reproachful because he was unable to join the active fighting. The South was weakening badly. The 55th Georgia had been rushed to Richmond, as General U. S. Grant pressed on two fronts. The local situation was unimportant. Perhaps the war was making Jeremy too bitter to love anyone. Caroline sighed. It was obvious that he had no love left to give her.

Turning away, Caroline saw Captain Wirz standing in the shadows, watching. His wounded right arm was stiffly anchored on his breast button. The Northern press called Wirz a vicious sadist, a monster. Could he and Jeremy, both of whom had lost so much, really be taking out their hatred of the enemy on these prisoners?

With revulsion, Caroline started away from the ugly scene. She glimpsed a doe-colored coat at the top of the stairs over the tavern. The man was brushing his shoulder as Berry often did. Perhaps it was Berry. They never knew when he was around.

Moving with uncertain steps, she quickened with joy when she saw the sweet face of Anne Head. Rushing toward her with outstretched arms, Caroline knew her troubles were over. Anne would take her to her home in Americus.

"Caroline, my dear," she said in delight as she embraced her warmly. "How lovely to see you."

"I'm so glad to see you," Caroline began, but Anne interrupted before she could pour out her problems.

"We are to be neighbors. We are just moving to Andersonville."

Relief flooded over her. "I'm so thankful—"

She interrupted again, and the agitation in her voice became more apparent as she chattered on, her words tumbling out. "Doctor is to be part of the additional hospital they are setting up in the prison. There has been a sharp increase in deaths, 135 the week of May 8; isn't that terrible?" She shook her black hair that was fast becoming gray. "They have just set another area of hospital tents in a shady oak grove southeast of the stockade. The bakehouse was completed in May, and that should help relieve the diarrhea from the food the prisoners have half-cooked over small fires. Oh, it's just terrible that they've sent so many prisoners before facilities were completed. Of course, they had to remove them from Richmond . . ."

Punctuated with "It's just terrible," Anne's words kept spilling out about the horrors within the prison. Caroline's little problem of a sick old lady whose mind was failing and a witch's spell seemed too silly even to tell her. Yet, if she would come and live with Anne and help her . . .

Anne saw that Caroline was no longer listening. Stopping her gory recital, she pointed. "That is where I will be living."

Andersonville boasted about a dozen houses and twenty or thirty permanent residents. Dismay became despair as Caroline's eyes followed her finger toward several poor shanties. Her house was a tiny two-room shack.

At that moment Penelope reappeared. Grumbling because Benjamin Dykes' stocks were so scarce and the prices were so high, she spoke curtly to Anne Head and told Caroline to get in the buggy.

There was nothing to do but return with her to the plantation. Approaching the house, driving through the avenue of magnolias, Caroline was sickened by the sweetness of their heavy perfume.

One thought crowded out all other problems: she had thrown herself at Jeremy Medlock, and he had repulsed her. How could she love a man who could be partially responsible for so many deaths? Maybe she had reached out to him because she had not had Shadow to warn her that cruelty might lie behind Jeremy Medlock's disarming smile.

Chapter 7

Fear was felt in every room of the beautiful house in the days that followed. Maj. Gen. William T. Sherman's name was on everyone's lips. Talk of the Yankees crept into every conversation. Chaddy's and Ret's round-eyed gaze followed Caroline everywhere. If she glanced quickly over her shoulder, she would catch them peeping around a doorway. Their tricks seemed laughable now beside fear of the enemy. Since Caroline had come from farther north, she wondered if Chaddy and Ret thought she was a Yankee.

The northwestern part of Georgia was now the scene of battle as the Confederate Army of Tennessee struggled with Sherman. So many prisoners were taken in the fighting that the already overcrowded facilities at Andersonville were packed with 25,000 men. Brig. Gen. John H. Winder replaced Colonel Persons as commander of the post. Winder found so much gangrene and scurvy that he recommended that the prisoners be removed elsewhere and that no more be sent. The heat of the battles, however, prevented his urgent messages from reaching their destination, and more prisoners poured into the horrible place.

Rain fell day after day as June became hotter. The steaming mud of the prison camp gave off an odor that could be smelled two miles away. Axes, spades, and shovels were issued to the prisoners to enlarge the stockade, but they could not keep up with the incoming stream of prisoners.

The plantation holders feared and the prisoners hoped that Sherman would come to set the prisoners free. There seemed no way for Caroline to leave the plantation. She calmed herself by taking a brisk, mile walk around the barn each day. Even though Shadow's hair was turning gray, her teeth were falling out, and she was stiff with rheumatism in the mornings, she responded to the walks with delight. After she made the first effort, her joints would loosen and she would bounce along happily. When there was a breeze blowing back her silky ears and the hair from her eyes, she would run ahead. Sometimes she lagged behind to investigate a rat hole in the barn. Then she became frantic trying to find Caroline. Too nearsighted to see across the way and too hard of hearing to follow Caroline's calls, she would scamper along with her nose on the ground, tracking footsteps. Often she would run the whole course before finding her mistress.

One morning as they started out, Shadow drew back, her whole body tense and her tail tucked down. Stopping midstep, Caroline swept the yard with wild eyes, searching for the blue coat of the enemy. Sighing with relief, she saw that it was only Robert Abernathy. The solicitor greeted her with cold politeness. When they returned from their walk, the lawyer was still closeted with Cousin Sophronia.

Berry appeared a few days later for one of his unexpected visits. His jovial company made everything more pleasant. The unsalted vegetables, bacon, and cornbread, the only food now available, tasted better with Berry's tales of adventure providing the seasoning. He lavished attention on his mother. Because Caroline felt an empathy for Penelope and her yearning to be loved, she was glad when she saw him walking with his aunt in the garden that afternoon.

Sitting in the gazebo, Caroline was shelling black-eyed peas to be dried for the time when the spring garden gave out. Seeing Berry and Penelope enter the brick-walled garden, she concealed her spreading calico skirt behind the shutters so that she would not intrude upon Penelope's moment of attention.

"... and because of that, Sophronia has changed her will!" Penelope's voice was agitated as they approached. "I've always worked to keep the plantation going to pass it on to you. How could she decide not to leave it to you?"

"Is the new will already in effect?"

"I'm afraid so."

"Couldn't you convince Abernathy that she's not in her right mind?" His voice was tense.

Caroline clutched the gum-wood bowl, realizing she had done the wrong thing by concealing her presence. Embarrassed, she was afraid they would think her intentionally eavesdropping on their private business.

"I tried to do that," Penelope answered, "but Dr. Head told him there is nothing wrong with her mind. He is treating her for heart dropsy. It is only when the congestion around her heart makes it difficult for her to get her breath and she becomes so ill—or she takes too much of her medication—that she hallucinates."

"Well, don't worry about it," he said as if it did not matter at all. "We are losing the war, and a plantation will soon be useless."

"But the land has been in the family since it was first cleared after the Indian treaty of 1825. You should demand it be yours." The anger in her voice was so strong that it seemed to remain suspended in the air as they continued down the path.

That afternoon, Berry invited Caroline for a drive. His cheery manner indicated he had not noticed her in the gazebo. Since the sisters were napping, Caroline decided to escape without the mourning outfit. Berry waited while she changed into an afternoon street outfit of fine cambric decorated with wide ribbon in a dramatic zigzag around the neckline, hem, and sleeves. Adding a straw bonnet and picking up a tiny fringed parasol, Caroline hurried to join Berry.

Enjoying the breeze on her face as the buggy rolled along, Caroline beamed at him. "It's so good to get away for a while! I wish I were a man and could go where I pleased as you do."

"I'm much happier that you're a beautiful woman," he bantered in his usual flirtatious way. "Don't you like plantation life?"

"Life here was pleasant before I became afraid. Now I must find somewhere to go."

"Nowhere in the South is safe the way the war is turning."

"I realize there's no place to run from the war." Caroline shrugged. "That's not what I mean. There's someone who doesn't want me on the plantation." Glad of the chance to talk with him at last, she told how someone had resorted to witchcraft. "Cousin Sophronia didn't want me here from the beginning. Perhaps when she has one of her spells, she—"

A harsh laugh interrupted her. "It's ironic you would think Mama would try to scare you away."

"I'm sorry, I—" Caroline stammered in embarrassment.

"Probably Ret did it. She spooks me the way she glides about so silently, but Mama loves her. Ret's jealous of the attention Mama gives you."

Joe stopped in the shade and began to eat tree leaves. Allowing the horse his head, Berry dropped the reins and gathered her hands in his.

"No so-called witch can really harm you," he soothed. "The danger from Sherman's men or an escaped prisoner is much more grave." He put his arm around her and pulled her close with a physical insistence she had never felt before. "I can't think of a safe place I could send you." He smiled and slowly his eyes assessed her from head to toe. "Marry me. We'll leave it all and go out West."

Caroline stared at him in open-mouthed surprise. Joe lurched forward to a mudhole to drink. Relieved that Berry's hands were busied keeping the buggy steady, she wondered if he was serious or jesting. Before today his attentions had seemed merely friendly admiration. He had made her feel alive, interesting; she had been guilty of flirting with him; but she had never thought of him in terms of love.

Uncertain of his intentions, Caroline was glad the willful horse forced Berry to get out and take the bit to turn him around. Struggling with Joe, he did not press a reply about marriage.

"Is Sherman really burning and destroying everything in his path?" she asked shakily. "Is fleeing West necessary?"

Berry described far worse destruction than she had feared. He confided that the South was losing the war. His proposal became submerged in gloom that the enemy would soon overwhelm the Confederacy.

Berry's high spirits returned that night as he entertained the women at supper. Afterwards over the card table, he winked and grinned. Caroline blushed since Cousins Sophronia and Penelope were also in the parlor.

Early the next morning, Caroline and Shadow started on their usual walk. Cousin Sophronia was on her hands and knees pulling nutgrass from around the two large hydrangeas that marked the entrance to the garden.

Charmed by the beauty of the day, Caroline greeted her with poetry. "And what is so rare as a day in June?"

"Then, if ever, come perfect days," Sophronia replied with a smile.

"Then, Heaven tries the earth if it be in tune," Caroline said, surprised that Sophronia knew these lines from a contemporary poet, James Russell Lowell.

"And over it softly her warm ear lays." She sat back. "I think Lowell's 'Vision of Sir Launfal' one of his best poems. Oh dear, how long it's been since we had a new copy of his *Atlantic Monthly*."

When her mind was clear, Cousin Sophronia seemed a kindred spirit. Caroline dropped down to help pull weeds. Shadow ran ahead, then turned to look back and give a bark that clearly said, "Come on." After several tries she became disgusted and trotted away. Laughing, they saw that she was following the usual route.

"I'm so glad you love the land as I do, my dear." Sophronia's cheeks lifted in a smile. "But you are staying outside too unprotected."

"I know there's danger," Caroline replied, "but we're probably no safer in the house."

"I expect that you are right as far as the 'unpleasantness' is concerned; however, I meant the protection from the sun." She coughed. "You are getting too brown. A lady keeps her skin looking delicate." The older woman held out her arms to demonstrate how she had pulled old stockings over her hands and arms with only her fingers protruding.

"Yes, ma'am." Caroline replied meekly. She changed the subject because she enjoyed the sun and hated to be covered up with hat, gloves, and parasol all of the time. "I love the huge blooms on these hydrangeas. Why is one so blue and the other pink?"

"Hydrangeas change color according to the soil." Sophronia smiled with pleasure at her interest. "I put clay at the roots to make the rosy pink. A box of bluing and soot from the cookstove turn the other one blue."

Lulled by the warmth of the sun on their backs, they worked in companionable silence tugging at the roots of the troublesome weeds. Suddenly a shadow fell across them. Caroline gasped in fright. It was only Penelope.

"Sister, you will overdo yourself and bring on a spell," she said sharply.

"I'll stop when the sun gets higher," she promised, pushing wet wisps of gray hair from her plump cheeks.

Snorting disgustedly, Penelope said, "Caroline, there is an error in the account books that I simply cannot find. Come help me."

Pleased that she respected her ability, Caroline complied at once, following her toward the neat building to the left of the garden that housed the farm's business office. A sharp barking from the vicinity of the barn made her realize Shadow had not returned.

"Shadow. Shadow, come back!" The barking became frantic, but Shadow didn't appear.

"Do you suppose she sees a snake?" Caroline called after Penelope, who was moving briskly ahead.

"There were snakes in Eden," she snapped impatiently. "They're part of life in the country." She frowned and began a harangue about Abernathy's demands for precise, accurate accounts.

Sighing, Caroline followed, hoping Shadow only wanted her for their usual walk.

The dinner bell was ringing when Caroline closed the books. She had not realized that the plantation was such a valuable property. Penelope managed it well.

Berry came to dinner with a frightening announcement. "Rumors are flying that Sherman's raiding party is near here. You had best make preparations, Aunt Nel. They confiscate or destroy everything in their path."

After a hurried meal, which no one tasted, Penelope left to tell the field hands to hide the horses and mules in the swamp. Sophronia began instructing a frightened Ret and Chaddy.

Caroline went toward the kitchen to feed Shadow. Normally when her mistress was not outdoors, she hid herself in a bed of lemon lilies. The dog was not there.

What if she had been barking at a rattlesnake? Some of the hands had seen one crawling near the quarters and had let it get away. Dreading what she might find, Caroline began to run. If Shadow had been bitten by such a poisonous snake, she might be dying.

Reaching the barn, she stopped fearfully. Shadow often went in to sniff at rat holes, but Caroline never followed. She stepped into the darkness. A waving finger of spider web stuck in her hair. Her eyes adjusted enough to see that spider webs hung from every rafter in festoons made thick with bits of hay. There were stalls and hiding places everywhere. An escaped prisoner could easily conceal himself. Gulping breath, her throat filled with dusty particles of hay.

"Shadow!" she squeaked and coughed.

Weak yelping answered.

Circling the barn, Caroline alternately called and listened for an answering bark. Tracing the sound to a clump of waist-high weeds, she parted them gingerly, looked, and listened for a snake. She stepped into enfolding weeds.

Eyes, wildly rolled back to the whites, looked beseechingly from below the surface of the ground. Shadow's nose searched for air. Dropping to her stomach, Caroline reached down into the hole. Evidently, someone had dug a post hole and never used it because the sides were completely vertical. The dog's tiny body filled the space, and her futile attempts to escape had only caused dirt to fall in on her. Drawing her out, Caroline hugged her sweaty body and received a coating of red dirt. Shadow was near exhaustion. Soon she would have been too weak to answer searching calls. Laughing and crying, Caroline cradled the dog in her arms. She had nearly lost the only one in the world who loved her.

Carrying her to the kitchen, Caroline found a wash basin. Three waters were required to wash the red dirt from the dog's black hair. When Shadow was clean at last, Caroline left her resting in the lily bed and started for the house to bathe.

A dry rustle as she stepped on the covered dogtrot stopped her. Clutching her dirty dress, she knew she was tired and letting thoughts of a snake spook her. She took another step. The sound, like a dry seed pod rattling, terrified her. Frozen, letting only her eyes move, she saw him.

The diamond pattern on his back partially hid his sinuous, three-foot body. Caroline screamed. The snake whipped into a coil with his three-inch head up, ready to strike. Flicking his tongue wickedly, he warned her back with a rapid staccato rhythm of the rattlers at the end of his upturned tail. Backing slowly, afraid she would fall, she could not take her eyes from the snake.

Feet pounded from all directions. A loud, quick bang exploded. The rattlesnake lurched forward and writhed in death. Someone pulled Caroline back. Peeping through her fingers, she saw that Berry had shot into the deadly coil with a large pistol. Penelope appeared with a one-eyed Joe. Although the snake was obviously dying, she flailed the hoe and chopped off its head.

The awful body continued to twitch, but Berry cut the string of rattlers from the snake's tail. Counting eleven rattlers and a button, he held it out to Caroline for a souvenir.

Shuddering, she shook her head, not wanting to touch it or hear the terrible sound. Laughing at her fear, Berry put it into his coat pocket.

"Thank goodness I didn't meet him at the barn with no help around," Caroline sighed. Suddenly aware of her bedraggled appearance, she related Shadow's plight and rescue.

"I should have told you she was out there," said Berry, "but it slipped my mind. When I stabled my horse, I saw her poking her nose into rat holes. She slipped into that old post hole, but I figured she'd get out."

Caroline tried not to think that he had deliberately risked Shadow's life rather than get mud on his clothes. She turned her back.

The sound of galloping hoofbeats stopped thought, movement, breath.

"Sherman!" gasped Sophronia, clasping both hands to her throat. "I haven't buried the silver."

Mesmerized, they watched horses and mules thunder down the lane. In the open, armed with one pistol and one hoe, they were helpless. Stunned, they slowly realized the animals were riderless. Loping behind them were the two young boys who had been sent to the swamp to hide the stock.

"St. John, what is the meaning of this?" Penelope asked the older boy sharply.

"Us heard the shot and thought the Yankees was here," St. John drawled. "Us wanted to see what Yankees look like." He grinned with flashing teeth.

The family sat down weakly, laughing hysterically. Exasperated, Penelope again detailed her instructions to hide the stock in the swamp and leave them there.

They relaxed momentarily as laughter soothed their overworked nerves. Then the incident sent them scurrying about the task of hiding valuables with fresh urgency.

Caroline followed Cousin Sophronia to the dining room saying that she would help with packing the silver as soon as she had washed off the mud. Something winked at her from the cherry sideboard. There by the silver tea service lay Josiah's brooch.

There was no mistaking the unusual hair brooch with its twisted gold thread around the shadow frame. Clapping her hand over her mouth to stifle sound, Caroline fled.

Leaning from the window of her room, she gulped air. Sophronia had accused her of stealing the brooch when she had it all of the time! Caroline had been fooled by her sweetness. Desperately wanting someone to love her, she had been blind to hatred. Now it seemed she could hear again Sophronia's first words, "Send her away!"

I'll go gladly. Now. In a city she would feel safe. No jumping at every shadow and sound. Calmer with her decision, she eased her grip on the windowsill. Marrying Berry was the only solution. They could go somewhere safe, have fun.

A horse whinnied. Berry galloped around the house on horseback and rode away.

Chapter 8

"Berry, Berry!" Caroline shouted, too late.

Letting pent up tears fall, she knew she had ignored his proposal. She must catch up with him, tell him she would go West with him. But even old Joe was gone now, hidden she knew not where. There was no way to follow Berry except to walk.

The shadowy road to Andersonville swam vividly in her mind's eye. Dense woods and thick undergrowth at the road's edge could conceal an escaped prisoner waiting to jump out. The thought of Sherman's army was worse. One lone woman could expect no mercy.

Weak with despair, Caroline threw herself across the bed and sobbed out her frustration. At last she sat up, straightened her shoulders, and clenched her teeth. She would not sit meekly waiting to die either from her country's enemy or from her strange foe within the house. Penelope would not be afraid. She slipped down the hall and knocked on the door to her room.

At the invitation to enter, Caroline stepped into a room entirely different from the rest of the house. She had admired Penelope's progressiveness, but she had not expected her domain to be decorated in the modern Victorian manner.

"As Grandma used to say 'my tired came down.'" Penelope laughed. "Sit 'til I rest a minute." She motioned to an overstuffed chair. Reaching for a pitcher of thick juice placed with a tray of matching glasses on a marble-topped table, she poured Caroline a drink and continued, "Refresh yourself with some peach nectar. Then you can go with me to the family cemetery."

"What?"

Penelope laughed. "You and I can dig what appears to be a baby's grave. That should do nicely to hide the silver flatware."

Laughing at Penelope's spunk, Caroline no longer felt alone as she looked at the warm clutter of this room. Faces, scenes, pictures large, small, rectangular, oval, were suspended on cords from the crown molding on every wall. Bric-a-brac crowded shelves and tables.

Sipping the tangy juice, Caroline pondered how to present her problem to Penelope. "After I help with the preparations for Sherman, I must leave." She hesitated. "If you'll help me find a way."

"I understand your fear, but Will and some of the others can protect us. You would be as safe here as—"

"No, no, you don't understand." She squeezed her hands against her temples, then blurted, "I have a confession to make."

Penelope considered her with snapping eyes.

"The day I came I overheard Cousin Sophronia tell you to send me away. She treats me warmly—until she has a spell." She shook her hair. "Then her true feelings surface. She must've had Ret consult the witch to—to frighten me away or—worse. She accused me of stealing the brooch, and . . . well, I saw it just now with the things she's packing. You see," she said with a sigh, "I shouldn't be here against her wishes. Just because you're my cousins, there's no reason to have to take me in. If you will help me, I'll gladly leave. If I had some funds, I could go—s—somewhere."

Unreadable emotion played over Penelope's usually expressionless face. She chose the same word Berry had used, "Ironic." Taking out a handkerchief edged with tatting, she blew her hooked nose. Then she spoke, slowly, precisely. "Sister's reasons for not wanting you here go back to an old enmity toward your mother."

Setting down her glass with a whack, Caroline gasped, "I thought she loved Mama."

Penelope shrugged. "She did love her, but—I'm surprised that you didn't know—*we* are not your cousins. Josiah was. Your mother was related to the Beardens, not the Greenes."

"She visited here so much; I just assumed... But, of course, she died when I was born. Papa never told me details about her family. Only about her being here when they met and fell in love."

"Yes." She frowned. "Well, all that is over and done and doesn't matter now," she said brusquely. Suddenly a smile lit her plain features. "What matters is that you are going to marry Berry. If you two will perpetuate the plantation, your welcome here is unquestioned."

Red popped into Caroline's cheeks and crept down her neck. If Penelope knew about Berry's proposal, he must have been serious.

"Don't worry about Sophronia," she soothed. "Her senses leave her completely at times, and she has everything and everybody confused. Adeline prays on her mind. It was suspected that her death was caused by a heavy dose of Sophronia's digitalis that she takes for her heart... But if you are Berry's wife, that will be foremost. You will be in no more danger."

Caroline stared, unable to speak.

"I'm delighted about Berry's choice," Penelope chattered on, not waiting for a reply. "You'll make him a perfect wife. You thought you were our blood kin because you are so much like me." She beamed. "You are strong, single-minded. A wife can make him shoulder the responsibility he's been shirking. Of course, boys must sow their wild oats." She laughed.

Penelope seemed unconcerned how Caroline felt in the matter. As they buried the family silver in the cemetery, Caroline's mind reeled. How did she feel? One thought kept popping to the forefront of the circle: Penelope had said that Caroline was like her. *Am I? Am I so concerned that love is passing me by that I think of no one but myself?* Was she, like Penelope, single-minded to the point that everything and everybody must suit her own purposes?

With Penelope's assurances that she must stay, Caroline stumbled through tension-filled days. Although it seemed certain that Sherman would take Atlanta, then Macon and

Andersonville, he might never notice this house, well secluded down a country lane. Caroline saw no harm in letting them think she planned to marry Berry if that would keep her safe.

The external crisis passed for the moment. The rumor that Sherman was near proved to be false. Dispatches confirmed that the general was still being held off by the Army of Tennessee north of Atlanta.

The sudden release of tension left them limp. Debilitation became extreme as the days became hotter. Perspiring heavily, with no salt to eat, they found it necessary to rest for longer and longer periods in the heat of the day. Although she was weak, Cousin Sophronia seemed to have less congestion and was coughing less these days. Her mind was clear.

One hot afternoon, Caroline found her in the wide center hallway with the double doors open at each end to capture the breeze.

Smiling, she looked up from a bit of fancy work. "I know I should be sewing for the war effort," she said, "but sometimes one must feed the soul." She held out the pretty sampler that she was cross-stitching.

"'Each day is a vessel into which a great deal may be poured if one will actually fill it up. Goethe,'" Caroline read the sampler aloud. "I'm not familiar with Goethe."

"Why, my dear, what have they taught you at that school? Goethe ranks first of German authors. His place is comparable to Shakespeare's in English literature. Surely you've read his masterpiece: *Faust*?"

"I guess my education has not progressed as far as I had thought," Caroline replied meekly. "My studies were devoted to French."

Sophronia laughed. "I suppose I am well versed in German because my tutor's grandparents were the Salzburgers who settled in coastal Georgia in 1734, a year after Oglethorpe's group of English settlers. The Salzburgers were German Lutheran immigrants seeking religious freedom." She applied her needle to the dainty stitches outlining the word *vessel*. "This line says so much to me: 'One should pour himself into a day by being helpful instead of asking to be helped, being lovable instead of waiting to be loved." She looked over her steel-rimmed spectacles like a scolding school teacher.

Caroline's cheeks reddened and she twisted her idle hands.

"I realize that when one is young it seems all important to be loved," Sophronia continued. "Poor Penelope never matured beyond that point. She holds a grudge for the merest unintentional slight and wallows in self-pity that no one cares about her. She goes through life with the attitude that 'I'll dance at your wedding *if* you do thus and so for me *first*.' Don't be like that. Don't ever say, 'I'll love you if' or 'I love you because.' It must simply be 'I love you.'"

"Yes, ma'am."

"Even with Berry, whom she really loves, she won't show any affection or kindness unless he does something to take the first step. The important thing in life is not that someone else loves you, but that you give your love to others. Are you a Christian, dear?"

"Of course." Caroline shrugged. "Papa taught me that Jesus is the Son of God, the Savior who died for our sins, from the moment I could talk. Besides that," she added flippantly, "we had Bible studies at college." Crossly, she imagined that she knew as much Scripture as Sophronia did; and if the whisperings about her causing Adeline's death were true, Sophronia was surely a hypocrite.

Cousin Sophronia fixed Caroline with a steady gaze. For a long moment she said nothing; then she spoke quietly, "I'm sure you have head knowledge, dear; that's fine, but you must also have heart knowledge. Jesus said if we would truly follow him, we must deny self and take up our cross of service daily."

Penelope was coming in the back door, and Caroline was thankful the lecture was terminated. She ached to cry out to this elderly lady that she did not know what it was like to be young and have no one to love you. She could only pour her longing for Jeremy's love into her journal each night.

"Sister," Penelope brusquely interrupted, "we simply must have salt to eat and to preserve some meat for winter. I'm drying vegetables and peaches with no problem, but the figs will not keep without sugar to put between the layers. And the smoked pork definitely will not keep without salt to pack it in."

"Berry can't get you any more sugar or salt?"

"No. He says the whole Confederacy is out of supplies. Already, people across the South are going hungry." Penelope's thin face was grim. "For now, we can subsist on what we're growing but we must plan for winter. Without salt to preserve the fattened hogs, we will starve!"

"I've heard that some of our neighbors have sent their most trusted servants down to the Gulf of Mexico to boil down sea water and dip out the salt," said Sophronia.

"We could trust Will to look after the job. He could take all of our syrup kettles on the wagon and collect enough salt to get us by." Penelope hurried from the room to set the project in motion.

The anticipation of having salt intensified their craving for it. During the days that followed, as they waited for Will and the others to return, everyone began to feel weak and nauseated as they sweated out body salt with none to replace it.

"The time has come to use the one ham I've been saving," Penelope said at last. "Go fetch the keys from the office and I'll meet you at the smokehouse, Caroline," she directed.

Watching as Penelope unlocked the door and lifted the heavy board that lay across it, Caroline said, "I've never been inside a smokehouse. Some townspeople have them, but since I didn't have a mother to look after things, we bought our meat."

She followed curiously and was soon sorry because the dark little house had no windows. Caroline glanced back to make certain the one door could not swing shut. She willed herself to shake off a terrible closed-in feeling in the dark, closetlike room. Mud daubed between every log left no crack for smoke to escape. Even though there were no green boughs of pine or hickory burning in the hole in the floor just now; the strong smell of smoke filled the room. Palms sweating, Caroline turned to leave; but Penelope began to explain the process.

"Normally, the house is filled with meat." She took down the one lone, spicy, greasy-smelling ham hanging from the joist just over their heads. "This has been here for three years. We rubbed it with black pepper and red pepper after the salt curing. Then we sewed it into the croaker sack and soaked it in lime water. That made the casing air tight so the ham is still good. I've hesitated to use it since it is the last, but with the prospect of salt to cure with when the weather turns cold, I guess we can eat this now."

"We spread the meat in here." She indicated the now empty hollowed log. "And rub salt into the flesh side of the meat. Then the meat is placed in that large wooden box by the door. It's packed in layers of salt with care being taken that one piece of meat does not touch another. It remains there for three weeks." She shook her skirts at a mouse venturing across the dirt floor.

Nails biting palms, Caroline backed toward the door.

"Then we wash off the salt and hang the meat to smoke for flavor—Oh, I have an idea!" She clapped her hands. "So much salt has been used in here over the years that the dirt floor must be full of it!" She hurried out shouting, "Chaddy!"

Her ingenious idea was to dig up the dirt floor and put it in an old iron pot with a hole in the bottom. Patiently Chaddy poured just enough water through the huge pot of dirt to let it drip through. She caught the salty water, put it in thin pans, and let it evaporate in the sun. Ecstatically, they ate the remaining salt with no thought to the dirt. They saved most of the ham because the vegetables were delicious with the satisfying taste of salt.

When Will and his men returned from the Gulf with the kettles of salt, they killed some hogs for fresh pork. With the weather too hot to attempt to cure any meat, most of the salt was carefully stored for winter. For now, everyone on the plantation was fed with fresh, salted meat. A few pounds were left to sell at Benjamin Dykes' store in Andersonville.

Feeling well fed, Caroline realized how long it had been since they had done anything except languish in the house. Excitedly, she bathed and dressed to ride to the market with Penelope, who suggested that they might meet Berry. Caroline knew as she carefully brushed her hair that she really hoped to see Jeremy Medlock.

Chapter 9

Humming a jaunty tune, Caroline struggled with the black taffeta mourning outfit as she climbed over the wagon side and up to the high seat. Laughing as she retrieved the fringed shawl and retied the heavy veil around her bonnet, she was too happy to be going into Andersonville to argue with the sisters about being properly dressed in public. Most of the women in the South were now wearing mourning.

The creaking wagon lurched and swayed as the mule plodded along. In a pleasant, talkative mood, Penelope explained that horses would break their hearts to please their master—unless they were old, cantankerous, and did not like their rider as in the case of Joe—but mules never hurried or worked themselves past what they knew to be their limit.

Caroline wiggled impatiently as the miles crept by, reveling in anticipation of seeing Jeremy. It was only when Penelope stopped with the load of meat in front of the general store that Caroline began to bite her lip nervously. Seeing him might be more pain than pleasure. She must not let her love for him show in her face or her voice.

A crowd, gathered at the top of the hill in front of the church, aroused Caroline's curiosity. Noticing as she neared that a dozen rifled muskets stood neatly stacked against the chimney of the church, she hoped Jeremy might be in the group. With a puzzled frown, she looked at the guns. Some were slung with white cartridge boxes marked CSA while others held black Union-issue cartridge cases. She shrugged off momentary alarm, feeling certain that they all belonged to Confederate soldiers. After three years of struggle, the supplies coming from Richmond were meager. Confederate soldiers used equipment salvaged from the enemy on the battlefield; they even used Yankee belt buckles, turning the US upside down.

Although the soldiers frequently held prayer meetings, the middle of a Tuesday morning seemed an unlikely time, and Caroline was about to question a bystander when the church door opened. Soldiers marched out, took up their gear, and formed a line on either side of the door. The officer called, "Arch sabers!" The ushers raised their blades, sharp edges up, points touching. Through this "arch of steel" walked a bride and groom.

The wedding march, wheezing from the pump organ, was suddenly muffled by the chugging of a locomotive. Backs stiffened against the sound that heralded another load of prisoners. The group turned as one toward the bride. Her simple brown calico dress disappointed Caroline. It spoke of difficult times; however, she clutched a nosegay of flowers, and blossoms nodded hopefully from her knot of yellow hair. As the bride and groom climbed into a waiting buggy and rode away amid shouts of good wishes, the honor guard shuffled wearily back to their duty.

"Oh, Jeremy, Jeremy," Caroline whispered. He would be busy unloading prisoners. Not wanting to see the enemy, she slipped through the disbursing crowd into the cemetery behind the church. Moving silently over the brown pine straw carpet, she threw back her head to breathe the fresh-scented air. The rustling pines seemed to whisper Jeremy's name, and churning emotions confused sensible thoughts.

Seeing this young couple who had found love even in the midst of this blood bath made her long the more for Jeremy's love. Smiling sadly, she remembered how his blue eyes had met hers across a space of other people, and they had communed alone even in a crowd. She would feel him reaching out only to draw back. Perhaps, she was mistaking gallant attention for affection. When he had thought she desired marriage, he had been swift with rejection. Walking blindly among the tombstones, she knew she did not want to believe what her eyes and ears told her about him; she wanted to believe her heart. Was it possible that he loved her but held back for some reason? With nothing answered, she returned through the empty churchyard. Stooping to pick up a fallen blossom, she thought again of the wedding and remembered Berry's proposal with a guilty heart. To feel safer on the plantation, she had let everyone think she had accepted him. Uncomfortable that even her most selfish, shallow part considered marrying Berry when it was Jeremy she loved, she commanded herself to be practical. Jeremy did not return her love.

Walking past soldiers in the pitiful, mismatched garb that passed for uniforms, she knew that she was weak enough to want to get away from the poverty and hunger of this war. Berry would find fun, freedom from responsibility, safety.

Yet, if Jeremy would only say something to show he loves me, Caroline thought, *I could face anything with him.* She searched for him in the crowd of soldiers that milled about the tiny village now that the unloading was finished. Had she missed Jeremy? Trying to appear casual, she strolled by the tavern, past the jail, and down the slope beneath a thick canopy of trees. Crossing the small stream that tumbled from the water wheel of the grist mill, she climbed to the spring that bubbled out of a fern-covered hummock and drank deeply of the cool water. The mingled music of water and songbirds created a peaceful spot. Might Jeremy come here seeking refreshment for body and soul? She lingered as long as she dared. She must not keep Penelope waiting. Circling back by the blacksmith shop, she sniffed the acrid smoke rising in a black cloud from the blaze in the brazier and paused a moment to watch the smithy. With a ringing musical rhythm as his left hand flipped a round iron rod on the anvil, his hammer-wielding right hand pounded it into a square. Myriads of tools hung from his work table and all about the shop. Caroline dawdled, pretending to look at them as she glanced about for Jeremy. He was nowhere to be seen.

Hurrying now, she sighed. If only she could talk with him one more time. If she knew for a certainty that he was a cruel man or did not love her, it would be foolish not to marry Berry.

Penelope was impatiently tapping the toe of her black, high-topped shoe when Caroline reached the wagon. Apologizing, Caroline climbed up beside her as she slapped the reins and started for home.

Bursting to talk, Caroline thought surely this lonely woman would understand. "Cousin Penelope," she blurted, "do you think Berry was serious when he asked me to marry him? He's given me lots of flattering attention but never any words of love. I thought perhaps he was jesting?"

"Oh, no, he meant the proposal," Penelope assured her. "We discussed the advisability of your marriage. It would definitely be the best thing for both of you."

"I'm just not sure. I . . . I really like him. He makes me feel pretty and smart and happy, but is that love? He seems to make all of the women around him suddenly aware of themselves."

"He's a very good catch for you, Caroline." Her nasal voice was intense. "You should not risk waiting until he falls in love with some woman who will carry him far away from here." Pain pinched her thin face.

"I'm afraid that maybe I just want to be married. The war has gone on for such a long time . . . all of us girls at school felt that love was passing us by . . ." Caroline stopped, realizing that love had passed Penelope by. The intensity of her voice had seemed to be concern that Caroline might lose Berry if she postponed marriage. Looking at Penelope through narrowed eyes, Caroline realized that concern was there; however, she suddenly understood that Penelope's fear of giving love stemmed from losing the one she had loved to someone else. Her teeth popped together as the wagon lurched over a rut. Hesitating, Caroline finished lamely, "Should I marry Berry when there is someone else in my heart?"

"Your fiancé is dead. You must go on living."

Sighing, glad that she had misunderstood and not realized that she meant Jeremy, Caroline knew since she had grown to love Jeremy that she had merely liked Samuel and enjoyed thinking that she was in love with a girlish yearning for love.

"Don't throw away your life on an impossible dream. You should marry Berry immediately." She spoke with a finality that ended the conversation.

That afternoon Caroline joined Cousin Sophronia in the ladies' parlor. The gold leaf mantel was carved with the head of a woman while over the fireplace in the gentlemen's area was the likeness of a man. Although Sophronia was back to heavy knitting, she seemed to be working in the dainty room to give herself a semblance of normal times. Ready to pretend with her that there was no war, Caroline chatted over the tiresome job of making a soldier's socks as though it were silken fancy work. She seemed to find the young woman's company as pleasant as Caroline found hers; yet, just when they seemed to be friends, Sophronia turned against her. Caroline could not solve the riddle.

"You will make such a good wife for Berry." She suddenly broached the subject Caroline did not want to think about. "With you to give him an incentive and help him with the planning, he can make Looking Glass Plantation prosper again as soon as this 'unpleasantness' is over. With times as they are—umh—no one would expect you to wait for a proper period of mourning for Samuel." She put down her work and directed a piercing gaze at Caroline. "It would be best for everyone if you married immediately."

Surprised that Sophronia was pushing her, she searched for a reply to put her off. "I'm not sure that I . . . should marry Berry . . . we are close cousins."

"The relationship is not that close," she began. Then her soft, pleasant face hardened and she continued, "Actually you are no kin at all. I thought you suspected the truth the day we were discussing the ambrotype."

Caroline blinked at the photograph enclosed in its leather box. Fingering the copper scrolls, she struggled to recall their earlier conversation. She could remember only that she had been flustered by Berry's unexpected appearance that day.

"I don't understand. Penelope explained that I was kin to your husband rather than to you, but still—"

"Humph." Sophronia laughed. "I suppose a sense of guilt always makes one think that others guess the truth. Maybe you should know," she said cryptically. "Perhaps one day I'll tell you." Then she launched a literary discussion that blocked further questions.

Late that afternoon, needing to stretch and relax, Caroline went out to walk Shadow, who usually remained hidden unless her mistress was outside. Chaddy called as they passed the kitchen that Berry had come.

"I'm fixing a special supper, and that no 'count Ret ain't nowhere to be found. I'm plum wore out. I need more of that cured ham. Miss Nel put it back in the smokehouse. Fetch it for me on your way back."

Resting her eyes on the far scene across the fields and woodlands and enjoying the exercise, Caroline was in a pleasant frame of mind when they returned by way of the smokehouse. Shadow bounced merrily over the doorsill and followed her into the darkness. *Being short makes everything a struggle*, Caroline thought. She stood on tiptoe to reach the joists and take down the remainder of the ham.

Bam! The door slammed shut. Whirling to open it, Caroline heard the cross-board fastener slide steadily into place and thunk solidly into its notch, barring the door.

"Wait! Don't! I'm in here," Caroline screeched. Beating her fists on the heavy wood, she continued to call to no avail. "Bark, Shadow," she commanded. "Bark." If the timid dog had been left outside separated from Caroline, she would have barked. As it was, she huddled under her skirt for protection.

Exasperated, Caroline pounded and called. Fists hurting and voice failing, she knew even a strong man could not force open the door with that heavy piece of wood barring it. Thoroughly annoyed, she must wait. Whether it was accidental or on purpose, no one here could know how badly being shut in a small space would affect Caroline. Her chest hurt as if she would smother. Gritting her teeth, she tried to concentrate on being angry. Chaddy would soon let her out. She would be disgusted and come for the ham herself when Caroline did not return.

It was nearly time for supper. What if Chaddy really did not want the ham? *Was it a pretext to lock me in?* Caroline fought a feeling of faintness.

A squeaking mouse ran over her foot. Shrieking, she stepped back on Shadow who yelped pitifully. In the total darkness, mice skittered everywhere. They could climb, but she remembered that the brine vat had seemed reasonably clean and clear. It would be preferable to standing with mice running over her feet. Lifting Shadow into the hollowed-out log, she climbed in, hoping there was nothing in the vat.

Lecturing herself on the foolishness of the fear of closed places, she dried her sweating palms and knew it was more than that. Since her childhood, when their house had caught fire, her subconscious always reacted even before she consciously smelled smoke. She tried to calm her breathing. No one would set fire to this place. Naturally, a smokehouse smelled like smoke. She could do nothing except huddle down with Shadow and wait.

Chapter 10

Time seemed as still as the air in the dark little room. With great relief, Caroline heard voices at last, coming from several directions, merging at the door. The wooden board slid up smartly, and the door squeaked open. Three faces peered blindly into the blackness.

"Caroline?" Berry called. As his eyes adjusted to the dim light, he saw her huddled in the brine bin and laughed.

"We finally decided the wind must have blown the door shut on you when you didn't come back with the ham," said Penelope.

Caroline uncoiled slowly, stretching muscles tense from crouching in the salt bin for so long.

Stepping gingerly across the dirt floor, Berry swooped her in his arms and lifted her from the table-high hollow log. Continuing to hold her, he nuzzled her hair and said, "I'm glad to find you safe and sound!" He squeezed her and brushed a quick kiss across her cheek before he set her down.

Surprised, Caroline drew back demurely and stammered her thanks. She could see more clearly than they in the dim light, and the expression on Penelope's thin face was clearly jealousy, even though she was the most insistent that they marry.

Chaddy's round cheeks shook with disapproval at the little love scene. Brushing by Caroline to retrieve the ham, she muttered, "Bad clouds. Ought to leave this here place fo' good."

Stepping into the fresh air, Caroline felt no wind to cool her sweaty face. She knew that the door had not blown shut. There had been no sudden slam and quick falling of the latch; the door fastened with a slow, deliberate sliding of the bar. Surreptitiously, Caroline searched the face of each of her rescuers to determine if one of them had also been her captor.

"I believe I'd better marry you right away. You need looking after," Berry laughed merrily. He continued to tease and steal little hugs as they walked back to the house.

Hot, dirty, angry, Caroline tartly asked permission to use Cousin Sophronia's hip bath. As she enjoyed the luxury of bathing from head to toe, she crossly reflected upon Berry's suddenly amorous behavior. Could he have shut her in the smokehouse in order to stage a loving rescue? He had thought it funny; but, of course, he could not know how much it would bother her. Probably, he imagined being in his arms would rush her decision about becoming his wife.

Nervous and still angry, she descended the spiral staircase on knees that shook. Suspicious of everyone, she felt this house to be a beautiful, gracious prison.

Supper was plain fare served on the ironstone and pewter normally used in the kitchen. The garden vegetables lacked seasoning. Everyone except Berry had only a tiny ration of the hateful ham. There was neither coffee nor tea, nor sugar nor flour for a dessert. Penelope decreed that they could have fresh peaches and cream since Berry was at home. Normally, she dried all of the fruit to save for winter. Repeatedly she warned that when they no longer had a plentiful garden and orchard, they might starve.

Caroline's unpleasant feelings were intensified by Ret's strange, sidelong glances while she served the meal. After supper, Caroline quickly slipped out and followed her along the dogtrot.

"Ret, did you shut me in the smokehouse," Caroline demanded, then softened her tone—"Just for a prank?"

Rolling wild, frightened eyes upward, Ret shook her head vigorously and babbled, "I wouldn't do nothing to you." She hunched her shoulder and covered her face with her hands. "I stay away from you. You're cursed!"

"Ret, I don't believe . . ." she began, but the girl fled.

Far into the night, Caroline lay staring at the canopy above her bed. Still angry and nursing hurt feelings, she pondered each person's actions in turn. Did one of them have reason to hate her? Or was it merely that none of them cared about her? She wanted to withdraw into herself and not care about any of them. If she could cease to feel, she would cease to hurt.

Caroline awoke the next morning with an aching band around her head, but she stubbornly resolved to get up and find some answers. She walked to the quarters to interrogate Patience. The old woman retreated into a deafness and senility that had not been there before. Caroline could not determine if she were the one who practiced witchcraft. Patience merely stared blankly when she tried to question her.

Feeling frustrated, she searched for Chaddy and found her in the kitchen yard making soap. Bending her bulk with difficulty, Chaddy added wood to the fires beneath two large, black iron kettles hung on chains from a log framework.

"Aunt Chaddy," Caroline pleaded, "please tell me why Cousin Sophronia doesn't want me here." She patted Chaddy's arm and tried to face her, but the old woman picked up a long stick and stirred a potful of hot grease left from cooking. Sighing, Caroline asked, "Is she having Ret play tricks on me to frighten me away?"

Chaddy began adding potash, which she had already prepared by evaporating the lye from wood ashes in the other iron pot. Making a show of taking great care in mixing the potash and hot grease, she kept her lips firmly pressed together.

Seeing that she must ask the right question to receive an answer, she tried again. "Why do you say since I'm young and pretty I should go away?" Gradually adding water to the bubbling mixture, Chaddy still did not reply. Losing patience, Caroline raised her voice. "If you loved my mother, why do you hate me?"

"Law, chile, I love you 'cause I loved your ma!" The loquacious woman could keep silent no longer. Words bubbled out. "I wants you to leave here to save your life. Your ma, she took her love, but she died young. The hate made her die when you was being born. Miss Adeline, she was blossoming one day; then her love died. She was grieving, just like you for your dead love. She was a' pining so bad she wouldn't eat my good cooking." Chaddy paused for breath. She pushed back her sun bonnet and wiped perspiration before she finished gravely, "Then of a sudden she just dropped dead."

Caroline stared at her across the bubbling mass that was turning into thick globs like jelly. Her predictions allowed no safety whether she found love or lost it. "Thank you, Chaddy," she said softly, "for worrying about me." She smiled and added brightly, "but I'm strong and healthy!"

Chaddy again clamped her lips together while she poured the mixture into a wooden box where it would harden to be cut into squares. Then she took off her calico bonnet and fanned herself with it. "Go 'way from here. Get on that train." The gold hoops in her ears danced in emphasis. "Go just as far, far as you can."

Caroline searched her face for a long time before replying slowly. "I wish I could, Aunt Chaddy." She did not try to explain that the trains were filled with prisoners. "I have no money for a ticket. I have no home. The war is everywhere. There is no place to go."

Chaddy shook her head sadly and clucked her ebony cheeks.

Feeling a great deal more depressed, Caroline walked around the house and found Berry taking leave of the sisters who looked flustered and surprisingly happy.

"Here is the bride, now," Cousin Sophronia said, smiling.

"Berry is going to leave word for the preacher when he comes back around on this circuit," explained Cousin Penelope. "Then you can set the wedding date. You two will be master and mistress of Looking Glass Plantation." She beamed with satisfaction.

Berry bowed and kissed Caroline's left hand. Before she knew what was happening, he slipped a ring on her third finger. She gasped in surprise.

"It's as blue as your eyes." Berry smiled. "Mama said we could have it for an engagement ring." He squeezed her hand and then let go with a warning. "It's been in the family for a very long time. Take good care of it."

"It's . . . lovely." Caroline's voice seemed to come from a long way off. Extending her hand stiffly she looked at a large sapphire set in carved gold flowers.

Swinging into the saddle, Berry reared his horse and called back, "I'll let you know as soon as I find out about the preacher."

Stunned by the swiftness of events, Caroline murmured polite replies to the sisters without knowing what she said. She had expected to keep postponing an answer until she found some way out of the maze, but Berry had taken her question about fleeing West as acceptance. Of course, the sisters assumed that if their darling boy wanted to marry her that was the way it would be. Now, her only clear thought was *I don't want a blue ring.*

Pleased and excited, the elderly ladies did not notice her reticence as she followed them into the house. Over sewing, they made elaborate plans, forgetting there was no food for entertaining. Biting her lip, Caroline tried to reason sensibly with herself that marriage was the only solution. Vaguely, she heard Cousin Sophronia listing guests who must be invited to the wedding reception: Dr. and Mrs. Head, friends from neighboring plantations, the officers from Camp Sumter . . . Wincing, Caroline stopped listening.

Stabbing her needle into the sewing, Caroline chided herself. She must not think of Jeremy. He had offered nothing. She must have shelter, food, some way to go on living. Chaddy's mutterings indicated that unhappiness and danger lay ahead even if she became Berry's wife. Surely if she married her son, Sophronia would be pleased to have her here and would see to it that the silly occurrences stopped. Fun-loving Berry would stay only if things were pleasant. He would have the means to take her away.

Whining wagon wheels interrupted the sisters' chatter and Caroline's chaotic thoughts. Hurrying to the veranda, Caroline was delighted to see the sweet face of Anne Head. As she ushered her into the parlor, she could tell that Anne was going through the customary practice of saying "Good morning" and inquiring after everyone's health as quickly as politely possible in order to get to the point of her visit.

"Miss Sophronia, I hate to speak to you of something unpleasant," she began, "but I really must tell you how dreadful things have become and enlist your aid."

Putting down their handwork, they gave her full attention.

"As I told you when I last saw you," she said as she looked at Caroline, "a new prison hospital for 800 was built the last of May, when Dr. Head and I came. Since June 20, it's been packed with 1,020 patients."

"So many sick?" Sophronia shook her sagging cheeks sadly.

"Yes, ma'am, not just sick but dying. The number of inmates has reached 25,000 because of the heavy fighting as Sherman closes in on Atlanta." Anguish lined her face, and she ran her fingers through her hair. "I hate to upset you, but men are dying with diarrhea, scurvy, and gangrene." She sighed heavily. "We have no medicine to treat them. We can get nothing—nothing—through the Federal blockade. The Yankees, themselves, are causing us to treat their wounded with roots and barks and sometimes nothing but water. We have no food to give them except coarse cornbread and field peas . . ."

"That's all we have to eat," snapped Penelope.

"I know that," Anne replied quietly, "but these men are sick. They need soft food."

"So does Sister. If I had better, I'd give it to her."

"Now, now, Nel," soothed Sophronia. She turned back to Anne. "I read in the *Sumter Republican* that U. R. Harrison, the surgeon in charge of the Sumter Hospital, was advertising for chicken, eggs, butter, and vegetables."

"Yes, the advertisement brought some response but not nearly enough for so many. We are in dire need of linens. Doctor has taken food and linens from our house, but of course, those were quickly used. He and Dr. David Bagley are treating men lying on beds of straw. We must have linen and cotton, and we also need wine and cordial—anything to relieve some poor fellow's suffering. I'm touring the countryside urging the ladies to give aid."

"Our trunks are empty," said Penelope. "We've given our own army everything we had. Our boys fight whole days without a morsel to eat. At best, they live on four crackers and a quarter pound of meat a day. Why should an enemy that has caused us so much suffering have better?"

Sophronia rose shakily to her feet without acknowledging Penelope's remarks. "Come," she said to Anne. "We should be able to find a few pieces of clothing and linen to spare. Penelope, umh—get some chickens ready. We can get by on vegetables."

"You can't be a Yankee sympathizer," Penelope called after her in a voice sharp with scorn.

"You know I'm as true as steel to the South," Sophronia replied, turning on the stairs, "but I will not let men die on my doorstep with no aid."

Penelope trailed behind. Sophronia slid back the bolt and entered the plunder room. Standing before the clutter of trunks and quilt chests for a moment, she began opening them with no apparent plan. Caroline saw that Penelope had spoken the truth. Many of the trunks were completely empty.

"Those were Mama's wedding presents," Penelope shrieked when Sophronia laid out a small pile of the beautifully embroidered linens. "You can't . . ."

"Then, it's time they were used," Sophronia replied firmly. From a trunk by the door, she lifted some men's clothing.

"No, no, not Berry's clothes." Penelope snatched them from her and replaced them in the trunk.

"Very well. Anne, I'm afraid that's all we have."

Caroline had stood back in the shadows. She stepped forward quickly. "You should not be traveling about alone, Anne. I will go with you on your rounds, if I may?"

"You might help the very one who shot Rufus," Penelope snapped.

The words hit Caroline in the stomach and sickened her. Her father's killer could be in the prison hospital. Wavering, she wondered if she could find it in her soul to do kindness for those who had killed Papa and Samuel and destroyed their world. Holding back until the wagon was loaded, she resolutely clapped on her bonnet, flung on her shawl, and rode away with Anne Head.

Raw hearts were scraped at every plantation they visited. Epithets like *ravishers*, *robbers*, *brigands*, and *highwaymen* were flung out to describe those Anne was trying to aid. Many echoed Penelope, saying it was treason to help the invaders. Every home they entered was in mourning. In one parlor draped with black crepe, Caroline saw four tiny bodies, children dead from the war-spread diphtheria.

Unflaggingly, Anne maintained her quiet sweetness. As she returned each morning to pick up Caroline and continue the canvas throughout the long, hot week, she gave no lectures, spouted no Scriptures. Even if the women railed against her, she responded with overflowing love. As they drove empty-handed from one house with a woman screaming after them that she would let her vegetables rot on the vine before she helped the enemy, Anne said reassuringly, "Her nonobservance of charity can certainly be excused."

Perhaps it was being away from the house that made it seem to change. When Caroline returned soul-weary in the evenings, the beautiful house held out welcoming arms as if it understood that she would soon become its mistress. Although Penelope remained angry because Caroline was "aiding Rufus's killers," she was caught up in the excitement of Sophronia's plans for the wedding. Too emotionally drained to think, Caroline let their happy chatter slide around her, wanting only to ease muscles sore from bumping in the wagon into her cream-draped bed.

Conversely, the visits that brought stinging tears to Caroline's eyes were those that filled the wagon with supplies. Watching most of the plantation mistresses respond with true Christian charity as they denied their own needs and gave to help their enemy, Caroline struggled with mixed emotions. She had taken being a Christian for granted. Believing Jesus is the Son of God and being baptized had seemed the beginning and the end of it. Now she saw that following Him might be quite another matter. Something as yet intangible began to grow inside her as she saw the moral courage displayed by these women in their deeds of mercy. Many packages were wet with tears as women clasped their treasures to them for a last moment before they laid them in the wagon to aid men who had caused their sorrow.

Caroline could not erase the picture of a tiny woman at their last stop who had lost both her husband and her son. She had given a tear-soaked bundle and stood, like a small black ramrod, waving until they were out of sight. Caroline clutched the wagon seat in stony silence, but Anne talked incessantly. Overwrought, she could not stem the flow of horrors as she had seen men shrunk to skeletons and living in filth.

When they returned to Looking Glass, Caroline was glad that Anne dropped her out and drove on. Dragging wearily up the front steps, she suddenly saw Jeremy Medlock step out of a shadow. Meeting him held no joy.

"Why don't you do something about the prisoners?" she lashed out, white faced with anger. "Are you conspiring to make them die for your family's revenge?"

"You know better than that," Jeremy answered in cold, grim sorrow.

She had wanted to hurt him, but the depth of the pain, the sadness that welled in his blue eyes made her collapse on the steps and drop her head in her hands.

His measured words came between set teeth. "The horror is so great it could never be imagined. We are receiving no supplies. We struggle to feed thousands of men, thousands with the little grown right here." He laughed a bitter, harsh sound. Caroline peeped through her fingers as he continued, "It's ironic that we have no vessels to serve what food we do obtain. The South's few factories have been burned. Ironic," he repeated. "We have a quantity of molasses, but we can't pass it out. We have no buckets!"

Through a blur of tears, she looked up at his vulnerable face, wishing she had bitten off her tongue instead of accusing him.

"Did you know that the Federal Government has made clothing and medicine—for the first time in the history of the world—contraband of war?"

Miserably, she shook her hair.

Once started, Jeremy was like Anne, unable to stop talking. "A group of Northern wives and mothers tried to bring hidden medicine to relieve their loved ones. The Federal authorities had them searched. Took the medicine from them."

"Anne said our doctors have only roots and barks. She tells of unbearable horrors . . ."

"All war prisons are torturous places! Inmates are better off dead." Jeremy sat beside her and looked into her face pleading for understanding. "We've had reports that, even though the North has plenty of resources, the death rate at their prison in Elmira, New York, is nearly twice ours at Andersonville. Diarrhea and smallpox are so bad there that the death rate is higher than the actual hostilities. One doctor claimed he 'killed more Rebs than any soldier at the front.'" Jeremy struck out with his fist. "I would to God . . ." His deep voice broke. ". . . that I were a whole man killing my enemy honorably on the battlefield instead of watching them die like animals in a pen."

Shadow bounced around the house. Having caught Caroline's scent, she presented herself joyfully. Caroline patted her absently.

"Can't you turn them loose?"

"Enemy soldiers sworn to kill secessionists loosed on the innocent, unprotected women of the plantations?" He threw out his arms wildly at her foolishness.

Caroline drew back, stiffened at the remembrance of the little ramrod woman whose only protection was sheer determination.

Mistaking their gestures, Shadow growled low in her throat. Arching her back she yelped fearfully, "Scree, scree, scree!"

"Hush, Shadow, hush!" Caroline scooped the dog into her lap and continued to press the conversation. "Why isn't there a prisoner exchange?"

"We've tried. Deaths are mounting with summer's heat. President Jefferson Davis ordered a delegation of prisoners to Washington to plead for exchange. So far their mission's been unsuccessful."

Miserable, Caroline hugged Shadow. She had forced a proud man to admit poverty and impotence in handling a terrible situation.

"I came here to buy soap, but Chaddy said she'd used her last grease. Lack of cleanliness is one of our biggest problems." He sighed deeply. "I was leaving but I saw you—now I wish . . ." He stood wearily. Looking down, he shook his head. "I never saw a girl sit and hold a dog like you do."

"Only when you're around." Exhaustion lit her temper. "She's scared to death of you!"

"I'm sorry you two think ill of me." Jeremy's voice rumbled. "Sorry you found out how bad things are." Trying to walk proudly without limping, he turned and added, "I hope you'll understand Captain Wirz is doing the best he can." He mounted his horse and rode away.

Burying her face against Shadow's silky ears, she sobbed. "I'm back where I started—no one loves me but you. You've got to be wrong . . . about him being a threat to me. I believe him."

Shadow licked at her tears. Shuddering, controlling herself at last, she set the dog down and tiptoed inside hoping to slip into her room.

"Are you all right, child?" Cousin Sophronia called from the parlor where she sat rocking and stitching her sampler.

"Oh, Cousin Sophronia," Caroline flopped on the stool at her feet. Knowing she had heard their angry words and her sobs, she wailed, "Why do men make war?"

Sophronia looked over her steel-rimmed spectacles and sighed sorrowfully. Stroking her wrinkled cheek thoughtfully, she said, "Our men feel they are fighting for their birthright. I guess the others feel—umh—that all the states must belong to the Union, no matter how dear the cost. Maybe someday men will find a better way than war, and women will be able to do more than sit and wait."

Spontaneously, Caroline kissed Sophronia's tissue-paper cheek. Excusing herself, she went to her room, poured water in the porcelain bowl, and washed off some of the tear streaks and grime. Untying the dotted swiss draperies from the iron and brass bedposts and letting the creamy folds fall loose to conceal her in case Ret or Chaddy walked in, she climbed into the bed. Exhausted, she lay staring wide-eyed at the canopy. She had hurt Jeremy dreadfully with false accusations. Knowing how bad things really were, she could understand. The experiences with Anne had taught the meaning of soul-weariness. Perhaps, Jeremy had no heart left for loving. If he thought of her at all, it was as a silly girl who sat and held a lap dog.

Squeezing her eyes shut, she envisioned Cousin Sophronia cross-stitching her sampler with her motto. What was it she had said? Oh yes, "Don't wait to be loved, be loving." *I do love Jeremy.* She stopped trying to push it back into a dark corner of her heart and let love flow out with the tears trickling onto the pillowslip. *Even if he never cares for me in return, I will love Jeremy.* Knowing he needed all of the love she could give, she relaxed. Happier, she slept.

Caroline awakened in darkness. The sisters would be upset because she was late for supper. Shakily, she lit the candle. Wind whipped the flame, casting huge shadowy fingers across the ceiling. Sighing, Caroline knew the women would be inconsolable when she told them what she must. She loved Jeremy, and even if he did not love her, she could not marry Berry.

Chapter 11

Blinking tear-swollen eyes at the glittering prisms of the Waterford chandelier over the dining table, Caroline joined the sisters, who were already eating. They sniffed in annoyance at her breach of etiquette in being late for supper and made no reply to her greeting.

"I . . . I apologize for my tardiness," Caroline said with her sunniest smile. "I was so tired I . . ." She laughed self-consciously as they still did not look at her. "I guess I'd have slept 'til morning if I hadn't been so hungry!" She bit into a fried cornbread patty.

"Yes, dear," murmured Cousin Sophronia.

Caroline ate a forkful of tasteless, lukewarm field peas and tried to think of a polite mealtime topic such as they expected from her, but she could not concentrate on mundane matters. She looked from one to the other. Sunk in a soft mound of flesh, Sophronia had a vague smile fixed above the sagging folds of her face and throat. Absently, she brushed wisps of thinning gray hair from her round face. Glancing through her lashes at Penelope's thin, craggy cheeks, snapping black eyes set in deep hollows beneath black brows, and slicked-back black hair, Caroline thought of a hawk. Nodding to herself, she knew that although they had not given her love, they had taken her in and shared what they had. She could not continue to let matters drift merely to assure her welcome.

With her appetite suddenly gone, she pushed back her plate and said softly, "Cousin Sophronia, Cousin Penelope, I must tell you my decision."

They put down their forks and looked at her expectantly.

Image in the Looking Glass

"I . . . I like Berry very much. I like him as a friend. He's great fun to be with, but . . . I cannot marry him." She pinched at her tense neck muscles, then blurted, "I love someone else."

"You're still children," Penelope said, with a shrill. "Love will come as you mature." She half-rose from her chair. "Emotions shouldn't outweigh reason. What matters is that you are a perfect match to perpetuate the plantation."

Sophronia's watery blue eyes focused on Caroline with a penetrating depth of understanding. "Perhaps you only think you love this young man because he cuts such a . . . romantic figure in his uniform," she said, panting. "You know nothing about him—umh. He might not be a husband suitable to your station."

"He's not thinking of marrying me," Caroline said, laughing ruefully. "But Anne Head told me a great deal about Jeremy Medlock. He was at the United States Military Academy at West Point, where he was due to graduate in June of 1861. Just one month before that, he and a great many other cadets resigned their commissions to fight for the Confederacy."

Pausing for breath, Caroline again looked from one sister to the other. Buoyed up by talking about Jeremy, Caroline refused to let them intimidate her. The emotion surging through her as she spoke his name made her know her feeling for him was no longer a girlish whim. He had plucked the deep chords of her womanhood. Remembering the dark sadness of his eyes, the proud way he tried to hide his limp, she resumed speaking softly through a mist of tears.

"Jeremy was wounded in battle. He was half-pinned to the ground by his dead horse. It's because he has such great pain in walking or sitting on a horse that he was assigned to work in Captain Wirz' office."

"Even if his family is in the same class with yours, he has nothing to offer you as Berry does," whined Penelope.

"No, everything he owned was destroyed by Yankee troops when they ravaged their way through North Carolina." Caroline shook her head sadly. "Besides he merely thinks me a silly girl. But my goodness . . ." She gestured with her fork. "It wouldn't be fair to Berry to marry him when I can't give him my whole heart."

"Ridiculous!" said Penelope.

Sophronia's silence smoldered. It made Caroline more uncomfortable than Penelope's shrill arguments. Squirming in a bright spot of light under the chandelier, Caroline felt that the rest of the house closed darkly around her, hating her again. Trying to shake off this foolish fantasy, she told herself that she must stop being childish. It was only because the candles had been left unlit in the wall sconces to preserve the precious tallow and beeswax that the room seemed dark and threatening.

During the days and nights that followed, Caroline could not shake the silly notion that the house was watching her with hate-filled eyes. Sophronia remained silent with her lips pressed in a grim expression, but Penelope followed Caroline about urging her to reconsider. When Caroline held firm, she said briskly, "Don't decide now," and set Chaddy to cleaning and polishing anyway.

Chaddy's attitude was the most unnerving. Glowering, she worked with furious strength, punctuating each lick or jab with such dark muttering that Caroline began to wonder if Adeline had suspected her of poisoning her food and stopped eating—too late.

Whenever possible, Caroline escaped the house and stayed in the garden. The soft June mornings stretched peacefully. The garden's protective green wall of crape myrtle bushes turned pink with huge clusters of blooms. If she sat very still, Caroline was often rewarded with quick glimpses of a hummingbird. The round green bird with his blur of rapidly beating wings would dart his needle beak into the deep throats of the orange lilies that grew as high as her shoulder. Tilting her head backward as he whisked to the top of a towering pine, she marveled wistfully that so tiny a bird could fly so high.

As warm, wet June came to a close, the days began to sizzle. Cousin Sophronia followed Caroline's lead in bringing her work to the gazebo. The blaze of the sun was felt early in the morning now, and insects increased with the humidity. By midafternoon, clouds of gnats flew about their heads; and the worrisome insects tickling an ear or snuffing up a nostril drove them back indoors. Caroline's thoughts drifted to the prisoners who must remain outside, pestered by the minute creatures.

The tension of the stifling air increased hourly until the charge exploded each afternoon about tea time. Black clouds suddenly lowered smotheringly. Gashes of lightning ripped them, releasing torrents of rain. Crashes of thunder reverberated around the house, shaking teeth and loosening raw nerve endings.

Berry appeared suddenly during one such dazzling storm. Wet, but cheerful as usual, he grinned at them and said, "We just missed the preacher! He'd gone on his circuit when I inquired, but I left word for him when he gets back."

"Berry, I . . ." Caroline plucked at his wet sleeve.

"That is, if he's not afraid to come back," he said in a voice pitched high with excitement.

Taking off his wet coat, drying his face, and tousling his black curls with the towel Penelope handed him, he talked on in his nonstop way of not listening to what others said. "The camp's a blaze of excitement! A breakout was planned 'bout the tenth of June, but some traitor told Wirz. He pointed thirty or forty pieces of artillery down on the prisoners. Either that quieted 'em down, or they got word that a raiding column is coming to free them." His body sagged suddenly in an expression of helplessness. "Prisoners are still shipping in—even though General Winder keeps sending messages to his superiors that no more be sent."

"What's Winder doing?" asked Penelope.

"He's planning some hasty defenses."

Caroline went to the window and looked out through the lace curtains. The war, which had been in a seemingly distant world, was lowering upon them like the black clouds. Sighing, she said softly, "I'm sure the oppressive humidity and drenching storms ferment the prisoners."

Berry looked at her over the sisters' heads with his glittering eyes adding a private message to his words. "Your friend,

Medlock," he said dryly, "and Wirz are not handling the problems of the inner prison. There's a gang of some 500 cutthroats who've organized a band called the Raiders. They prey upon their fellow prisoners, pouncing upon them, taking the clothes off their backs—often killing them." His voice rose intensely. "The situation's about to boil over . . ."

"There's nothing we can do." Sophronia patted his arm in her usual quiet manner. "We're in the Lord's hands. Right now you need dry clothing and food."

Berry was soon on his way again without Caroline having to face a private encounter. Talk of marriage was totally forgotten, made unnecessary by the frightening danger of a prison break.

The next day galloping hoofbeats drew them to the door. A boy jumped down and handed Penelope a message. Caroline watched her tanned cheeks go white as her hawk eyes scanned the note. Without a word, she thrust it into Caroline's hand.

Andersonville, Georgia
July 3, 1864

Dear Miss Sophronia and Miss Penelope,

A virtual war within a war has begun as hundreds of prisoners are fighting among themselves. It started when a new shipment of 350 prisoners from West Virginia arrived bringing news of the near termination of the war. The gang called Raiders proceeded to rob them of their valuables.

The cutthroats are coming out ahead. The prisoners are about to rise up and break away. They have sent up a shout for Wirz.

Stay well guarded.

Your obedient servant,
Robert Abernathy

Caroline clapped her hands to her mouth and stood trembling with fear for Jeremy. The accusations Berry had planted grew to thistles pricking her heart. Were he and Wirz callously ignoring their charges, letting them kill each other?

Penelope sent Caroline to help Sophronia into the house while she set the lanky boy, St. John, as a guard and dispatched Will to the hill overlooking the prison to see what was happening.

Will returned wild-eyed with fright. "The battle is a-raging," he gasped, swallowing hard. "They is fighting with great big clubs they say Cap'n Wirz gave 'em. They say the Cap'n order no mo' food be gibben."

It was July 4. The plantation's guards were lackadaisical as they were accustomed to the "Fourth Day" being their big holiday.

The next day a cryptic message came from Abernathy. "Things are quiet but tense. Court is in session. Stay guarded."

For the next several days they could barely breathe from the heat and the tension. Chafing from lack of communication, Penelope sent Will off again. When he returned, all he could report was, "Them Yankees is holding court."

Early in the afternoon of July 11, the women heard a horse galloping up the drive. Seated in the central hallway trying to catch a breeze, they were in the open, defenseless. Penelope rushed to slam and lock the front doors. Cautiously, she peeped through the side glass. "It's Berry," she cried, throwing open the doors.

"There's been a hanging!" he shouted, jumping from his horse and bounding to the porch. He flung his arm around Caroline's waist. "In fact, six men were hanged." He grinned down at her.

Caroline swooned in his arms.

When she opened her eyes, they were standing over her with smelling salts and fans. Blinking, Caroline wondered if she had said aloud the one word which pounded in her brain, her heart, her whole being: *Jeremy!* Clutching her head with both hands as she fought for control, she gasped, "Is the palisade broken? Have they hanged Jeremy?" She strangled, coughed. "And Wirz and Winder?" She tried to cover her heart-thoughts.

"No, no," Berry laughed. "There was nearly a lynching among the prisoners, but old Wirz came through. He issued an order no food be given until the ringleaders of the Raiders were arrested. He furnished clubs to the orderly prisoners who formed a police force. They arrested all the Raiders—oh it was some battle." He gestured wildly. "And then they conducted court and tried their own men. It was a fair trial, a defense counsel and everything." He laughed.

Caroline sighed in relief. Feeling better, she sat up and listened as he told the details of the trial with glittering eyes.

"Most of the men were condemned to light punishment; set in stocks, strung up by thumbs, thumb screws, head hanging. That sort of thing." He shrugged. "The six ringleaders were hanged this morning at eleven o'clock."

"Wirz had a scaffold built inside the prison," he continued. "He withdrew the guards and let the Yankees perform their own execution. It was quite a show. Curtiss, a stout fellow from Rhode Island, managed to get his hands untied. He jumped off the scaffold and made for the swamp." Berry laughed gleefully. "But they caught him and brought him back. Each man made a long speech about how honest he had been before starvation and evil associates had driven him to commit the crimes. I was standing on a high platform with Wirz and the guards looking down into the prison. It was the first hanging I'd ever seen. Moseby's rope broke and he fell to the ground with blood spurting from his ears. He begged to live but they lifted him back to the swinging off place. Sarsfield drew his knees to his chin and jerked and the veins in his neck—"

"Berry," Sophronia commanded sharply. "I know you are overwrought, but spare us the details."

"Yes, ma'am." Berry let out his breath. "I will tell you they had a priest. They buried the six a distance from the graves of the honorable prisoners. Good order has prevailed since the hanging. The men have settled right down to the business of dying, with no interruption."

With the ferment inside the prison stilled at last, they sank into a week of quietude. Tumult erupted again as the combat 150 miles to the north of Atlanta became more savage. Major General Sherman's name was a curse again on everyone's lips. On July 18, the CSA sent Gen. John B. Hood to replace Gen. Joseph E. Johnson as the commander of the Army of Tennessee. Hundreds of Yankees were captured in the battle of Atlanta on July 22, and sent to Andersonville. The residents' fears multiplied again with the swelling numbers.

Early one morning, Cousin Sophronia's solicitor arrived with a warning to increase precautions. "Andersonville is surely a magnet drawing Sherman's raiding column to free the prisoners," Robert Abernathy said. "Maj. Gen. Lovell Rousseau's raiders have wrecked the Montgomery and West Point Railroad eighty-five miles northwest of Atlanta. Confederate authorities believe the release of the prisoners is Rousseau's goal." The elderly gentleman fidgeted nervously. "General Winder has thrown up breastworks for defending the prison, but you must increase your security."

Watching him drive away, Caroline felt this to be impossible; however, Penelope seemed undaunted. Arming herself with the large pistol, their only weapon, she commanded them to stay close to her side at all times. Will was called in from supervising the field work to set up a guard around the house; nevertheless, they moved about the necessary work in a state of numbness. Each day dangled in an agony of suspense.

The clatter of a horse's hooves just after dawn one morning drew them together in fear. Trooping down the stairs, they prepared to face the enemy. Clutching her nightclothes to her breast, Caroline seemed to stop breathing as the horseman alighted and limped to the door.

"Jeremy!"

"Ladies, I'm sorry to disturb you so early." He took off his hat as he bowed and averted his eyes from their dishevelment. "But we've received word that Sherman and George Stoneman have made plans to raid Macon and Andersonville."

"Macon? Oh, my beautiful college," Caroline wailed.

Jeremy looked at her for a long moment without replying. Watching his lean face work with frustration, she knew he was right. She was a silly girl to be worrying about a school building when the enemy was now possibly ninety miles from this plantation, moving this way.

Jeremy turned back to Penelope and spoke in an urgent tone, "Captain Theodore Moreno has arrived to lay out better fortifications. We'll keep the area as safe as possible, but it would be best for you to leave. Every route is cut off except directly south. Do you have any friends or relatives who could take you in?"

"We have nowhere to go," replied Sophronia, "but even if we did we could not leave our home unguarded."

Jeremy continued to try to impress her with the seriousness of the matter. Although his frantic gaze sought aid from Caroline, she did not join him in urging her to leave, knowing Sophronia could not stand the trip. The increasing heat and humidity left her struggling to breathe. Sophronia spent most of her days now lying weakly in bed.

Some kind soul in Americus would surely take her in as a lone refugee, Caroline knew, but she could not find it in her heart to abandon the helpless old woman. After Jeremy left, Caroline straightened her shoulders and marched back into the house. Could one really hide from an advancing army?

Each day the sisters repeated the same conversation. They reassured each other that the invaders would not burn their home around them. Caroline knew that they would. She had heard many reports of the enemy burning and destroying everything. The thought of fire terrified her even more than the idea of facing enemy soldiers. Firmly, she resolved to fight them for her life, her honor.

Caroline was spending yet another hot afternoon beside Cousin Sophronia's bed bathing her face with cool water when she heard a horse. Tiptoeing to the window, she cracked the shutter and peered out.

"It's Berry!" Running to meet him, Caroline threw her arms around his neck in relief. He lifted her off her feet and swung her into a gleeful dance.

"The crisis has passed," he shouted. Then he laughed, "The Yankees are here."

Caroline drew back from him in shock. Was he a traitor?

"The Yankees are here," he repeated, reaching for her again. "Safely behind the palisade."

"How?" she cried in disbelief. Dodging his grasp, she repeated, "How?"

"On July 30, just two miles east of Macon, Gen. Howell Cobb, with only a motley force, outfought the Yankees and repulsed Stoneman. The next day Brig. Gen. Alfred Iverson routed the main raiding column at the village of Hillsboro." He clapped his hands in glee. "He captured General Stoneman and 500 men. So you see, they got to Andersonville after all. They're prisoners!"

Caroline stared at him, unable to believe the glad news. Sitting down, smiling as she gradually absorbed the fact that Macon had escaped ruin, she clapped her hands that they all were safe. Jeremy would not have to do battle.

Berry chattered on in high excitement. "The Yankees won't last long there. The prisoners are dying like flies. The Northern press is charging that Wirz and his lieutenants are deliberately murdering them in cold blood. They're calling him the 'Fiend of Anderson-vile,' a 'brute who tortures and kills.'"

Everyone had heard Berry's noisy arrival. Penelope rushed in, and Ret sidled up to whisper that Sophronia wanted him at her bedside. Caroline followed behind as he began the story again. She tried to join in the rejoicing that the crisis had passed, but she stood back in the shadows, washed with the horror of the dreadful accusation that implicated Jeremy.

The fieldhands were singing at their work as August became white with the cotton harvest. Caroline tended to forget her problems and burst into song at her tasks also, with the great relief that the raiding column had been defeated and they could send their guards back to the fields. Caroline was caught up in the happy excitement that filled the plantation as everyone from the youngest children to the oldest women began to work between the shoulder-high cotton plants. She was surprised at the costumes they wore in the heat: layers upon layers of clothing that covered them wetly from the broiling sun. They plucked the fluffy white bolls that matted about oily gray seeds and deposited them in bags, which they wore slung over their shoulders. When the bags were full of cotton, they took them to the ends of the long rows and emptied them on jute squares known as cotton sheets. The corners of the filled sheets were brought up and tied into bundles.

Berry surprised her by supervising the harvest. She smilingly agreed with Penelope that he was growing up at last. His presence made them relax. By flirting with Caroline and teasing the sisters, he made mealtimes fun even though food was scarce.

Cousin Sophronia was up and about now; however, she moved with short, shuffling steps and Shadow snapped at the flapping of her soft, satin slippers. It was silly to think of this weak old woman meaning anyone harm, and Caroline wondered if she were equally foolish in attaching significance to Shadow's growling declaration that Jeremy Medlock was her enemy.

In the daylight hours, Caroline wavered toward the pleasure of Berry's fun-loving company; nevertheless, in the darkness of the night, it was Jeremy's tender smile she saw. She had firmly told them all that she would not marry Berry, and they had ceased to bring up the subject of wedding preparations. Enjoying the increased activity on the farm, especially her small job of riding to the field each evening to tally the weights as the tremendous bundles were hung on a balancing scale then piled high on wagons, she let everything else drift around her. Escaping Chaddy's scolding finger herself, she took no notice of Ret, who was washing windows and sweeping yards. Even Cousin Sophronia found strength to snip dead blossoms and groom her parched garden.

Suddenly, Caroline realized that they were all making preparations for her wedding. The thought hit her with a physical force that turned her mouth to cotton and her knees to water. Sinking to the nearest chair, she stared at Berry, who had just arrived from the village, and hoped, prayed, she had misunderstood.

"Next week this time," he repeated, "you'll be Mrs. Berry Bearden." He leaned down, placing his left arm around her shoulders, his right hand tracing the neckline of her dress. He kissed her possessively. Drawing back with smug satisfaction, he explained, "The preacher is due on the Andersonville circuit this week. We will be married on Sunday."

Gasping, struggling to push him away, she whimpered, "Don't Berry, no!" She hid her blazing face with her hands. "Oh, Berry, I told you I can't be your wife. We're not ready for marriage now! Let's just be friends," she pleaded. "I don't want to hurt you, but . . ." She slipped from his grasp and backed away.

Anger, not hurt, flamed Berry's face. "I've made all of the arrangements." His voice rose shrilly. "You must marry me on Sunday!" He gulped, tried to cover his anger, and placated. "Mama can't live too much longer." He grasped her arm and brought his face close to hers. "We have to marry before she dies."

"I know she'd like to see you married . . ." Caroline tried to squirm away, but his thumb bruised her forearm. ". . . while . . . while she's living, but . . . but . . . she's improving again. We can't rush into—"

"But the preacher is arranged for." Fire snapped from his dark eyes. "He won't be back at this church for another month," he insisted.

"No! No, Berry," she shrieked. "I can't marry you now!" She wrenched from his grasp and fled to the sanctuary of her room.

Over the next few days, he alternately pressed her with attempts at lovemaking and cajoled her with delights of a honeymoon far away. When she continued to refuse, he bombarded her with tirades of guilt-inflicting words that she was going against the wishes of those who had sheltered her. Although she disliked disappointing the sisters, who remained silent through it all, Caroline felt strengthened in her resolve because Berry's behavior made her more certain of her decision.

Sunday passed with little note, except Berry settled into childish sulking. When Monday morning arrived and Penelope announced it was time to take the cotton to the gin house, Caroline felt a weight had been lifted from her shoulders.

Ginning the first bale of cotton was always an event. Cousin Sophronia dressed festively in rustling lavender taffeta far too heavy for the heat and too opulent for the occasion. *Overdressing is the prerogative of the elderly*, thought Caroline, sniffing at her scent of lavender. Cousin Sophronia dried the aromatic gray leaves to perfume her clothing. Thinking that Sophronia looked sweet and pretty, Caroline was delighted that she seemed stronger than usual and was able to enjoy an outing. Chaddy, splendid in snow-white apron and red bandana, helped her to the carriage. Penelope had fastened a fichu of lace to her rusty black dress with a pearl gray cameo. The still-sullen Berry wore a bright new cravat.

Feeling that she could not bear the black silk mourning dress and slippery shawl, Caroline had waited until the last minute and put on her coolest white, flower-sprigged muslin. Old, oft darned and mended, the frock would allow her to have fun. She chose her smallest daytime hoop and daringly donned only two petticoats.

Running out at the last minute, Caroline shook her head when the four started to make room for her in the carriage. She climbed up on the wagon and settled amid the bumps of the bulging cotton sheets beside Ret, who was giggling. Perched around them in the fluffy, greasy cotton, the children from the quarters laughed and chattered. The bundles of cotton were piled so high that, even though they were submerged in softness, they flirted with danger and squealed with delight as the wagon swayed behind the plodding mules.

Image in the Looking Glass

Excitement and singing filled the air as the entourage approached the gin house. Having grown up in town, Caroline had never seen a cotton gin before. The mélange of man and mules and machinery hinted at danger just enough to make it exciting. Sliding down from the wagon, she hurried forward eager to see it all.

The gin house was a large two-story affair. One end was a solid structure, but the greater part of the building jutted out over an open area with no sides except for supporting posts. Caroline leaned in to see what was there. Two sweating mules circled briskly. Shackled to a shrieking wooden wheel, they turned endlessly. Their force moved a wide belt that slanted upward and disappeared through the ceiling. Wanting to see what happened next, Caroline scampered up the steep stairway at the end of the building and entered the dim room closely set under the roof.

Standing by the doorway until her eyes adjusted to the unlit room, she saw that the belt came through the floor and attached to a small, whirling wheel mounted on a wooden box.

"This is the actual gin, missy," remarked the man attending it when he noted her curiosity.

"That little thing?" She had heard so much about Eli Whitney's marvelous invention that she was disappointed at the sight of the shoulder-high box about as wide and deep as she could spread her arms.

"It looks like my dressing table—except that cotton seeds are falling out the front." She grinned at him.

"It works on the principle of a saw pulling the fibers through ribs," the ginner explained as he emptied another basket of cotton over the top and poked it gradually into the opening. "No!" He warned her back as she reached out to touch the cotton. "It'll cut your hand off!"

Caroline watched in fascination until the cotton dust began to cling in the damp golden ringlets about her forehead and tickle her nose. Needing fresh air, she threaded through the crowd of men who were milling about, talking loudly of the fair to middlin' harvest. The noise of the stuffy room and the trembling of the floor made her reach out for the open doorway. Already drawing a deep breath, she started out.

Nothingness yawned beneath her foot. Grabbing frantically for the doorframe to catch herself, Caroline gasped at the sheer drop to the ground far below. There were no stairs. Ropes and pulleys hauled up bundles of cotton. Reeling dizzily from the near fall, Caroline drew back. Hands pressed her shoulders.

As she wrenched around, she saw a wagon piled high with cotton passing below and considered jumping. Then she realized it was only Berry.

"Better be careful," he shouted, pulling her into the room. "Did you see where the cotton comes out of the gin?"

Berry led her to the stairs. Thankful that he was behaving normally again, she followed around to the closed end of the building where the tall, narrow room was filling with luminous puffs of cotton floating like clouds as it came from the tiny gin under the eaves.

"It's so white now and linty." Caroline scratched her nose and stepped backwards into the path of another circling mule. "This is not the safest place I ever saw." She laughed, scrambling out of the way.

"No, it isn't," agreed Berry evenly.

Penelope called to him, and as he joined her, Caroline moved to a safer spot to watch the wooden screw press. This building had a shingled roof but no sides at all. From beneath a pagoda-like extension above the roof, two long log shafts protruded. Again, two mules were circling, this time outside the perimeter of the building. Caroline followed a man who took a split-oak basket of cotton lint from the gin house, carried it across the mule path, climbed the steps under the shelter, and dumped it into the press. High above their heads the tremendous log, chipped out in circling notches to form a screw, was coming down, down, down with each step of the mules. When the cotton was compressed sufficiently for handling, the ram was raised and the wooden doors were swung open on each side. The finished bale was pulled out to be placed on a wagon.

Caroline moved closer to watch as the men fitted the opening with more jute bagging and then slipped the metal bands in place beneath it. Cotton was poured in, the mules were prodded, and the huge screw descended again. Caroline was about to turn away when something displeased the workers, and they opened the door to check the half-finished bale. A boy about her size climbed into the opening that was as long as he was tall and about three feet wide. He stamped around pressing the cotton with his feet.

A shout that the shaft might break drew all of the men away. Caroline bent down to see the huge wooden block that moved as the screw turned.

Hands pushed sharply against her shoulders. Caroline's feet flew up. Her face plunged down, buried in the cotton. Choking on a mouthful of fuzzy lint, she could not cry out as the door swung firmly shut. Intense blackness filled the small space. Wood squeaked against wood as the screw began to turn again bringing the ram down, down, down, making the bed on which she lay nearer and nearer the size of a coffin.

Floundering, struggling, coughing, Caroline fought for breath enough to scream. Rolling on her side, she flailed her fists against the thick wooden walls. The squeaking of the turning screw drowned out her shrieks.

Taut muscles quivered, collapsed. Lying limply, Caroline prayed in snatches, *God, oh dear God, save me, save me!* Hearing the heavy, solid block groaning, pressing down upon her, she knew with terrible dread that with each step of the mules, it descended closer, closer above her face. Death was certain. Papa's teachings seeped through the murk of her brain.

Dear Jesus, take my soul, my spirit. Screams snatched from her throat unbidden. Renewed, she beat the unyielding door with failing strength.

Dazzling golden light streaked into the tomb. *Heaven? Is this heaven?* The door swung wide. Hands pulled her out. Faces swam crazily around her. She focused on one. Jeremy's.

He always sees me do something silly, she thought irrelevantly, then fainted.

Cool water bathed her face. Stirring, she flung out her hand, felt a bed of cotton, struggled and screamed.

"Hush, darling." Jeremy's voice soothed against her ear. "Open your eyes."

Fluttering eyelids let in blessed light. Jeremy bent over her with Berry close behind. Penelope was seated beside her on the cotton sheet bathing her face while Sophronia, Chaddy, Ret, and Robert Abernathy gathered around.

"Thank goodness you heard me," Caroline whimpered at last when she had drunk enough water to relieve fits of coughing.

"We wouldn't have heard you over all the noise," said Jeremy, "if we hadn't been looking for you."

"A piece of your skirt tore and hung outside the door," said Penelope.

"You owe your life to worn out muslin," rasped Berry. "If you'd been wearing your silk dress," he laughed, "it would've slipped right through—"

"Are you hurt anywhere?" interrupted Cousin Sophronia.

Thinking about it for a moment, feeling herself, she realized that she was unhurt and surprisingly calm. "No," Caroline replied. "I'm just embarrassed and . . . too weak and tired to move."

Berry lifted her in his arms and took her to the carriage.

"I'm sorry I spoiled our holiday with such a silly accident," she whispered weakly.

"You are a very careless girl," admonished Penelope.

"Please take care of yourself now," Jeremy said, following behind with his face full of loving concern. His blue eyes locked with Caroline's and spoke eloquently across the widening distance as the carriage drove away.

When they reached home she sank wearily into bed and immediately fell into a deep sleep. Whenever her eyes fluttered open, she saw one of the family group sitting at the bedside. Straining to waken, she apologized again to each one for being so careless. Night fell, and still her strength had not returned. Letting go, she slept.

Screaming and struggling and beating her fists against the pillow, Caroline once again fought death in a cotton-lined coffin. A streak of light came toward her. Chaddy was bending low.

"Hush, chile," she said. Setting the candle beside the bed, she grabbed for a basin as Caroline bent to vomit.

The nightmare and the retching reoccurred throughout the night. When daylight finally came, she breathed a thankful prayer that she had been spared and joyfully watched the sunrise. Gingerly, she moved sore muscles. Pain stabbed, wakened her fully and drove the fuzz from her brain. Recalling the episode with clarity, she clapped her hands over her mouth in horror. She had not stumbled and fallen into the press. She had been pushed.

Trembling violently, Caroline relived that instant when hands had pushed sharply. Sinking into the feather bed, she knew that she had discounted all of the things that had happened since she came to Looking Glass Plantation. There was no discounting those hands. Someone was determined to kill her.

Chapter 12

Berry's hands had been at her back only minutes before the accident, Caroline recalled. Clutching the bedsheet up to her chin, she gnawed her fingers. Had he been about to push her out of the second-story doorway? *Did he pull me back instead when he saw the wagonload of cotton move beneath me to break my fall?* The idea seemed too ridiculous to consider.

Bitterly she knew she should not have let him assume she would marry him. Twisting the sheet, she chastised herself for embarrassing him by waiting to speak definitely until he made arrangements with the preacher. She pushed back her tumble of hair with sweaty palms and tried to control her galloping emotions. Berry expected the granting of every whim, but a small setback would hardly give the fun-loving boy motive for murder.

The bedroom door eased silently open. A watery blue eye peeped through the crack. Seeing that Caroline was awake, Cousin Sophronia shuffled into the room and sank heavily onto the chair beside the bed. Smiling sweetly, she drew a rattling breath and asked, "Are you feeling better after your accident?"

"Yes, ma'am, thank you." Caroline sat up against the pillows and studied Sophronia. Her trembly, blue-veined hands lacked the strength to have pushed her down. Massaging her throbbing temple with her thumb, she tried to remember what Jeremy had said about Sophronia being possessed of sudden vigor when her mind became unbalanced. Berry had also said something about his mother and Ret, but what? Weak, feeling unbearably alone, Caroline needed to reach out to someone.

"Cousin Sophronia," she whispered, "I . . . I . . ." Suddenly, her trusting heart opened and she leaned toward the old lady. Wild-eyed, pale, she let the awful thoughts tumble out. "My senses are clearing—I realize—oh, Cousin Sophronia, it wasn't an accident," Caroline rasped hoarsely. "Someone pushed me!"

Sophronia's faded eyes stared in disbelief. "Huh!" She laughed uncertainly. "Pushed you?" She coughed. "You must be mistaken."

"No. No, I'm not." All doubts were gone from her mind. "Two hands pushed me sharply and slammed the door—just as the door to the smokehouse was deliberately shut. The first time was merely unpleasant. This thing could have—would have killed me . . . if someone hadn't seen my torn skirt hanging out the door." Clutching her head, she tore at her hair. "I just can't understand why someone wants to kill me."

With a long shuddering sigh, Sophronia straightened from her soft folds of flesh. Her eyes hardened, shuttered her thoughts. Speaking with uncharacteristic firmness, she said, "You are such a sweet and lovely girl that it could only be because of your inheritance."

"My inheritance?" Caroline's voice squeaked. She laughed a harsh sound. "Why everything my father had was lost. Even when the war ends, I will have absolutely nothing."

"You will have Looking Glass Plantation."

"Oh," Caroline whimpered, sinking into the feathers. *The poor dear's mind is slipping again.*

"I'm afraid I put your life in jeopardy." Her sagging, wrinkled cheeks jiggled as she shook her head. Sophronia continued in a perfectly rational voice. "I discussed my new will with Robert Abernathy in a place where we could—umh—be overheard."

Chaddy entered with a breakfast tray. Cousin Sophronia moved to the window and commented on the gathering clouds while Chaddy puffed out her cheeks and fussed over setting the tray properly. Watching her suspiciously, Caroline wondered if Chaddy would not want her to become mistress of the plantation? She appeared devoted to Berry. Naturally, she would want it to be his. Even so, she could hardly care enough to kill for it. Caroline reeled in total confusion.

"I don't understand what you're telling me." She picked up the conversation when Chaddy had gone out. Wondering what level Cousin Sophronia's mind was on now, she hoped for the best and asked, "Surely the plantation should go to Berry?"

"No-o-o." Shaking her head, Sophronia returned to her chair. "No, there are two reasons why it should not be his." She coughed. "The first is surely apparent to you. Whenever taking on responsibility is required, Berry runs away. He would lose the homeplace in no time at all." She pushed back straggling wisps of gray hair and spoke reflectively, sadly. "I can't blame Berry really. It's my fault for always taking the easy way out instead of teaching him discipline. I allowed Penelope and Chaddy to spoil him shamelessly," she said, sighing. "Josiah died just about the time Berry became old enough to really need a man's strong hand. Josiah was never much help anyway." She shrugged. "He gave him his name and a home, but he never really loved him."

"Gave his name?" Caroline shook her head. She could not seem to follow Sophronia's line of thought in her weakened state.

"Yes, I thought surely you realized when you examined the ambrotype and commented on the dissimilarity that Berry was not Josiah's son." She paused for a moment and looked at Caroline. "But *you* are blood kin to Josiah, and the plantation should stay in the Bearden line."

Looking away from her to conceal her shock, Caroline saw Penelope standing in the doorway. Sophronia followed her gaze and changed the subject to the approaching storm. While the sisters discussed the weather and the state of Caroline's health, she tried to digest the fact that Sophronia's husband was not the father of her son. Her enigma was complete. A woman of her breeding and character would never be the subject of such indiscretion.

Watching them covertly, Caroline realized that this was the second time Sophronia had stopped talking about leaving her the property. Since Penelope seemed delighted at the prospect of her becoming mistress of the plantation and continuing the work she had begun, Caroline decided that she must not know of Berry's parentage. The picture Sophronia presented was the soul of propriety. Relieved when they left together, Caroline sank into the feathers, glad to postpone discussing the will further.

The four walls seemed to press closer, closer, and by afternoon Caroline could stand the room no longer. Sliding down from the high bed, she folded to the floor like a rag doll. Forcing quivering muscles to grab and hold, she stood hanging on to the bed curtains until she steadied. With trembling fingers, she fumbled to put on the layers of her clothing. Sitting in the chair by the window, she tried to reason with herself that these walls protected her. The unknown assailant would not have the temerity to attack the safety of the bedroom. A footstep in the hall made her gulp breath and watch the door with frightened eyes until the sound died away. Exhaling, she dropped her head in her hands, then shook herself and straightened her shoulders with determination. She must escape the confines of the room.

It could only have been Berry who pushed her. Much as she dreaded to face him, she had to know. Gingerly, she stepped into the hall. Ret glided around a corner. Obviously, she had been watching. Unnerved, Caroline stumbled back into the room. Her pale face stared back at her from the looking glass. Madly curling blond hair stuck out in all directions. Chiding herself for foolishness, she brushed and smoothed her hair on the chance of encountering Berry.

Why did her emotions continually vacillate where he was concerned? She wanted to flee from him. She sighed and grimaced as she whacked the hairbrush on the marble-topped dresser. Yet she wanted to run away with him.

Wandering into the library thinking a book would calm her, she looked through the shelves well stocked with rare old volumes and the latest magazines published before the war interrupted further acquisition. Silence pushed the enemy spaces of her mind, set her scalp tingling, forced her to seek sound. The music room beckoned. Rippling chords over the mother-of-pearl keys of the beautiful piano, she began to relax, filling her mind and the lonely cavities of her soul with a Mozart sonata. Reaching for a treble passage, she glimpsed movement behind her right shoulder. Banging the keys with a jangling, teeth-sharpening pling, she whirled.

Berry stared sullenly, wordlessly. Silence shivered between them. Standing with his hands behind his back, he forced a left-sided smile as he tried to pull his charm into place. Failing, he whipped out a newspaper, rattled it under her nose, and laughed harshly, cracking the silence into fragments around them.

"Your friend, Medlock, has gained notoriety—in the North." He jounced from one foot to the other and spoke jerkily. "What was he doing . . . at the gin yesterday . . . anyway?"

Silently, Caroline took the paper he shook at her. Edging away from him where she could see him better, lessen his power over her, she glanced at the article that he had indicated with a thumping finger. With buzzing ears and pulsing throat, she read the Northern newspaper's scathing indictment of Captain Wirz and his cohorts. She bit her lip painfully. Jeremy's name was on the list. The paper charged them with maliciously, willfully, and traitorously conspiring to impair and injure the health and destroy the lives of soldiers of war to weaken the armies of the United States, in violation of the laws and customs of war. Casting sidewise glances at Berry who danced nervously about the room, Caroline hurried over specific charges against Captain Wirz of thirteen murders: three shot, one stamped to death, one beaten to death on the head with a revolver, two confined in stocks until they died, one bound neck and feet with chains and iron balls, four ordered shot by a sentinel, one pursued by ferocious dogs to his death. All thirteen were unknown prisoners. She wiped her eyes and forehead with her sleeve and shuddered with revulsion at the horror.

"Is this really true?" Caroline whispered through nausea rising in her throat.

Berry shrugged. "What does it matter?" He plinked, plinked, plinked one note on the piano.

Wanting to scream, to shout at him, Caroline prowled the room picking things up, putting them down, fighting to control her temper, her tongue. Studying him through narrow eyes, she saw his petulant lower lip curl as he slouched over the keyboard. Back straight and chin up, Caroline felt suddenly secure in her superior maturity. She was no longer afraid of him.

"Jeremy doesn't . . ." She cleared her throat and leaned on the piano. Waiting until he looked up into her face, she repeated, "Jeremy doesn't enter into what's between us." She flashed a dimpled smile and touched his sleeve. "I like you too much as my cousin to think of you as a—a lover," she inflected as much teasing lilt as she could muster. "You're fun as a friend . . ." Seeing his set jaw soften, she hurried on. "Did you shut me in the smokehouse," she laughed, "to affect a romantic rescue?"

"Heh, heh, heh," he chuckled guiltily.

Frowning as she considered the admission, she still could not imagine him pushing her into the cotton press. Knowing she could hardly ask him that question, she began an indirect approach. "Your mother's just told me about her will. Berry, surely you realize that I knew nothing—"

"You wasted no time ingratiating yourself to her."

"I had no ulterior motive." Caroline pressed her palm on her forehead and tugged at her curls. "I would love her dearly . . . if . . . if I could be sure how she really feels about me. Berry!" She clutched his sleeve as he swiveled the stool away to avoid her scrutiny. "You know she didn't mean it. She must've made the change in one of the times her mind—"

"No!" he flung out bitterly. He looked at her with hard, glittering eyes. "She intended to do it! Aunt Nell agrees that you'd make a far better plantation manager than I." He pulled away from her and stalked to the window, muttering, "Since the war, women are beginning to run things."

For long moments they stood in silence. When he turned to face her, his agitated movements ceased and his charm had taken surface control. "No matter!" The corners of his mouth lifted. "Mother is leaving me other assets. I don't care about—" He shrugged nonchalantly, "—a pile of dirt."

"But the plantation is your home!" Caroline insisted. "I have no right—"

"Better take it and be glad," he interrupted. "You seem determined to pursue that murderer, Medlock. He has nothing to give you."

Anger flared and she stood trembling, fists clenched, knowing he had bested her.

He strolled from the room, then thrust his head back in the door to add bitterly, "The Yankees will soon crush the Confederacy. All of this beauty . . . is chaff!"

Weakness drained her. Quivering from the encounter, Caroline sank to the stool and laid her head against the piano. The world she had known was crashing around her. Remembering the security of her childhood, she longed for her father to take her by the hand and show her which way to turn. She could not judge. Nothing here was ever as it seemed. Crumpling the Yankee newspaper with angry fists, she groaned through clenched teeth. Almost against her will, she smoothed it out and reread the horrible accusations. Suddenly unable to control her tears, Caroline fled into the garden. Heedlessly, she plunged along bisecting paths and collapsed in the shelter of the gazebo. With her sobbing drowning sound, she heard no footsteps. A shadow fell across her.

"Caroline!" Jeremy gasped. With an involuntary groan of pain, he dropped to one knee before her and pried her fingers from her face. "Darling, darling," he blurted anxiously. Holding both hands, he brushed his mustache across them as he kissed each fingertip. He searched her tear-streaked face. "What's wrong?" When she could not control her tears to answer, he sat beside her, cuddling her small body in his arms, stroking her hair, and murmuring soft sounds as if she were a child.

The sweet scent of his breath, warm against her face as he kissed the ringlets on her forehead overwhelmed her with longing. Forgetting the terrible accusations, she nestled into a secure world, the circle of his arms.

"Oh, Jeremy, Jeremy." Pressing against the rough material of his uniform jacket, she felt the hard muscles of his arms as her hands moved upward and twined sweetly around his neck. His enfolding embrace tightened, sending currents surging through her. Lifting her innocent face toward his, she gazed wonderingly into his darkly troubled eyes. Sighing, she lowered her lashes and received his kiss with trembling lips.

"Caroline. Caroline, my darling, I . . ." His mouth sought hers again, and he kissed her responsive lips urgently. For long moments they existed alone in a joyful, golden world.

Reluctantly, he released her. "My angel," he whispered huskily. "Tell me . . ." He held her away to look into her face with eyes that had lost some of their own misery in tender concern for her. "Tell me what's wrong." He cleared his throat of betraying emotion. "Were you injured more seriously in your accident than I thought?"

"It . . . it wasn't an accident," Caroline stammered. She pressed her hands against cheeks she knew to be blazing as she felt twinges deep within her body that she had never experienced before. Pushing back damp ringlets from her forehead, she held back with the sudden realization of decorum. "I told you of—of the strange things that've happened since I came here."

"Yes." He nodded and his hair tumbled over his forehead. "That someone was trying to frighten you away. But surely—"

"No, no, I'm certain of this. Someone tried to kill me! Since they couldn't get rid of me by making me leave . . ." She drew in a deep, shuddering breath. ". . . they chose a . . . permanent way."

"If only I had a home to offer you," he whispered hoarsely as his fingers clutched her arm.

Ducking her head away from his pained eyes, Caroline ached with hope that he meant more than mere refuge. She longed to cry out that all she needed was his love. Instead, she whispered, "I have nothing either."

Drawing in his breath openmouthed as if to say more, he shook his head. In a flat voice he said, "You must be mistaken. No one would want to harm a dear, sweet girl like you."

"I'm not mistaken. Someone pushed me sharply and shut the door! Berry as good as admitted that he locked me in the smokehouse. I embarrassed and angered him by refusing to marry him. But this—I can't believe he—"

"If he loved you enough to ask you to marry him, he wouldn't hurt you."

"There's more." Blushing again, she looked down at her twisting hands. "Cousin Sophronia has changed her will . . . to leave . . . Looking Glass Plantation to me." She gazed up at him, pleading for understanding. "I didn't know about it until today . . . and, of course, Berry should have it, not me . . ."

Jeremy's jaw muscles twitched. Otherwise motionless, he did not move physically; yet, a desolate sensation washed over her as he seemed to draw away.

"Now that I know about this," Caroline hurried on, "I can see that any or all of them could want me dead. Even Cousin Sophronia. She's been better recently, but her mind does such . . . strange reversals."

They sat stiffly, self-consciously looking away, staring through the doorway of the gazebo at the light rain beginning to fall. Protected by the shingled roof and shutters, they huddled together, yet apart, fully infected with misery.

"I don't know what to do." Jeremy sighed. "I want to take you with me this minute! Perhaps the will does provide a motive. I need to get you . . . somewhere safe." He kissed her clenched fists and surveyed her with worried eyes. Driving rain pricked through the latticed wall of the gazebo. "I'm on horseback. After the shock your system's had in the last twenty-four hours, you might become ill if you were soaked with rain. I could come back in the morning with a carriage and take you to Robert Abernathy. Perhaps, he will help us find a solution."

"I hadn't thought of him. He doesn't seem to like me," she murmured, "but he may know the answer."

"The problem is tonight." He waved his hands in a helpless gesture. "How can we keep you safe?" He stood, towering over her. "Maybe Miss Sophronia will allow Ret to stay in your room."

"I'm more afraid of Ret than anyone else." Caroline laughed ruefully. "I'll keep Shadow in my room. She's so old that she usually sleeps more soundly than I, but maybe she would growl if an enemy came in . . ." She paused, embarrassed.

"I didn't know she disliked anyone besides me." Jeremy laughed gruffly. "It's fixing to pour. Come on. Let's get you in the house before you get too wet."

Watching Jeremy ride away down the rain-drenched avenue of magnolias, Caroline told herself that Berry and Shadow must be wrong about him. She waited until he was completely out of sight before going through the hall and out onto the dogtrot to call Shadow from her lily-bed hiding place. Even with the faithful dog under her bed, Caroline knew she would spend a sleepless night fearfully watching the bedroom door. It would be many hours before Jeremy would return.

Chapter 13

Morning came at last, but Jeremy did not return. The mournful tattoo of rain had continued throughout the sleepless night. Reassured by the scent of Shadow, Caroline had lain smiling, reliving the warmth of Jeremy's embrace, the excitement of his kisses, the declaration of his love. From the first light of dawn until midmorning, she sat by the bedroom window and watched the dripping black-green magnolias. But Jeremy did not appear.

Gnawing in her stomach told Caroline it was nearing noon. Worry rats chewed the cords of her newfound love. Jeremy had not said he loved her, she now recalled. He had not hinted a marriage proposal. Pacing the goldenrod carpet, she clasped and unclasped her hands. His whispered endearments had been tender, sweet, comforting. Touching her lips, she felt again the thrilling kisses. "Oh, Jeremy," she moaned. She stood still. Feeling that she was blushing to the soles of her feet, Caroline relived the unladylike way she had thrown herself at Jeremy Medlock.

Clopping hooves and squealing springs sent her flying to the window. A fringed-topped carriage swayed up the drive. Snatching up her bonnet and reticule, Caroline bounded down the stairs two at a time. "Oh, Jeremy, I worried that . . . ," she babbled as she ducked under the fluttering top. Astounded, she stopped with one foot on the carriage step. The driver was not Jeremy.

Swallowing disappointment and fear, Caroline searched her memory. The boy looked familiar. Her shoulders drooped with relief. He had come with the Wirz family to the barbecue. Tall and thin, he looked as though his whole body had been drawn with a single stroke of a pen; and she judged him to be about sixteen. She supposed he must be Wirz's son.

Dropping back to the ground as the carriage lurched, she greeted him with a pleasant, "Good morning."

Without returning the customary salutation, he tugged at the nervous horse and replied in a voice that twanged harshly on her ears, "Miss Caroline Hannah?"

"Yes," she nodded.

"I got a word from Lieutenant Medlock." He handed her a note.

Camp Sumter
August 9, 1864

My Dearest Caroline,
I am terribly sorry that I could not come in person. The heavy rain yesterday undermined a stretch of the palisade wall. We have crews working in the rain to repair the stockade, and I could not leave with such a threat of mass escape.
This lad will conduct you to see Solicitor Abernathy.

Your obedient servant,
Lt. Jeremy Medlock CSA.

Oh, Jeremy, I need you, I need you, she thought, hugging both hands to her shoulders and rocking miserably. She had no idea how to approach the stern-faced Mr. Abernathy.

"Perhaps I'll wait until the weather..." Caroline murmured. Wiping raindrops from her face, she stumbled backward. A burning sensation of eyes upon her back made her whirl. Chaddy stood on the veranda, openly watching. Torn, afraid to go without Jeremy but more afraid to keep staying in this house, she decided swiftly. She raised her voice with a confidence she did not feel. "Aunt Chaddy, please tell my cousins that I have business in Andersonville."

"You know Miss Frony won't want you a-going with this here stranger," Chaddy muttered, scowling.

Caroline wavered uncertainly on the carriage step.

"I cain't leave Ol' Miss," said Chaddy as she twisted her apron in dismay. "But I'll send the girl wi' you. Just you wait now," the old woman commanded.

The moment Chaddy turned her broad back, Caroline jumped into the carriage and motioned the boy to leave. The last thing she wanted was Ret along, spying.

Resolutely, Caroline faced the wet road ahead. They drove silently for the first miles as she tried to collect herself and plan a course of action. Still weak and confused from the accident, she could not think clearly. She knew only that she must fend for herself from moment to moment.

Turning to look at the boy for the first time, she began an idle conversation about the unusual amount of rain. He replied in a voice with no trace of the foreign accent so prevalent in Captain Wirz's speech. She surmised that he must have grown up in this country when Wirz was a physician in Louisiana. She wondered, however, why he spoke rapidly with no trace of Creole, no polished manners. Puzzled about his origin, she changed the subject to the lack of food.

"Yeah, all we've had lately was milk, cornbread, and sear-ip," he said from the side of his mouth.

Her ears pricked; and suddenly her attention, which had been totally self-centered, turned fully upon him. He had said milk, not sweetmilk or buttermilk as most folks did. Just milk. Stunned, she blinked, swallowed. He had pronounced syrup, "sear-ip." Every Southerner she had ever known said "sur-up."

"Where are you from?"

"New York."

A Yankee! He must be an escaped prisoner, taking her hostage.

The carriage was rolling swiftly down a steep grade. She could not jump. Wishing she had listened to Chaddy, she clutched the arm of the seat and looked about for some means of escape. Woods closed darkly about the road, slippery, boggily wet. Breathing in excited jerks, Caroline wondered how he had gotten Jeremy's note.

The note. Frantically, she untied the drawstrings of her reticule and fished out the paper he had handed her. Jeremy had mentioned the boy. Limp with relief, she turned questioning eyes upon her driver.

"Who . . . are you?" Her voice sounded sharper than she intended.

"I thought ya knew." He shrugged. "Skinny Hendryx. Drummer boy for the Seventh New York Volunteers." He puffed out his chest with pride. "Captain Wirz felt sorry for me. Being in the prison, ya know. He took me into his home. Didn't nobody tell ya? I stay with his wife 'n three little girls."

Dumbfounded, Caroline stared at him. She continued to clutch the seat and cast sidelong glances into the forest.

"Com' on." He grimaced shortly. "Ain't nothing going to hurt ya." He added soothingly, "Lieutenant Medlock knows the Captain trusts me. I ride his old gray mare and take 'em his prison keys." He grinned broadly and scrubbed at his nose with a dirty finger. "Com' on. The lieutenant trusts me to take care o' his lady."

Blushing and confused, Caroline could think of nothing to say. His tale of kindness at the hands of the Commandant was a true picture of the man she had seen at the barbecue—a man who bore no resemblance to the monster in the Northern newspaper articles. Dared she hope this proved them wrong?

When they drove up the hill into Andersonville, Caroline saw Anne Head crossing the street and told Skinny she would take leave of him there. "Anne, Anne," she called excitedly with the hopes raised that she might offer refuge. Holding her hat, she ran to catch up.

"Caroline, dear." Anne turned and embraced her warmly. "How lovely to see you. How is everyone at Looking Glass?" Her voice lifted sweetly, politely, but her face was lined with a harried expression, and her eyes sought a spot over Caroline's shoulder.

"Everyone . . . is fine," Caroline panted, ready to pour out her troubles, tell her of the accident and her certainty that someone was trying to kill her. "We all went . . . to the gin . . . and something happened that—"

"That's nice," she interrupted with a distracted look. "Things are terrible here, terrible! When you and I were out collecting supplies, our hospital had a thousand patients. Now we have two thousand. The death toll is staggering." She pushed back gray hair bristling from the black. "I wish I could visit with you and hear about your fun at the gin, but Doctor is waiting for this." She indicated the basket on her arm. "These roots and barks and old home remedies are all of the medicine we have." Anne Head hurried away, clicking her tongue and repeating, "Terrible, terrible."

Caroline stood with unused words hanging on her sagging lips. She had not wanted to believe the newspaper, but it must be true. If so many men were dying here, the accusations against Wirz must have foundation. Not knowing what to believe, she anguished that Jeremy shared the blame.

Having thought Anne a true friend, Caroline felt deflated that the doctor's wife was too caught up in her own duties to listen to her fears. The only hope of aid lay with Robert Abernathy. Asking directions to his house, she staunchly marched down the street. A spattering of rain spotted her rustling black skirt.

Her knock was answered by a bent old manservant. He beamed at her with surprising recognition and conducted her into the solicitor's office.

"Good afternoon, my dear." Abernathy rushed forward graciously and seated her with a flourish. "Zebulon, get Miss Caroline some refreshment." With a relaxed air that attending her needs was the most important part of his day, he beamed at her from behind an enormous desk. Patting his fingertips together, he asked, "Now, what does Miss Sophronia need to bring you out on such a rainy day?"

"Uh, well, sir," she stammered. Her carefully rehearsed speech flew from her brain like a frightened bird. "Cousin Sophronia . . ." she cleared her throat. "She didn't send me. I . . . I need your help." Seeing his thick, white eyebrows bristle into a frown, Caroline hurried on. "I know she depends upon you, and I didn't have anyone else to turn to . . ." She leaned forward and her black silk shawl slipped to the floor.

"Yes? What is it you need?" His voice became crisp with impatience now that he knew she was not here on behalf of his client.

"I wondered if you could . . . help me get some funds. Surely there's something from my father's estate—or some way I could borrow against . . ." His stern expression intimidated her completely. She dared not mention inheriting from Cousin Sophronia. "I really must leave Looking Glass. I'm not wanted there."

Silently, the lawyer surveyed her with a contemptuous frown. He opened his mouth as if to speak, then pursed his lips as he assessed her. The insistent ticking of the grandfather's clock echoed in the silent room.

Caroline's fingers clutched nervously at the netting of her reticule, shaking it. The jingling of a few coins reminded her this was the extent of her entire fortune. A bright red spot shone in each pale cheek as she realized that he did not intend to reply. "Cousin Penelope invited me for a visit . . ." She floundered, gritting her teeth with determination to explain the situation. "But from the first moment they saw me, I felt unwelcome."

"I don't wonder." He leaned back in the chair with his hands fastened in his coat lapels. "You closely resemble your mother."

"What possible difference does that make?" she exclaimed.

"None really." He smoothed back his white hair. His mouth twitched as he obviously held back words he wished to say.

Disconcerted, losing confidence, Caroline bit her lip. "It's more than feeling unwelcome." She sighed. Looking at the heavy dust on everything except the tops of the furniture, she surmised that there was no woman in this house. Discouraged that she would find neither understanding nor refuge here, she gave up. Rising to leave, she realized that she had nowhere to go. Her knees buckled and she sank back in the chair. She must try again. As quickly as possible, she described the episode of the witch.

". . . of course, I don't believe in witches," she finished, "but, but fright—or harm was intended. And then I was locked in the smokehouse. Oh, Berry half-admitted doing that too . . ." she paused, blushing. "But the accident at the gin. That was serious. I could have been killed."

He narrowed his eyes. "You are a very careless young lady."

"No, sir. You must believe me. I was pushed! There is someone on the plantation who wants to be rid of me. Suddenly, she remembered his face in the group around her. "You were at the gin when it happened. Did you see who was close to me?"

Livid, he lost control of his polished manners. "The people at Looking Glass have been highly respected throughout the generations." He bit off his words angrily. "There has never been a breath of scandal about any of them. Miss Penelope's a fine woman. Brilliant. And she gave you a home even though she pegged you as a fortune hunter." His voice rose shrilly. "I will not allow you to malign this family."

Anger outdistanced fear, good sense. "I am not a fortune hunter!" Caroline stamped her foot and shook her fists. "I don't want the plantation," she shouted, near hysteria. "Berry should have it! I didn't even know 'til yesterday . . ." She swallowed and tried to tone down her vehemence. ". . . that Cousin Sophronia had willed it to me. It's all your fault! You should not have allowed her to change her will. Her mind is not right. One moment she loves me and the next she forgets who I am and starts accusing me of evil deeds . . ."

"Did you come here thinking I'd declare that fine woman insane?" He jumped to his feet. "She was wrong to change her will in your favor. But there are ways to get around that. And if you think I'll turn the plantation over to you now, you're sadly mistaken." He stamped across the room and flung the door open.

Caroline saw Zebulon entering the hall carrying a silver tray laden with food. Her empty stomach gurgled hungrily as he stopped in astonishment when Abernathy waved him away.

Image in the Looking Glass

Bowing stiffly, the distinguished gentleman opened the front door himself.

"Frantically, she tried one last protest. "You misunderstand. I feel my life is in danger. If I could just have enough money for train fare to Macon, some of my Wesleyan friends would surely help me!"

Watching him purse his thin lips and narrow his eyes, she could tell that he would never listen to her pleas. Swinging her reticule, Caroline tried to look him in the eye with her chin jutting proudly as she went by him at the entrance. He refused to meet her gaze. As he slammed the heavy door behind her, she felt he had closed her last avenue of escape.

Standing in the street, which was now a rushing river of red mud, Caroline looked at the deserted town in a daze. Hunger gnawed so sharply that her only thought was anger that she had been dismissed without the promised refreshments.

A streak of lightning split a sky as black as her mood. Clouds ripped open. Water dumped upon her as if someone overturned a bucket. Running toward Benjamin Dykes' General Store, she stumbled inside. The rumble of voices and coarse chuckles ceased suddenly as the group of men, seated in rocking chairs or perched on boxes, tapped one another and motioned toward her.

"May I . . . wait out the storm—here?" Her voice squeaked with timidity as all eyes focused on her wet form.

"Sure thang, ma'am." A slight fellow grinned around a cheekful of tobacco. "Patui . . ." He spit. ". . . come in."

"Here, miss, have my chair." Another man jumped up and waved her into a rocker set slightly apart from the group.

Self-consciously, she looked around the dimly lit store as the conversation, punctuated by streams of tobacco juice, resumed halfheartedly. A mélange of merchandise hung on nails driven into the unfinished walls or swung from ropes tied to the rafters. Many shelves were empty, thick with musty dust. Spider webs curtained a space marked "Coffee."

Caroline's nose twitched at the mixture of tobacco and oiled floorboards and from the potpourri of smells picked the aroma of cheese. Her mouth watered as she looked at the inviting round wheel of cheese, but she hesitated to spend the few coins in her reticule. She rubbed her stomach and tried to forget hunger.

Time seemed measured by the rain thundering on the tin roof. The watch pinned to her bodice had shown three o'clock when she entered. Now it showed four, and still there had been no letup. The men shifted, as uneasy in her presence as she was in theirs. Shivering, she stared out at the storm.

She had left her shawl at Abernathy's, but she resolved never to return for it. She supposed she would have to go back sometime to Looking Glass Plantation to retrieve her belongings, but she did not want to spend another sleepless night there.

Even when the rain ceased, what could she do? Anne Head was her only friend. Although she was busy and distracted, Caroline had nowhere else to turn. She paced to the door and looked out. No light emanated from the small shack Anne had pointed out as home. Caroline had no idea where to find her. Gritting her teeth, she thought she had never seen it rain so hard.

Suddenly a soldier burst through the door. "We need every able bodied man," he yelled. "The palisade is washing away! All the prisoners will escape!" He waved a summoning arm. "Y'all come on."

Every man jumped to his feet except the aproned shopkeeper who drawled, "What happened, Zeke?"

"The branch rose five feet. Water rushed across the naked ground of the pen and undercut the wall." Zeke waved both arms excitedly. "A hundred feet a' the west wall was swept plum away, clean as a whistle!"

Just as the men rushed for the door, a loud blast made Caroline jump. A second echoing blast sent her away from the door, nearer to the shopkeeper.

"The officer-of-the-day must have fired the two cannon in the Star Fort," he said in a drawn out syllables, "to prevent a mass escape."

His words gave her no comfort. They remained in anxious silence broken only by a pang, pang, pang, as drops from a leak in the roof hit a tin plate.

Another man stamped in slushing mud from his boots. "We need more shovels," he said. "It's bad! The officers are standing with arms at the ready in the downpour. Troops and working parties will spend a sleepless night trying to mend the breach." He wiped rain from bushy eyebrows and shook his head.

"What of the prisoners? Are many escaping?" asked the shopkeeper.

"Most of 'em are standing back laughing." He took off his hat and scratched tousled hair. "They've started a singsong taunt. 'That is good for you, Rebs. That's the way your Confederacy'll fall. Grant and Sherman are making . . . bigger holes than these.'"

With a whimpering cry, Caroline burst into long-held-back tears. The ruddy man glanced at her over his shoulder and hurried out into the rain. Embarrassed, the shopkeeper rubbed his hands on his apron.

"There, there, miss,' he soothed. "Our boys'll handle 'em. Don't you fret now—" The roar of a cannon made him wince.

"I must get back to Looking Glass Plantation." Caroline gulped sobs, surprised at the sound of her own voice. "My cousins won't know about this. They won't be on guard."

"Miss Penelope's a strong woman. She'll manage." He shrugged and added offhandedly, "There's always danger these days."

"But not like this,' Caroline wailed. "It's different if one or two slip away through the woods. If they escape en masse, they could murder my family in their beds and ride away on the mules." A nearly hysterical giggle escaped her as she thought that they would not get far if they took old Joe. "I must go to them! Cousin Sophronia is so frail."

Suddenly she knew. She loved Sophronia dearly. Even if the confused woman was trying to kill her, she could not help what she did when her mind went wrong. Pacing between the barrels in the shadowy store, Caroline clutched and unclutched her hands. She had been thinking only of herself, wanting someone to love and care for her. She still longed for their love and respect, but that did not matter now. She was young and strong. She would manage. What mattered was that they needed her love and care. Even Ret.

Snatching up her bag, she started for the door.

"Where are you going?"

"I must go home. The rain is slackening. I'm strong enough to walk a few miles. I don't care if I ruin this old black dress. I hate the ol' thing anyway." Caroline laughed shakily trying to bolster her courage.

"I cain't let you do that," he said tearing his apron in a frenzy. "What if you meet the enemy all alone?"

Caroline's hand froze on the latch. Her blue eyes widened in horror as she visualized his thought. She must get home. But how?

Image in the Looking Glass

Chapter 14

The door banged open. Chilled with terror as she pictured frenzied escapees besetting her, she whirled.

It was only the lad, the Yankee drummer boy.

"Lieutenant Medlock sent me . . ." He grinned and scrubbed his nose. ". . . to see 'bout ya. I've been looking everywhere. Heh-heh-heh." He laughed in boyish uncertainty.

Jeremy must love me if he thought of me in the middle of this crisis. Caroline clasped her hands to her heart and trembled with relief. She studied Skinny Hendryx. Dare she ask him to take her home?

Sighing heavily, she could think of no alternative. There was no one else to ask except Abernathy. Stubborn pride would not let her return to him. Narrowing her eyes, she recalled that he had been at the gin and seen the accident for himself. If he did not respond to her fears after that, there was no further use asking for his help.

Caroline turned to the lanky boy and spoke quickly before she lost courage. "Can you take me home? I can't impose on this nice man any longer." She smiled at the shopkeeper.

"Sure." Skinny shrugged. "I'll get a rig."

The gloomy day was sliding toward night when he returned. She climbed into the buggy that he had made as snug as possible by fastening up the leather sides against the rain. The shopkeeper insisted upon giving her a lap robe, but even though they huddled under it, they were thoroughly soaked before they had gone halfway. Trees hunched over the road, dark, dripping. Fearfully, she peered this way and that into the murky depths of the forest. Her breathing came in excited jerks as she expected every moment to encounter escaping masses of soldiers.

Blam! A cannon blast made her jump so hard she hurt.

"Lieutenant Medlock has unlimbered sixteen cannon," he said. "Six of them . . . are twelve-pound howitzers."

"What's a howitzer?" she queried, needing anything to relieve her tortured breathing, her knotted stomach.

"This war's most efficient killer, that's what." He preened, pleased to display his knowledge. "They shoot at short range when charged with a canister." He looked at her for a moment and lifted the lower half of his face in a faulty grin. "Com' on. Your lieutenant'll prevent a mass escape."

He was assuming far too much, she thought, rubbing her stomach. "But how . . . how many will slip away unnoticed in the rain?"

Pressing her fist to her mouth, she visualized the gaping hole in the palisade wall with frenzied, prison-crazed men rushing through. "They could slaughter us all." She gasped, forgetting for a moment that he was one of them. Suddenly her lashes fanned back from wide blue eyes, and she seemed unable to hold back her words. "What about you?"

Hurt washed over his innocent face. "Captain Wirz trusts me. He's been kind," he replied soberly. "Heh-heh-heh. Com' on! How would the likes of me find the way through these woods and swamps back to New York?"

Creak! Creak! The buggy careened and Caroline hung on to the side as it lunged down in a path worn deep between high red clay banks. Water erupted through a gully midway down the hill turning the roadbed into a rushing stream. At the bottom Skinny got out and led the horse by the bit through the red muddy flow. They completed the trip in tight-lipped silence broken only by the howling wind and sluicing rain.

When at last they reached the magnolia-lined lane to Looking Glass Plantation, Caroline asked the boy to stay the night. He refused, saying that Cornelia, Susie, and little Cora all had measles and he must return home in case Mrs. Wirz needed him. He grinned away her thanks and turned back into the swirling rain.

Caroline rushed up the wide brick steps. As she reached for the door, it opened. Chaddy had heard the buggy. She scowled darkly, but Caroline flung herself into the comforting enormity of her broad, soft body in a tremendous hug that jingled Chaddy's gold earrings.

"Oh, Aunt Chaddy," Caroline exclaimed, "it's good to be home! Is everyone safe?"

Cousin Sophronia stepped into the drafty hall. "Caroline, dear, we've—umh—been worried to death!"

Caroline hugged her tightly and kissed her soft, wrinkled cheek. "I'm sorry I worried you. I couldn't get home until the storm let up a little!" Looking over Sophronia's head at Penelope, Caroline mouthed words to Penelope. "I came as soon as I could to warn you of the danger!"

Penelope stood at the door to the parlor, apart from the others. Noting her self-imposed isolation, Caroline remembered Sophronia's words, "Don't hold back, waiting to be loved. Give your love where it is needed whether or not you are loved in return."

Caroline crossed quickly to Penelope and hugged her, too, even though there was no response. Back rigid, arms dangling, Penelope listened as Caroline whispered what had occurred because of the cloudburst. Nodding mutely, she strode purposefully through the door at the back.

Discovering that Caroline had not eaten all day, Cousin Sophronia sent Chaddy outside to the kitchen to get whatever she could find in the pie safe. By the time Caroline had exchanged her wet clothing for a warm wrapper, Chaddy had returned with cold field peas, fried cornbread patties, and a plate of lefts and rights. Even though the tough, brown peas were congealed and the rough-grained cornbread was cold and greasy, Caroline devoured the welcome food ravenously. It surprised her that Penelope had allowed Chaddy to use any of the precious dried peaches to make the lefts and rights, but she consumed the delicious half-moon pies without question.

Cousin Sophronia watched quietly while the hungry girl ate. When she had licked the last flaky crumb from her fingers, the elderly lady shook her sagging cheeks and chided, "You should not have gone into—umh—Anderson all alone. It was unsafe as well as unseemly. What on earth," she said, coughing, "made you do such a thing?"

What indeed? Caroline pushed back her chair and looked into her sweet, concerned face. After the terrible day in town and the long, frightening ride, it seemed so much like coming home that she had quite forgotten how desperately she had wanted to leave this morning. The hands that pushed her into the cotton press belonged to a nightmare from another age after this eon of a day.

"I . . . well, I . . . went to see Mr. Abernathy," Caroline said, searching for tactful words. "I asked him to find out if there is anything at all left from my father's estate." She could not meet the watery eyes. "I cannot keep imposing upon you, Cousin Sophronia, and I do want to go back to Wesleyan and finish my education." She brushed frizzling curls of damp hair away from her cheeks, which turned pink with embarrassment. "My father's death left me quite without funds."

"I should have inquired if you needed any money." Sophronia clicked her tongue. "These days there is nothing to buy. I just didn't think—umh—about your worrying." She shook her escaping gray hair, reached out, and patted Caroline's hand soothingly. "If you needed funds, you had only to ask."

"I've instructed Mr. Abernathy to make arrangements for you to return for the fall term. That is . . ." She struggled for breath. ". . . if the school can remain open with all of this unpleasantness. Until then, my dear, this is your home." Her face wreathed in smiles. "What I have is yours."

Penelope returned at that moment with her hawk eyes darting excitedly. "Will and St. John can guard us best if we all stay together in the morning room," she said briskly. She half-lifted Sophronia to her feet and assisted her to the other room without fully answering her vaguely murmured questions.

Caroline followed them. *Until the dangerous situation at the prison is under control, I won't be alone,* she thought. After that, she must simply be wary. Today was the ninth of August. The fall school term would soon begin. If she felt threatened again, she would merely ask Cousin Sophronia for train fare on the pretext of going early to visit a school chum.

They settled Sophronia as comfortably as possible on a couch. Caroline pulled a chair close beside her. Rubbing sandy eyes, she determined to stay awake. She smiled down at Sophronia, so frail, so hard of hearing. If the enemy came, she must be there to help her stand the shock. Caroline dozed and wakened with a listening start as a board creaked. It was a process repeated throughout the long night.

Morning came at last, but the sun did not shine. In an agony of tension, Caroline stood looking out at the gray skies. She could not stop thinking of the now 30,000 wretched men completely exposed to the elements. Pacing, she wondered if Jeremy was still in control.

The door to the morning room squeaked open. It was only Penelope coming back after making a check of the guards. The tension was becoming unbearable, and Caroline decided to suggest that they try to get to Americus. They would certainly be safer in town than out here alone. Thunder made her jump before she could speak. Brilliant streaks of lightning split the sky. Again rain poured. Looking at Cousin Sophronia lying limply on the couch, Caroline knew that she could not stand the ten-mile trip into town in a storm.

Resolutely, Caroline knelt on the hearth and built a small fire. It was not cold, but the blaze would add cheer and keep the lightning from being such a startling contrast. With cymbals of thunder for accompaniment, she read poetry to the ladies until tension drew the muscles between her shoulders and her head ached.

She returned to the window to rest and rub her neck. Most of the backyard, which was bare dirt swept daily, was now a large red puddle. When she sat down again, Cousin Sophronia handed Caroline her Bible and asked her to read the book of Luke. Caroline's voice was becoming hoarse when she reached the passage in the ninth chapter where Jesus asked his disciples who he is and received the great confession that he is the Christ, the Messiah sent from God. Slowly she read verses twenty-three and twenty-four, "If any man will come after me, let him deny himself, and take up his cross daily, and follow me. For whosoever will save his life shall lose it: but whosoever will lose his life for my sake, the same shall save it."

Caroline looked up at the sisters. Sophronia had fallen asleep. Penelope, who had moved to the window, was obviously not listening to her. Reflecting upon the conversation she and Sophronia had had so long ago, she was embarrassed to remember how she had thought Sophronia a hypocrite. These words had seemed impossible. Surprised, Caroline realized that she had begun to put Sophronia first without thinking about it, simply because she loved her. Sophronia was right that sharing God's kind of love means seeking the highest good for the other person.

Like an inchworm, the day crawled infuriatingly into another night spent huddled together with no way of knowing what was happening in the prison or the village. Caroline's whole body seemed numb with this idle, passive waiting.

Another day dawned at last, the eleventh of August. Torrents of rain still enclosed the house in a gray sheet. How long would it hold them captive? A band of nerves closed tightly around her chest, strangling breath.

When the storm abated on the evening of the twelfth, Caroline ventured onto the veranda. Stretching toward the joyous colors of a rainbow, she smiled at its promise. As she watched it, the figure of a rider was etched against the glow. Again fear leaped.

"It's Berry!" Penelope shouted in her ear.

He whooped and waved his high silk hat as he neared. "The situation is under control!"

"You always come with good news!" His aunt broke her accustomed reserve to kiss his cheek.

After the current danger is averted, Caroline thought to herself.

Berry greeted them with exuberant hugs. "Old General Winder 'bout lost his nerve." He grinned. "Yesterday he telegraphed Adjutant General Cooper that the two days of tremendous rain had damaged the stockade so much that he didn't know if the whole force could save it. He told him not to send any more prisoners." He waved his hands excitedly and spoke in a rush. "Can you believe that another trainload arrived today?"

"Why in the world do they keep sending them?" Caroline demanded. "When it's already so horribly overcrowded?"

"There's a food shortage in Richmond," he explained as they went into the house. "The only answer is to construct another stockade here. The trouble is . . ." He reached out for her, but she side-stepped. ". . . it's taken everything right now simply to repair the breach. The nearest steam-powered sawmill is at Smithville. That's twenty-three miles away!"

The tinkling sound of delicate china breaking drew them down the hall into the morning room. Cousin Sophronia's arm dangled from the couch. She stared straight ahead unmindful of the broken cup at her fingertips. She had barely eaten during their self-imposed confinement; yet, her face and neck and hands looked fat.

Feeling her own gaunt cheek, Caroline realized suddenly that Sophronia was swollen rather than fat. Bending over the couch, she asked softly, "Are you all right, Cousin Sophronia? What can I get for you?"

Peering unseeingly, turning her head, squinting blurred eyes, she mumbled incoherently.

Caroline spoke loudly and distinctly hoping to pierce her confusion. "Berry is here. He brought good news. Our danger is over. Your son is here."

Berry knelt beside her and patted her hand. "I'm here, Mother. What do you need?"

"Not—my son," she said weakly.

Taking the lifeless arm, Caroline searched for her pulse. When at last she located a fluttering throb, she was unable to make a count. She could tell only that the heartbeat was irregular. "Berry," she whispered, "you'd better try to get Dr. Head."

"Yes, Berry, you must hurry for the doctor," echoed Penelope close behind. "Hurry," she emphasized. "We'll get her into bed. Make her more comfortable."

Straightening aching shoulders, Caroline looked at Penelope. On the occasions of the other attacks, her face had been set. She had remained her usual calm, detached self. Now her eyes showed obvious fear and her ministering hands shook.

Standing, Berry grasped Caroline's arm with biting fingers. "Caroline, she may be about to die. Please say you will marry me right away while she's living."

Sophronia's head rolled back. Her mind grasped his words even though she could not seem to speak connected sentences. She focused her eyes on the stunned girl. "Don't—die, Adeline—die. Go—go-o-o." She sank into unconsciousness.

"Berry is right," Penelope said solemnly. "She may not live to see it unless you are married immediately."

Chapter 15

"No! No, don't speak of that now." Caroline recoiled. "Hurry for the doctor." Shoving him with flattened palms, she emphasized her command. He did not budge, and her voice shrilled into a wail. "I don't want her to die."

Berry's cold-eyed stare paralyzed her for a seeming eternity; then he whirled away. Caroline dropped into a chair and buried her face in her hands. She did not want to lose Cousin Sophronia. She knew now that she loved her no matter what hateful words issued from her mouth when she was out of her head. Shivering, straining, she needed to cry. Emotionally drained, she was bereft of soothing tears. Too numb to realize she was biting blood from her lip, she washed in the utter loneliness of being without Cousin Sophronia, her one kindred spirit.

Watching Berry ride into the dusk of evening to fetch Dr. Head, Caroline knew with a certainty that she could not marry him even though it seemed evident Jeremy would not ask her. She had been so charmed by Berry's pleasant smile and happy chatter in the beginning that she had excused his irresponsibility as simple immaturity, just as everyone did. Now she saw him for what he was. Nodding grimly to herself, she gave him his due. His charm was not faked. He really became as joyfully excited about small pleasures as a child. He noticed and appreciated details of beauty, but . . . She smiled sadly.

Pesky ringlets escaped around her dainty face as they always did in heat and humidity. Taking out the tortoiseshell combs, she repositioned them to capture her golden hair more firmly. Head high, she thought as she marched back into the house, *Poor Berry. He will always walk away whenever he is called upon to give anything in return or to shoulder responsibility.*

Determinedly climbing the stairs, Caroline dreaded to see Cousin Sophronia's condition. Chaddy sat beside her bed forcing her to take sips of buttermilk.

Leaning her head against the bedpost, Caroline wondered how Berry could talk of a wedding with her in this condition. He loved his mother, but saying that he wanted her to die happy did not ring true. He kept insisting that he did not care about the plantation. She sighed and shook her head. The fact that she was to inherit Looking Glass must be the only reason he was pushing her to marry him. She went to the window and leaned out, letting her eyes move lingeringly over the beautiful grounds. Even though she had turned him down, it pricked her pride to know that he did not really love her. *Of course,* she thought, *I hurt his pride, too.*

Darkness fell, and they began another long night of fear. Only the source of dread was changed as, relieved from the threat of the enemy's escape, they faced the loss of Cousin Sophronia. Taking turns sitting beside her and giving her sips of nourishment each time she stirred, they vexed themselves that in anxiety over the prison wall's collapse, they had failed to be sure she kept up her strength.

With the first streaks of dawn, Chaddy muttered, "This be the thirteenth! Unlucky!" She shook her dark jowls and muttered morosely, "Bad clouds, bad clouds."

Caroline began a vigil at the window. She had begun to doubt that Berry would return; however, he appeared with Dr. Head quite early. The gentle doctor stayed with Sophronia for a long time. His eyes were grave when he emerged from the room to report to the gathered family.

"She has severe heart dropsy," he said. "Her heartbeat is very slow and coming with two beats together. Possibly her dose of digitalis was too strong . . ." He rubbed the puzzled creases of his forehead. "When she stopped eating, her heart slowed drastically. We'll do what we can . . . and pray." He returned to his patient.

Caroline's cheeks smarted that she had to be reminded to pray. Chaddy's mutterings turned into a chanting wail that drove the distraught girl into the wet garden even though the skies were as black as her melancholy.

Wandering past sadly drooping hydrangeas, Caroline did not realize she was being followed until a fallen branch snapped beneath a footfall.

Turning, she saw Berry behind her on the path. Stretching a welcoming hand toward him, Caroline smiled, hoping to rekindle their early friendship. The vulnerable sag of his boyish cheeks made her readily forgive his anger at her refusal of marriage. She had been so glad to see him, with his good news that the palisade was repaired, that she yearned for his former companionship.

Berry joined her with a wan smile, and they silently strolled the garden path. "I've never seen Mama this weak before." He sighed. "I'm afraid she's dying."

His indifferently drooping shoulders suddenly tensed as they moved beyond huge boxwoods which screened them from the house. He planted one foot solidly in front of her, the other behind. "We should stop postponing our wedding," he declared firmly. "Let's go into Anderson and find a justice of the peace or someone to marry us immediately so we can tell her before—"

"No. No!" Caroline shrieked. She flung her hand up to protect her neck from his hot breath. The insinuating pressure of his body enflamed her fears.

Swallowing convulsively, Caroline drew and held a calming breath. Forcing her face into a smile, she said as sweetly as possible, "I know your mother might be pleased to see us together—and Cousin Penelope wants us to continue the plantation . . . but, oh, Berry, we're young. That's not what I want to base a marriage upon." She laughed lightly and eased carefully back a step. "I thought I had made you understand that. I don't—we don't love each other." With a lift of her shoulder, she laughed again and tried to turn aside. "As soon as Cousin Sophronia is better . . . ," she said, tossing her curls airily, ". . . I'm going back to school."

"You don't need any more education." His voice growled with a petulance that always surfaced when his wishes were thwarted. He grasped her arms with fingernails that tore her tender skin. Pulling her roughly against him, he forced a bruising kiss.

Unable to move as he bent her neck painfully backward, Caroline became limp in his arms until he relaxed his grip for a moment. Twisting her head away, Caroline searched his dark eyes fearfully. She saw no love, only anger that she had failed to succumb to his charm.

"Berry, I know it's Looking Glass you want, not me." She struggled against his encircling arms. "You know it's yours—not mine, and . . ."

He dropped his arms disgustedly. "I've told you I don't care about a pile of dirt. Unless we act quickly, it makes little difference," he flung out bitterly. "I'm just back from trying to bring quinine through the blockade. I couldn't get hold of enough to cure my—to cure a single headache." He spread his hands in a gesture of hopelessness. "Our boys are still fighting. A few war heroes like your . . ." His lip curled disdainfully.

Caroline knew he meant Jeremy. As he paused and looked at her through narrowed slits, she could see that his nerves were tightly strung, but he believed what he was saying.

". . . still say we'll win the war," he finished slowly. "But they're putting up a brave front. I've traveled enough to see that the Confederacy is on her knees! Our troops have no food, no medicine, no weapons—nothing left but valor."

They stood staring at each other for a long moment. Then he took her hand and stroked it gently. "Let's take what we have," he spoke placatingly, "while we still have something to take." He flashed his most disarming smile. "We'd have fun in Mexico!"

Escape to Mexico! Innocent blue eyes wide, mouth open, Caroline stared at the handsome man holding out his hands ingratiatingly. How good it would be to run away, away from this place where she was not wanted; to flee the terrible tensions of the prison; to leave behind the war that each day closed inexorably tighter around them.

Motionless, Berry held her gaze, waited.

In the stillness of the garden, Caroline seemed not to breathe. The sun scorched her brain as she remembered how she had thrown herself into Jeremy's arms and yet received no vows of love. Should she place her fate in Berry's hands?

Seeing that she wavered, he grinned triumphantly and flicked a bit of lint from the shoulder of his immaculate coat.

"Berry, I . . ." She swallowed. Behind him, streaks of lightning ripped across the Northern sky just as her searching shredded her soul. The girl who had come four months ago, centered only in herself, would have left the people here without a thought. Now, something was stirring within her that she could not define.

Wham! Blinding light, deafening thunder shook the earth beneath their feet. Blackened skies lowered around them. Pelting rain plastered their hair and clothing as they ran for the shelter of the dogtrot. Clattering along the wooden floor, she wondered if this storming within and without would never cease?

Penelope and Dr. Head, conferring in the entrance hall, looked up in surprise as the noisy pair entered. Bewildered, Caroline lifted her wet skirts and started toward the stairs. Berry's hand flashed out, grasped her wrist painfully. Startled, she whirled to stare at his questioning eyes, his snarling lips. She had not wanted to believe him capable of the viciousness at the gin. Now, his coldly menacing demeanor stabbed her heart with fear. Wrenching away, she ran to her room where propriety would not allow him to follow.

When this latest storm was over, she watched from the window until she saw Berry riding away with Dr. Head. Only then did she emerge from the confining walls of her room.

Sunshine was turning her bedroom into a bowl of rich cream when Caroline awoke the next morning. Miraculously, Cousin Sophronia had begun a recovery when she had taken her turn at the sickbed during the night. Happily Caroline dressed and went out to greet the morning.

A rider rounded the far curve of the drive. Afraid Berry was returning, she lifted her hoops to run. A fluttering sensation drew around her. Her heart spoke before her eyes could distinguish Confederate gray. Jeremy!

Longing to fly to meet him and fling herself into his arms, Caroline stood holding onto the column, clinging to her fears.

Swinging down from his horse, Jeremy smiled, crinkling his eyes in delight. Arms outstretched, he sprang forward and engulfed her in a secure circle as she melted against him. For one shimmering moment her world held only sunshine. Fears banished, she released herself into the happiness of his embrace. Burrowing her face against the rough material of his jacket, she shivered as he kissed the crown of her head. Tiptoeing, she twined her hands about his neck and lifted her joyful face for his kiss, but the corner of her eye caught movement. Blushing, she whispered, "Someone's watching."

Laughing self-consciously, they strolled hand in hand into the formal garden.

In the seclusion of the gazebo, Jeremy tenderly kissed her lips, her cheeks, her eyelids, as though he had lost her and wanted to memorize her face again.

"I've been so worried about you," he said at last. "When Skinny told me he'd brought you back here, I was frantic." He kissed her fingertips. "But I couldn't come to see about you. If I'd left my duty, holding off the prisoners . . ." His brow furrowed and his eyes pleaded for understanding. ". . . you'd have been in more jeopardy."

"It's all right," Caroline patted him soothingly. "I understood. We were frightened, but we survived." She exhaled and laughed shakily.

"You do understand, you do—that I couldn't leave?" he insisted. "Captain Wirz is so crippled from his wounds that he can't raise his right arm. I guess that's why we're assigned together. I'm the arms, he's the legs. My body had to stay in the Star Fort, but my heart has been with you." He smiled tenderly and kissed the soft curls at her temples. Suddenly, he leaned back and cleared his throat. "Why did you come back here?"

Caressing his dear face, stroking his hair, she related being in the general store and hearing of the prison wall's collapse. "I had no choice. I had to return to warn my cousins."

"You're so sweet, so caring, but that was far too dangerous! You—"

"Don't paint me too angelic," she interrupted, laughing. "I had no place to go. Abernathy refused to give me any form of aid." She lowered her lashes. "He ordered me out as a fortune hunter."

"What!" He drew back in disbelief. "I felt so sure we could count on Abernathy. He's not the man I thought him." Dropping his head between his hands, he sighed. "What can I do? I share a wretched officers' quarters. I have nothing to offer you. I cannot leave my duty just now," he mumbled in an agonized voice, "much as I wish I could."

"It's all right." Caroline stroked his hand. "Cousin Sophronia needs me. I can't leave now either."

"How can I let you stay here?" His eyes dulled with pain as he lifted them to her face. "I'll be frantic after that attempt on your life."

"Don't worry," she soothed sweetly. "I'm sure it was only Berry. He's just a spoiled child." She laughed offhandedly. "I'll be watchful when he's around. You can be sure I won't give him any more chances."

"I've never felt so discouraged, so helpless." His voice was husky with emotion. With a stiff, halting gait, he paced about the small gazebo.

Feeling that he had purposely drawn away from her, she clenched her nails into her palms and watched him, not knowing what to say. Hating to reenter the world with its problems, she yearned for the feel of his strong-muscled arms shielding her. If only he would speak of love; instead, he was unburdening himself of the horrors of his duty assisting the commandant of the prison. Caroline pursed her unkissed lips into a pout and shut out his horrible tales of skeleton-like men crowded into filthy pens like animals. Slowly she realized he had stopped pacing. She met his forlorn gaze and listened again to his words.

"It's more than a human can bear," he said with his tensed body vibrating with his plea for understanding. "In the last seven days, I totaled 633 dead."

She gasped involuntarily. "Then Captain Wirz is really murdering them as the Northern papers say?"

Jeremy sank to the bench across from her. "Of course not. You've seen the man." His lips stiff, his voice hollow, he spoke as from an unreachable distance. "You know he lacks the size, the strength, for the beatings and stampings they are accusing him of. He can't even raise his arm to hold a heavy gun for the shootings they've fabricated."

Caroline's heart opened to him. At last she understood why he was speaking to her of these horrible things when she longed to be cuddled and consoled. Her cheeks burned that even she had questioned his integrity. Watching a twitch in his tanned cheek, she saw that he knew everything said about Wirz reflected upon him.

"I know people who don't have all the facts are blaming us." The muscles of his lame leg quivered beneath the worn, butternut trousers. "But, Caroline, you must realize we now have 33,000 men in a small prison. We have almost no medicine." His voice dropped hopelessly. "No food."

Hurt emanated from every inch of his body. How had she ever believed him capable of the atrocities of which he was accused? Fanning back her lashes from tear-filled eyes, she thought bitterly that she had wasted all of their summer together when she could have been a comforting friend.

Seeing him sitting head down, body drawn with misery, she ached with sudden empathy. *How foolish I have been to wait to see if I was loved before I gave my heart!*

Not caring whether it was the proper thing for a lady to do, Caroline went to him across the few feet of floor, across the great gulf that had stretched between them. Whatever his reasons were for not declaring love, she would not press him. What mattered now was that he needed all of the love she could give to help him through the agony he was experiencing.

Kneeling before him, she wrapped her arms around his body, which was rigid with the pain he was bearing.

"I understand," Caroline whispered, kissing his bowed head. "I know you are doing the very best you can."

Jeremy flung his arms around her and clung tightly. Absorbing her stalwart strength, he relaxed as some of his misery flowed away.

"You do see," he said with his face against her tear-wet cheek. "You do know—it's . . . it's not like they say?" He held her back, and his eyes beseeched her to believe in him.

"Yes." She dabbed at her tears. "It's just hard to conceive of 33,000 people you have to feed—and without buckets." She laughed shakily, trying to make a small joke.

"Oh, we are trying," he emphasized, needing to tell her about it, needing to be sure she no longer doubted. "We give them field peas and cornbread." He lifted his shoulders expressively. "But they don't like that."

"Why? That's some of our favorite food," Caroline asked, trying now to listen, to share his problems.

"Yes, but Northerners aren't used to it or to the hundred degree heat as we are. But then, our Southern men can't survive either." He held both her hands in his and spoke slowly. "Disease takes a terrible toll. My guards are dying before my very eyes. Just like the prisoners. There's scurvy, dysentery, gangrene."

Caroline waited quietly while Jeremy looked out across the garden as if to erase the picture.

"General Winder's trying desperately to transfer the prisoners to other points because . . ." He paused and assessed the courageous tilt of her chin. "You'll have to know soon anyway, Caroline." He gritted his teeth. "The Confederacy is falling around us."

Berry had been speaking the truth, she realized. Her hands flew to her face, and she turned away from Jeremy. *Perhaps she had misjudged her cousin. No, he was not her cousin. Maybe that was the problem. She had spurned his kisses because her first feelings for him had been love for a near kinsman. She had felt the same way even after Sophronia admitted they were not related.* Her cheeks reddened when she thought back over how wishy-washy she had been with him. *She had not given him a fair chance and now...*

"I'm sorry to be the one to tell you." Jeremy's deep voice interrupted her thoughts.

Turning back to face him, Caroline saw he had misunderstood her agitation. She exhaled softly. "I'm glad this horrible bloodbath is ending."

"But our cause will be crushed," he replied bitterly. "We'll be ground beneath the enemy's heel."

She searched his face with questioning eyes. "If it's nearly over couldn't you exchange the prisoners?"

"A state of war still exists and the North continues to refuse." He sighed. "I told you President Davis sent four prisoners to Washington to plead for exchange. They explained how bad conditions are. It's unbelievable—" He popped his fist against his palm and said earnestly, "But the Federal Secretary of War, Edwin M. Stanton, said he would not exchange 'skeletons for healthy men.' I must tell you how honorable the four Yankees were. They kept their parole and returned here to stay in prison with their comrades."

"That took courage."

"Yes," he nodded. "Our Commissioner of Exchange, Colonel Ould, made an offer two weeks ago to deliver fifteen thousand sick and wounded without requiring an equivalent in return. So far, the Federals have not sent transportation for them." Jeremy's voice remained deadened with despair.

"Surely they will soon." Caroline tried to assuage his grief.

The time had come for Jeremy to return to his duty. As they strolled hand in hand down the garden path, bright butterflies fluttered up from brilliant blossoms refreshed by the rain. They paused for a moment to share the beauty.

Jeremy smiled tenderly and squeezed her hand. "One wonderful thing happened yesterday. The lightning struck in the prison during that storm..."

"I thought it must have struck nearby. It scared me to death!"

Jeremy laughed. "Yes, it was about midway between the north gate and the stream. A spring had been there. In fact," he said, as he moved a fallen branch from the path, "one of the reasons the prison was located here in the first place was that source of water. During construction, the flow became a mere ooze into the creek. Anyway, when the lightning struck, a tree uprooted, debris washed away, and a spring of pure water burst out strong and clear."

"How wonderful! Pure water will help so much!" Caroline snapped off a crimson rose as they left the garden. Smiling radiantly at him, she gently wafted it beneath her nose, savoring its heady perfume.

"Yes," Jeremy replied, his voice rich and warm again. "The prisoners are calling it 'Providence Spring.' They say, 'Our cries of thirst rang up to heaven and God sent sweet water gushing forth.'" His smile lifted his cheeks and shined from his eyes. They stopped beside his horse. Silently communing, they needed no words to voice the thought that the bubbling spring was a harbinger of good to come.

Delaying parting, they stood tremulously waiting. Hoping for a good-bye kiss, Caroline stood on tiptoe, her eyes as bright as her cornflower blue muslin dress. Against the black velvet of the horse's neck, her hair glinted like pure gold.

"You are so beautiful . . . ," he said, his voice catching, ". . . to me." His large-boned hands hovered yearningly near her tiny waist, then dropped to his sides as the sudden creak of a shutter told them someone was behind a window.

Swinging into the saddle, he bent down to whisper, "Be on guard if Berry comes around."

Smiling and nodding a promise, Caroline lightly kissed the rose and held it up to him. Taking it, he galloped away. Motionlessly, she stood watching until he was out of sight. He had to return to that terrible place; yet, Caroline felt so intoxicated with the joy of loving him that she waltzed back through the garden singing. He had not verbally declared his love, but he had showed it was waiting in his heart. "And, oh how I love him!" she sang, hugging herself, whirling giddily.

Suddenly ravenously hungry, she detoured to the kitchen.

"Us got a special treat," said Chaddy, beaming in answer to her question about dinner. "That Will, he's been leaving bait near the 'simmon tree and caught us a 'possum. I've roasted it whole and ringed it round with sweet 'tatoes, and my, my," she said, smacking her lips, "it'll be good eating."

Caroline knew the persimmons were not ripe enough for even opossums to eat until September. Her nose twitched. That meant the bait was some putrid carrion. She held a whispered conference with Penelope, who assured her that since opossums did indeed eat snake skulls and dead birds and decayed animals, they were always put in a pen and fed for a while before they were cooked.

"You'd better be glad to have some meat for a change and eat hearty," Penelope admonished when they sat down for the noon meal.

Chaddy carried in a large platter with elaborate ceremony. In a bed of sweet potatoes, the opossum reposed whole in the manner of suckling pig. Caroline's mouth turned down at the sight. With an apple in its mouth, the ratlike creature seemed to be grinning at her. Her stomach flopped, and she knew Penelope was right. They had been a long while without meat.

Trying to block off her thoughts, she held out her plate as Penelope served her a slice. Gingerly, she bit into the meat. She chewed. It was fat, greasy, and sprang back in her mouth. The bite seemed to grow larger and larger. Simpering, she tried again because everyone was watching. Managing only a few swallows, she pushed the meat about the plate, trying to hide it under her peas.

"You know about persimmons, I guess?" asked Cousin Sophronia, who was enough better that she had been half-carried to the table to encourage her to eat.

"I know they have an orange, pulpy fruit." Caroline swallowed a lump. "But I've never tasted one."

"They're sweet if they're ripe, but never try to eat one before first frost." She waggled her finger gaily and giggled.

Image in the Looking Glass

"They are so bitter—umh—they will turn your mouth inside out!"

Penelope interrupted in her strong, sensible voice. "The bitterness comes from the tannic acid, the same substance used to turn rawhide into soft leather."

"I remember a young girl," Sophronia continued, chuckling, "who was expecting a baby in September. Someone gave her an unripe persimmon—umh—it drew her mouth so badly that she went right into labor." She laughed and fanned, obviously enjoying herself. "That little boy appeared before his time was due."

Penelope's heavy brows drew down. She shook her head at Caroline and her grimace clearly expressed that when people get old, they say things they should not say in polite company. Penelope sternly continued her discourse. "Tannic acid is also the substance that is released through rotting vegetation and colors the swampwater black. That's what gives it the mirrorlike quality."

Distracted, Caroline struggled to comprehend as they bombarded her with two different conversations at once.

"That big swamp on the backside of this place," Penelope was saying, "is what suggested the name of Looking Glass for this plantation."

"I didn't know that." Caroline wiped her mouth gingerly on her napkin. "I thought it was because of all of the petticoat mirrors and other looking glasses you have here."

"We've got a field we call the persimmon cut." Sophronia continued on her subject, oblivious to words pounding in Caroline's other ear. "One night in September—umh—when there's a harvest moon, we must go and sit by the big tree in the middle of the field until an opossum comes. It's a sight to see one silhouetted against a yellow moon . . . ," she said, coughing, ". . . holding a persimmon in his little front paws as he dangles upside down from a crooked limb—umh—swinging by his long, hairless tail."

Caroline laughed and pushed her chair back comfortably for it seemed evident that Sophronia was about to go on and on about persimmons in her weak, gaspy voice. Snorting disgustedly, Penelope excused herself to ring the bell and start the field hands back to work.

Caroline and Cousin Sophronia were still sitting at the table when Berry bounded in unexpectedly, exclaimed over the opossum, most of which remained on the platter, and began to eat hungrily. Knowing she could in no way eat any more, Caroline was glad so much meat would not be left that Chaddy's and Will's feelings would be hurt.

After the meal, the young people helped Sophronia to her favorite rocker. Caroline excused herself saying she would leave mother and son alone for a visit. Entering her room, she clung to the doorjamb as the walls whirled and the floor dipped. This giddiness was not joy from seeing Jeremy, or fear from Berry's arrival, it was from the opossum. Clasping her hand to her mouth, she fell across the bed on her stomach. How could she contend with Berry if he decided to stay? She tried to get back up to lock the door, but her dizziness worsened. Sighing, she thought that Berry never stayed very long. He would leave soon. She would feel safe again. Shutting her eyes against dancing spots, Caroline drifted into dream-haunted sleep.

When she awoke, her sickening sensations had gone. Because of Berry, she remained fidgeting about her room. After about two hours, the four walls could no longer contain her joy from Jeremy's love.

Peeping out fearfully, wondering if Berry was still around, she tiptoed down the stairs and slipped silently out of the house. Softly, she called Shadow from her hiding place. The fuzzy lap dog nuzzled her happily, joyfully ready for a walk.

The wet ground squished beneath Caroline's feet. She stretched her arms luxuriantly toward the brilliant blue of the freshly laundered skies and smiled approvingly at the glistening emerald green of the lush growth along the roadside. When they were out of earshot of the house, Caroline began to sing liltingly, "Oh, we'll all feel gay when Johnny comes marching home."

"Pretty! Pret-ty! Pret-ty," came an answering song.

The scarlet flash of a cardinal startled her as it flew from a sprangling weigela bush covered with blood-red, trumpet-shaped blossoms.

"Pretty! Pret-ty," began another singer from the other side of the lane, but the notes changed to copy Caroline's melody.

She glanced around and spotted his gray feathers. "Ah, Mr. Mockingbird, you thought you fooled me." She laughed.

Shadow, prancing along with her little head held high, darted daringly ahead. Suddenly she sank breast deep in a hole filled with muddy water.

"Come out of there, Shadow," Caroline scolded. "You'll get so dirty!"

Unmindful, the tiny dog lapped her small pink tongue into the thick red stuff.

Lifting her skirts above the water, Caroline edged carefully around a large wet privet bush. Off balance, she brought her foot down on a protruding leg. Pitching forward, sprawling in squishing mud, she flailed her hands, touched soft material, felt flesh. Her dripping fingers flew up, smearing her face, stifling her screams.

Chapter 16

Caroline's screams stuck in her throat. Unable to move, she peered through her dripping fingers. The trousered leg also remained still. Was this an escaped prisoner fallen along the wayside, sleeping?

She swallowed convulsively. Dead?

She drew back, unglued her fingers from her face, struggled to focus her eyes. There was no mistaking the doe-colored coat, the black hair.

"Berry, oh, Berry!" she screeched. She strained to turn him out of the mud. Red dripped from her fingers. Frantically, she felt about his head and chest but found no wound. Trembling violently, she realized that the red streaks she was smearing over herself were not blood; they were only Georgia clay.

Berry's skin felt soft, his body warm as she shook him, patted his cheek, called out to rouse him. Gradually a prickling crept up her spine, covered her scalp. She leaned over his mouth, then sat back weakly. Berry was not breathing.

Springing up, she began to run. Halfway to the house, her knees buckled and she sank to the ground. She must not allow herself to think, to cry, only to act. Gathering strength, she reached the kitchen and collapsed onto a bench.

"Chaddy, something's wrong with Berry! I think he's . . ." She looked at the woman, whose eyes had rolled back wildly, and finished lamely, "I . . . don't know . . . just go and prepare his mother."

Leaving Chaddy twisting her apron, Caroline began a frantic search for Penelope. Highly agitated, she blurted without thinking, "Oh, Penelope, I think Berry's dead!"

Stiffening with horror, the tall woman snapped, "What are you prattling about?"

"I found Berry lying in the mud, and—" Caroline's voice rose in a shriek.

Penelope grasped her shoulders and shook her. "Show me quickly, you foolish girl."

Running to follow Caroline with surprising speed for her age, Penelope flung herself in the mud and tried to revive Berry. Patting his cheeks, sprinkling water in his face, she pleaded for him to awaken. Then she fell upon him, screaming and crying, wildly hysterical.

Frightened, Caroline stepped back from the woman who was usually so calm, so controlled. Not knowing what to do, she sighed in relief when she saw Chaddy puffing down the lane. Running to meet her, Caroline sought to fling herself into Chaddy's large, comforting arms.

Chaddy pushed her away. Seeing Berry, she began to squall and howl, "Oh, lawdy, lawdy, lawdy, my baby, my baby." She lost herself in a loud chant.

Covering her ears against their wails, Caroline knew she would have to take charge. Running again, she came to the cotton field, climbed the split rail fence, and signaled Will.

The strapping man loped toward her grinning, "What's za matter, Miss Caroline? Ha-ha. Find another snake? Lawdy." He gasped as he came near enough to see her pale face. "You look lak you done seed a ghost!"

"Oh, Will," she rasped hoarsely, "Berry's hurt. Dying. Dead! Oh, I don't know. Send St. John to fetch Dr. Head." It was all she could think to do.

Exhausted, she flopped down on a pile of cotton poured out on a burlap sheet. When her breathing came more easily, an alarm began ringing in her brain.

"Will," she gasped, rising on shaky legs, "get some men and search the premises. Look everywhere. It might be escaped prisoners who killed Berry. They might still be here."

The huge man looked at her in wild-eyed fright, but he set about to do as she instructed.

Cousin Sophronia had only Ret to look after her, Caroline realized. Panting for breath, she plunged towards the house. She met the old lady struggling along the road, leaning heavily on Ret. Caroline had hoped to wait until Dr. Head arrived, but Sophronia questioned her sharply about the commotion. As gently as possible, Caroline broke the sad news. Wordlessly, Sophronia fainted.

With the reassurance of Dr. Head's presence, Caroline settled back into a state of numbness. Detached, she half-watched, half-listened, half-comprehended.

Dr. Head was not certain what caused Berry's death. There was no evidence of a blow to indicate that someone had struck him down, and Will found no sign of intruders. There seemed to be nothing missing from his possessions, but they found a bottle of quinine in the skirt pocket of Berry's coat. It could have been intended for delivery at the hospital; however, it was only half full. Dr. Head speculated that Berry might have been taking it himself.

Caroline thought he had not seemed sick. How vitally alive he was, she remembered, when he devoured that opossum.

The sheriff arrived, leading a blind man identified as the coroner. Startled, Caroline aroused from her stupor, wondering how a blind man could possibly determine anything. Surprisingly, he conducted an inquest with efficiency. Dr. Head testified that a heart condition ran in the family. The group of jurors rendered a verdict of death by natural causes, just as they had done when Adeline died suddenly. The men left shaking their heads and telling each other it seemed a shame that members of this family often died young.

With a great many tears for her baby, whom she had nursed and cared for, Chaddy bathed and dressed the body and laid it out in the parlor. The sight of the wooden coffin, wide at the shoulders and narrow at the feet, burned an image behind Caroline's eyes that would not go away. Friends and neighbors began arriving with bouquets of flowers and dishes of food from what they could scrape together. Many remained to take their turns at the custom of "setting up" with the corpse through the long day and night.

The next afternoon they followed the coffin to the family cemetery on a shady knoll about half a mile from the house. Watching through a blur of tears, Caroline thought how different this was from the day she and Penelope had buried the silver.

She should have felt relieved that her attacker was gone; instead, Caroline felt bereaved as the men lowered Berry's coffin into the earth. Again attired in Adeline's mourning costume, Caroline felt that she, herself, was not a part of the scene.

Only the fact that Jeremy had come, gave her any sense of reality. Standing at her elbow, he exuded a quiet strength that sustained her through the funeral. When the ordeal ended, she whispered, "Thank you for always being here when I need you."

Cousin Sophronia's mind remained off balance through it all. She did not recognize Caroline, and the distraught girl could not make her understand who she was. Caring for her tenderly, Caroline sat by her bed to feed her. From the picture on the writing table in Adeline's room, which was now Caroline's, she could tell that she resembled Adeline slightly. She decided, however, that it was not as much the resemblance as the fact that Cousin Sophronia's mind had moved back in time. Oddly enough, with her mind gone, her body strengthened. She did not gasp for breath as much; consequently, she giggled and laughed and wanted to talk about old times.

Grieving that the elderly lady would think that she had left her in her hour of need, Caroline gave up trying to explain her presence and accepted the role of Adeline. Sophronia wanted to talk about Adeline's beaus, and when she asked a question Caroline could not answer, she laughed heartily at Caroline's silliness in forgetting.

The infinite sadness of these encounters left Caroline drained; however, Sophronia's mental lapse was easier to contend with than the change that came over Penelope. After all of the friends and neighbors had gone and a ticking quiet settled over the house, Penelope went from the deadly calm that had followed her immediate hysteria to venomous behavior toward everyone in sight.

One evening as the family sat in the parlor and Caroline read aloud, Cousin Sophronia suddenly shook her finger in Caroline's face and sharply scolded her supposed Adeline for some offense Caroline did not understand.

"Her true feelings toward you come out when her mind is unbalanced," Penelope sneered spitefully.

"She thinks I'm Adeline," Caroline whispered.

"Not always!" she snapped, looking down her hawk's beak nose. "Sophronia acts as sticky sweet as molasses. She's got you fooled. When her mind goes over the brink and she can't plot what she's saying, she lashes out at you, doesn't she?"

Caroline pressed her clenched fist against her lips and did not answer. In Penelope's very evident sorrow at the loss of Berry, the sunshine of her life at the plantation, she was being malicious. Caroline tried to excuse her.

Penelope's nasal voice relentlessly continued, "What makes you think she loves you? She didn't even love Berry as she naturally should. Oh-h-h," she said, tossing her head contemptuously, "she left him well fixed with other holdings. But she hurt him by leaving you the land."

The agitated woman went to the window and stared unseeingly. Her deadened voice seemed to come from a far, far distance. "The land is all that matters. The dust of our ancestors is here. Even when times get bad and crops fail and taxes make the land a millstone about our necks, spring will come again with a whole new start. With land you can always believe next year will be better."

It was a long speech for Penelope who was usually reticent. Suddenly, she began to sob hysterically and call out Berry's name. She created such a commotion that it penetrated Sophronia's fog.

"Caroline, tell me what has happened?" Cousin Sophronia focused her eyes at last.

Penelope bolted from the room, her hands covering blotchy cheeks.

Sophronia wept quietly when Caroline explained, and she seemed to return to her normal self. Her blue-veined hands trembled helplessly, and she summoned Ret who appeared instantly as always. Wearily, Caroline smiled at the thought that this girl was the personification of the term "hand" because she would do anything the pitiful, dropsy-swollen woman told her to do.

When they had settled her in bed, Cousin Sophronia thanked Caroline sweetly. Glad that Sophronia was herself again, Caroline waved away her thanks.

As she brushed her hair her usual hundred strokes in preparation for bed, Caroline kept losing count as she wondered what Sophronia's true self was. Caroline had excused Penelope's accusations as a result of her bereavement, but she had to admit her cousin had spoken the truth: whenever Sophronia lost control over what she was saying, she reacted violently toward her.

Blowing out the candle, she lay tensely in the darkness. The wind tossed the curtains and they cast menacing shadows about the room in the moonlight. She had thought she had nothing to fear with Berry gone. Now, drawing a ragged breath, she wondered. Was it merely good breeding and fine manners that made the normal Sophronia act pleasantly toward her? What made her change so drastically? Sophronia was helpless; it could not have been her hands at her back.

Caroline sat bolt upright. *Ret is her hands!* The girl was strong, supple, like a willow tree with her long arms constantly moving in the wind. Shivering, Caroline lit the candle again. The thought of Ret gliding silently about was too ominous to bear in darkness.

Pacing the room, Caroline debated if Penelope was right that Sophronia acted with less than mother love toward Berry by leaving her the land or if Sophronia did it to keep the property for him through Caroline's efficient ability. She leaned her hot cheek against the cool brass bed.

Chaddy would know. She possessed a great deal of intelligence and shrewdness, and her eyes took in everything that happened here. She could give the key, if she would. Caroline had noticed that if asked a direct question, Chaddy would say what she thought you wanted to hear instead of literal truth. *I must approach her craftily!*

Climbing back into the high bed, she pulled the counterpane up to her chin. She could not believe that Cousin Sophronia knew what she was doing when her mind slipped. Caroline felt certain that she must have loved Berry and that she must love her. Realizing she was exhausting herself by letting her mind go round and around and her fears run out in all directions, she picked up a book and forced herself to read by the flickering candle until her eyes became so blurry that she could not stay awake.

When Caroline awakened, her head ached, and she wished they still had coffee or at least tea. Her fears of the night before seemed ridiculous by the light of day. She had scarcely tasted the meager dishes brought by the neighbors the day before and at the moment she was more interested in food than in answers.

Entering the dim kitchen, she found Chaddy singing a mournful chant as she bent over the hearth. Tears trickled down her round cheeks as she brushed the hot coals from the lid of the Dutch oven and took out crusty brown biscuits.

"Last winter's wheat near 'bout gone," Chaddy said without looking up.

Caroline slathered the precious biscuit with pale butter. "I hope the cow lives and the corn meal holds out," she said fervently, thinking that when she had eaten, her brain would function better to parry with the obstinate old woman.

Watching Caroline eat hungrily, Chaddy sighed and sat down heavily on a sawed-legged chair. "You got to go way from this place. I told you. You be too young, too pretty! Now you see my baby's gone. I birthed him, and nursed him, and loved him the bestes. He wuz sech a pretty baby, so fat and fine."

She rocked herself back and forth and lamented in a loud singsong. Fresh tears streaked her dark cheeks.

Suddenly she wiped her glistening face on her apron and scooted her chair closer. With her face inches from Caroline's she whispered ominously, "I done told you. Miss Adeline died and Miss Mary Lillian—"

"But my mother—"

"You wouldn't listen. You wouldn't leave. Now this here thing happened. It wuz meant to be you. Yo' time's run out. You got to go away. Now!"

Chapter 17

"Aunt Chaddy, you will just have to stop telling me that. I have nowhere to go," Caroline began firmly, but Chaddy's wildly rolled back eyes made her falter. "I . . . I know you are distraught. I wish I could leave this minute! But I'm—you must see I'm needed here right now." She held out her hands placatingly and said sweetly, "Let me stay a few more weeks. Then I'll go back to Wesleyan."

"You won't never go back to that there school." Chaddy poked out her lips and prophesied dolefully. "A few weeks'll be too late."

Patting her plump hand, Caroline tried to soothe her. "Don't you worry now. I'll be fine." She forced more confidence into her voice than she felt. She must not let herself be frightened by Chaddy's superstitions that were no doubt set aflame by the family trait of dying young from inherited heart problems. Caroline squared her shoulders and pulled herself to all of the height and courage she could muster as she got up from the bench. "I can't leave just yet. Cousin Sophronia and Cousin Penelope need me. They must have someone to love them and help them through their grief."

Chaddy's face worked with emotion. She shook her bandana-bound head until her earrings jingled, but she made no reply.

Caroline smiled reassuringly at her. Jutting out her chin with determination, she stepped into the brilliant sunlight, stretched, and considered what she most needed to do with her day. Chaddy was too upset to be questioned about Cousin Sophronia's motives. For the moment they were not the most important thing.

What she had just told Chaddy was true. Whether or not they loved her, her cousins needed her. As long as Sophronia's mind stayed in balance, Caroline felt safe. She resolved to keep all senses alert when Ret was around.

Returning along the dogtrot to the house, Caroline was surprised to realize that returning to school did not seem important now. Proving her intelligence no longer held top priority. All of her friends at Wesleyan were silly girls whose only thought about this hideous war was that it took away their beaus and left them feeling that love was passing them by. She stopped midway along the covered walkway and nodded ruefully.

She had been like that when she came here. Her only worry had been that she had no one to love her. That spring day when she arrived seemed a very long time removed from the heat of this summer.

Going to her room, she untied the ribbon that had held back her curls and let them tumble around her shoulders like a little girl. Twisting the hair up in back, she piled it high in fluffy bangs. Surveying herself in the looking glass, she smiled. She did look taller, older. She dressed quickly in crisp organdy, yellow with a muted plaid of pink and blue.

She hurried to the plantation office because she realized that Penelope had not even rung the bell to call the hands for the day's work. Until Penelope felt better, she would act as mistress. She had helped enough that she knew how to go through the motions of control, but she suddenly realized that it was a great responsibility to have so many people depending upon you to supply the necessities of life.

Tired but satisfied with a morning well spent, Caroline wandered to the gazebo to rest at midafternoon. She opened all four of the green shutters to let in every breath of air and sat on the bench by the white latticed wall. The days shimmered with heat now, and the roses had almost ceased to bloom. Only the hardiest flowers, especially the crape myrtle bushes, remained undroopingly a blaze of pink to rival the brilliance of the sun.

Shadow lay at her feet panting as Caroline idly waved a palmetto fan. Both of them had lapsed into a heat-induced doze when suddenly Shadow whirled around screaming, "Scree, Scree, Scree!"

Jeremy stood in the doorway. They had not heard him coming. Shadow alternately screamed and snapped her teeth even though Caroline cuddled and cooed. Jeremy's face sagged with exhaustion, and he limped badly as he came into the gazebo. Annoyed that Shadow's behavior caused him embarrassment, Caroline patted and soothed, but the dog continued to cry out plaintively.

He apologized loudly above the din. "I'm sorry I startled you again."

"I guess you came upon her unexpectedly this time, but there's something more than that," Caroline shouted. Shadow's screams quieted into a menacing growl, and Caroline spoke more evenly, "I can't figure out why she dislikes you."

Jeremy shook his head ruefully and remained on the opposite side of the summerhouse. "The very first time she saw me, I frightened her; but you're right. It's more than that." He took off his hat and raked his fingers through brown hair grown ragged and in need of cutting. "I've heard that dogs sometimes behave this way out of jealousy. Every time I come around, she acts like this." He grinned crookedly. "Then you pick her up and hold her and give her lots of attention. Does she do it now to keep us apart? To keep your attention?"

Caroline laughed. "It could be that. She's much smarter than she looks with her little mop of hair." She put Shadow down and spanked her lightly. Shadow continued a low rumbling. "Bad dog. Hush. Jeremy won't hurt you." Caroline spanked again. "Hush!"

Shadow glared beneath bristling brows. Then she slunk under a bush and peeped out as they sat down, still slightly apart with a strain between them.

Caroline felt guilty that she had ever let the dog's behavior toward him arouse suspicious thoughts. That was a foolish young girl who had been afraid of him because of a silly dog. She was a woman now. She would never remind him that she had questioned his intent in the treatment of the prisoners. Looking at him sitting dejectedly, she knew he held no guilt, only sorrow.

"Has there been any answer to your request for the Federals to take the wounded prisoners?" Caroline asked softly, hoping to shoulder a little of his suffering.

"No," he replied. Sensing the concern in her manner, he covered her hand with his.

Shadow edged back closer, crawling flat on her stomach. Her monkeylike face wore an expression of chagrin. Laughing, they let her settle cozily at their feet while he told her the latest news.

"Ulysses Grant is the general in charge of all the Union armies. He issued a statement on August 18—here, I'll show you." He searched in his pocket and handed her a crumpled paper.

"'It is hard on our men held in Southern prisons not to exchange them,'" Caroline read aloud, "'but it is humanity to those left in the ranks to fight our battles.'" She frowned, uncomprehendingly, but continued, "'At this particular time to release all rebel prisoners North, would insure Sherman's defeat and would compromise our safety here.'" She looked up at Jeremy in shock. "I can't understand this. How can he leave his men to such suffering? The two governments exchanged prisoners in the beginning."

"Yes, but Grant believes exchange would help the South, with its desperate want of manpower, more than it would help the North." He gestured despairingly, "The word has gotten to the prisoners, and they're bitter toward their government."

"I don't wonder," she exclaimed, "when more than 600 died in a week."

"I don't know what we're going to do with them all. We must move some of them somewhere." Again he tugged at his hair. "It's the worst thing I've ever had to deal with."

The depth of melancholy in Jeremy's eyes told her he needed her strength. Gladly, she sat quietly holding his hand, speaking no words, needing none. Watching the butterflies fluttering over the tall heads of phlox that echoed the pink of the crape myrtle, they tried to absorb the quiet peace of the garden.

She had planned to discuss her problems when next she saw him and tell him about Chaddy's insistent warning to leave, but now she thought only of his needs. She would not add to his worry. With Berry dead, Jeremy was content that she had a secure home.

Knowing he could not offer his love, Caroline asked for nothing. Her heart felt heaped up, pressed down, spilling over. She sat smiling softly, comfortingly at Jeremy. Feeling her overflowing love, he turned to take her face in both his hands and kiss her tenderly. For a long while they sat with her head nestled against his shoulder. There was no sound except the singing of the birds and the quiet breathing of Shadow sleeping at their feet. For one brief moment, time suspended.

When Jeremy returned to his duty, Caroline floated to music that swelled within her. All of the horror Jeremy was encountering and all of the hostility she was feeling could not engulf her joy. She went back into the house hoping Cousin Sophronia would like her to play the piano. She ached to release her inner music into the air.

When Caroline found her, Cousin Sophronia was mentally alert; however, she was cross and acting uncharacteristically peeved and upset.

"I've been ringing and ringing for Ret. The naughty girl has chosen not to appear all afternoon. She knows I can't do a thing without her hands."

"What can I get for you, dear?" Caroline asked sweetly as she stopped to pick up the sewing that had fallen in a heap beside Sophronia's rosewood rocker. Noticing that she had finished the sampler she had been cross-stitching with the line from Goethe, Caroline read aloud, "'Each day is a vessel into which a great deal may be poured if one will actually fill it up.'" Caroline looked at her with shining eyes. "That is so true. I didn't understand when you first tried to explain it to me. But now I do, and it makes me very happy to give—"

Image in the Looking Glass

In no frame of mind for philosophy today, Sophronia interrupted, "I'm hot and thirsty. Please bring me something to drink. And find that worthless Ret. She knows I need her to watch."

Her crossness could not dampen Caroline's spirits, and she went about her errand singing. When she reached the kitchen, there was another opossum in a small pen outside the building. She shuddered. The creature reminded her of a huge rat. She hoped Chaddy had something else to serve because she did not want even the gravy cooked from him. Berry had really enjoyed the other one though, she thought, shuddering again.

Opossums ate dead things. She stopped wide-eyed. What if the first one had eaten a rattlesnake and the poison in it had killed Berry? Chaddy was in the kitchen, and Caroline asked her about it.

"'Course not. Folks eat 'possum all the time." She was wiping perspiration and speaking crossly, too. "Eating a 'possum wouldn't naturally kill a body." She stopped her motion, looked straight in Caroline's eyes, and asked accusingly, "You didn't eat any did you?"

Caroline squirmed under her scrutiny. "I tried to. I know how hard you work to keep us fed." Her cheeks reddened in embarrassment. "I ate a few bites, but I just couldn't." She hurriedly changed the subject. "I came to get Cousin Sophronia a drink."

Chaddy handed her a glass of buttermilk. "So my baby," she said, peering at her narrowly, "ate most all of it?"

"Yes. Do you think—" Caroline's hand jerked and she slopped milk on her skirt. Chaddy's earlier words rang in her ears. She had said, "It was meant to be you." Not taking her too seriously because of her superstitions, Caroline had thought it a friendly warning. Had she meant it as a threat?

Caroline stared at her in dumb horror. Had Chaddy known the sisters would not eat the thing and expected her to eat it because of her normally healthy appetite? No one had anticipated Berry's arrival for dinner that day. Dabbing at her wet skirt, she stammered, "Uh, have you seen Ret?" She faltered,

"Cousin Sophronia says she... hasn't been around all afternoon."

Chaddy scowled. "That no 'count girl is supposed to be watching. You go to Ol' Miss' and *stay* with her. I'll find Ret."

Hurrying back to Cousin Sophronia, Caroline let her mind roam back to Berry. Immediately after his death, she had felt all of her danger was gone. She had been certain that he was the cause of her problems. Berry had almost admitted locking her in the smokehouse. It had been easy to believe that he placed the witch's curse to frighten her away before his mother might will her the plantation.

Caroline stopped along the dogtrot and considered. She had thought him capable of murder to keep the property, but after her morning's work, she wondered if he *had* wanted it. Perhaps he was telling the truth about not wanting the plantation. She realized more of what overseeing involved now that she had spent the morning deciding what jobs to put each of the hands to doing. Someone had to determine what crops to plant next and what market to find for the harvested cotton. Caroline had been very glad to turn the work back over to Penelope this afternoon when she appeared to be herself again. She had felt proudly equal to the task; however, she could understand why Berry might not have accepted the responsibility.

If Berry did not care about the plantation, it was highly unlikely that it was he who had tried to kill her. Panic had ebbed when he died. Now, she felt it rising in her throat. What could any of the others have against her?

Reaching the parlor, Caroline made a choice. She did not want to believe Cousin Sophronia was her enemy. She would divulge her suspicions about Chaddy.

Chaddy had motive, Caroline thought tensely. Her devotion to her "baby" could have made her want to get rid of an interloper. She had even opportunity to poison the food because she did all of the cooking. A person could not stop eating. Or could they? Caroline tried to remember what she had said about Adeline. "She quit eating my food, but she died." That was it!

Caroline's hand shook as she gave Cousin Sophronia the buttermilk. Watching her drink it, she tried to form words that would not upset her too much. Sophronia asked to be helped to the couch. Before Caroline could decide how to tell her that Chaddy might have killed Berry with poison meant for her, Sophronia fell into a deep sleep.

Caroline sat beside her as Chaddy had instructed. She fidgeted with her wet plaid skirt. Turning at a sound she hoped was Ret coming to relieve her, she saw Penelope. There was actually a smile on her plain face.

"I wondered where you'd gotten off to." Quite calm again, Penelope spoke pleasantly.

"Did you have a job for me?" Caroline inquired. "Ret seems to have disappeared for the afternoon, so I'm sitting with Cousin Sophronia."

Penelope laughed lightly as Sophronia snored. "She'll probably sleep 'til suppertime. You said you didn't know where the plantation got the name of Looking Glass. Now would be a good time to show you because it surely must be a little cooler down at the cypress pond,"

Caroline stood up gratefully. Then she hesitated. "I told Chaddy I'd stay here . . ." Minding a murderer was a childish thing to do, she realized. A walk to the pond would give her a chance to tell Penelope her suspicions.

Chapter 18

Heat rose in shimmering waves dancing always just before them down the field road as Caroline and Penelope began their stroll to the cypress pond. The blistering sun beat upon their parasols. Finding it difficult to breathe in the heat and humidity, Caroline hoped Penelope was right that a visit to the pond would give them a cool respite. She decided to wait until they could sit in the shade before she disclosed her suspicions about Berry being poisoned.

As they passed a spot where a hole gaped in the middle of the field, Caroline pointed to it questioningly.

"Why, that's a lime sink that has occurred since I've been out this way!"

"A what?" Caroline laughed, following Penelope across the crusty field, struggling not to turn her ankles on the ridges of mud baked hard by the semitropical heat. At the edge of the hole, some ten feet wide, she looked down and gasped. "It drops straight from the rim like a well!" Bending over carefully, she looked down at cotton rows lying in perfect formation fifty feet below. Interested in the unusual sight and relaxed by activity, Caroline forgot her worries for the moment. Smiling companionably at Penelope, she exclaimed, "I've never seen anything like this!"

"Sinks occur frequently in this area of limestone aquifers," explained Penelope. "That simply means this ground lies over porous rocks and sands in water-bearing layers—You'll understand when you see a big one. Any spot, large or small, can suddenly sink straight down. The hands sometimes work across the field and come back to find the very row they had picked has dropped out of sight."

"How strange. How frightening! Has anyone ever had the ground fall out from under him?"

"No, but animals are lost occasionally."

They moved quickly toward the inviting shade where towering water oaks rimmed the field. Spanish moss festooned the limbs and beckoned in the slight breeze. Stepping from the dazzling glare into the deep shadows, Caroline closed her eyes and leaned against the trunk of an ancient tree. Sighing, she rested limply as damp coolness kissed her cheeks, caressed her perspiring body. When she opened her eyes and blinked to adjust them, she saw that Penelope had moved silently onward over the thick carpet of decaying leaves.

"Eeee! My feet sink down with every step!" Caroline exclaimed as she tried to follow across the spongy ground. "Is it safe to walk here?"

"Oh, yes," Penelope replied offhandedly. "The cows come along here to drink from the pond. That's what keeps the underbrush clear enough to walk through. Snakes usually get out of your way. Just stay on the path. But watch for holes. And cypress knees. The bald cypress spreads it roots widely for support," she explained as she waited for Caroline to catch up, "and sends up kinks to get air."

"There's something I need to talk with you about," Caroline said slowly, intent upon placing each foot gingerly. She stopped short at the edge of another lime sink and held onto an exposed root as she looked down. This sink was old, and the steep banks had become craggy. Green moss glistened from the sides and on the tumbles of lime rock far below. Intrigued by the unique place, Caroline leaned cautiously over the edge and heard the echoing sound of rushing water. "Is this the spring that feeds the pond?"

"No, it's the other way around. The overflow from the pond pours into the lime sink."

"What?" Caroline looked at her with a puzzled frown. "I don't understand."

"It's an underground stream," Penelope explained. "A pig fell in here once and came out miles below on the next farm."

"It was drowned, I guess?"

"No." Penelope shook her head. "It must be a pretty big cavity. It was still alive. But hogs are tough creatures."

"That makes me think of the opossum." Caroline sighed, hating to return to her problems. Edging away from the deep hole, Caroline followed Penelope as she descended the steep hill toward the pond.

"What about it?" Watching her footing, Penelope did not look back.

"Well, I asked Chaddy about it. It seems that she was expecting me to eat it, but I didn't. And then Berry came in and ate most of it."

"Berry ate it?" Penelope stumbled and fell. Even though she had warned Caroline against them, she had been tripped by the jagged edges of cypress knees protruding through the leaf mold like miniature mountain ranges.

Caroline hurried to help her up, but she shook off assistance.

"Berry ate the opossum?" Penelope stared in disbelief.

"Yes," Caroline replied slowly. "Don't you recall how he enjoyed it. He ate most all of it." Reflectively rubbing the firm, two-foot cypress knee, she reconstructed the day. "Oh, I remember. You had gone to ring the work bell, but Cousin Sophronia and I were still at the table when Berry came in unexpectedly."

"I didn't know he came in time for dinner." Her voice was devoid of inflection, dead.

They had reached the level of the black water, and Caroline stood wondering what to say. It had been a mistake to come to the cypress pond. Cypress was the emblem for mourning. Cypress was used for coffins.

The stillness and mystery of the swamp so strongly suggested death that Caroline feared Penelope would be overcome with grief for Berry. Her calmness lay like a dry and brittle leaf, waiting for the slightest breeze to sweep it away, the smallest spark to rekindle the flames of her hysteria.

Chattering, Caroline tried to divert her. "I can certainly understand where the name of Looking Glass comes from. The blackness of the water makes a perfect mirror." She waved her hand nervously toward the reflection where the ring of tall cypress on the far distant shore stood up-side-down before her in the still water.

Penelope said nothing.

"It's a beautiful sight." Caroline's voice sounded strident against the tension in the quiet air. There must be many wild animals here, predators lurking in the waiting stillness. Penelope remained deathly still, excruciatingly quiet. Caroline shifted uneasily. To her right a dozen tremendous cypress trees waded in the water. "With their trunks spreading at the bottom like crinoline," Caroline said, trying to keep her tone light, "and their gray lace shawls of Spanish moss, they make me think of dowagers. See," she said, pointing, "the knees pop up like little brown children around the widows' skirts."

Even her fantasies spoke of death. Caroline pressed her lips firmly together and stole a glance at Penelope. No tears were falling. Her face remained as hard and set as the cypress knees. Forgetting about Berry was impossible. Needing to enlist her aid, Caroline took a chance on upsetting her.

"I hate to remind you of Berry . . ." Caroline hesitated. "But it's important to know. Do you think Chaddy could have poisoned the opossum?"

This roused Penelope, and she looked up vaguely. Still she said nothing.

"Oh, I don't mean she meant to kill Berry." Caroline's tongue seemed to rattle with increasing agitation. "She considered him her baby, and she wanted him to have the plantation. But from the first moment I arrived, she's tried to frighten me away, and now . . ." She caught her breath and intoned each word. ". . . she said this death was meant for me."

"So that's what happened," Penelope said at last in a voice barely audible. "I was beginning to believe in Chaddy's superstitions myself." Grief pulled her skin tautly over her craggy features. Her mouth hung open and her chin shook with silent sobs.

Feeling sorry for the bereaved woman, Caroline dropped her eyes from Penelope's agony. Her own reflection lay in the black water straight below. She had wondered why they were not mirrored out across the water. Some trick of refraction made her face look back from directly below her feet. The image was amazingly clear. The yellow of her dress shone brightly. Silently, the tall gaunt woman in black stepped into the scene.

The image in the looking glass was plain. Her body no longer sagged with grief. With her hawklike features intent upon her prey, she hunched her shoulders and spread her bony hands slowly, slowly toward Caroline's shoulders.

Mesmerized by the evil on her face, Caroline could not move. Feeling herself to be asleep in the throes of a nightmare, Caroline willed herself to shatter the hypnotic spell of the black water. As she wrenched around to face her, Penelope's hands dropped. Not knowing what Caroline had seen, she pulled a masking smile across her face.

"I must get back to Cousin Sophronia," Caroline said as she edged away. Surely she had misread the image just as she had misread everything else on this plantation, but every nerve silently screamed at her to get away.

Mounting the hill as swiftly as she dared, knowing she must not reveal her terror, she prayed that she would not fall over a cypress knee. Penelope climbed close behind with an agility surprising for her age.

"There's no hurry," Penelope cajoled. "Sister will sleep 'til supper." She continued with drawled-out sweetness, "Let me show you where the pig went into the underground stream."

Moving with her in the direction of the lime sink, Caroline tried not to show that her suspicions had been aroused. Even though Penelope's manner toward her had always been gruff, Caroline had thought her a friend. Proud that Penelope respected her ability, Caroline had believed that she wanted her to be mistress of the plantation.

Near the top of the hill, the deep crevasse of the old lime sink loomed. Biting her lip, Caroline thought she was not as tough as a pig. She would never come out from underground. This time the blind coroner would have no body to examine.

Springing suddenly forward, Caroline began to run.

Screams split the silent air. "Wait. Come back. The death is meant for you!" Penelope pursued swiftly.

A rustling in the dead leaves to her right alerted Caroline that someone else was here. The missing Ret, she supposed. It must have been Penelope she was helping all along.

She could not fight them both. Cutting sharply to the left, she made for the top of the hill. Looking back at Penelope instead of before her, she plunged into a briar that grabbed her skirt with biting bony fingers. She snatched it free only to snag it in another spot. Penelope was catching up.

"You can't have my baby's land," she screeched hysterically. "You've tried to take everybody's love just like Mary Lillian stole my Rufus. I won't let you! I won't!"

Reaching the rim of the hill, Caroline rushed out of the dark woods into the blazing sunlight. Puffing for breath, running with difficulty in the heavy air, she glanced back again. Penelope's long-legged strides had closed the gap.

The mournful baying of hounds echoed in the distance and mingled with the rasping of Caroline's breathing. A prisoner must have escaped. She ran blindly, feeling kinship with the poor man who was pursued.

The new lime sink lay ahead. She veered, hoping she was running away from it. She must get far from this terrible up-side-down place. When she reached the outbuildings, she had gained slightly on Penelope.

"Chaddy, Aunt Chaddy!" Caroline stumbled into the kitchen screaming. She was not there.

Clattering along the dogtrot, Caroline entered the quiet house. Cousin Sophronia was not on the couch where she had left her. She was not in any of the downstairs rooms.

Gasping, her chest bursting, she mounted the spiral stairs. Flinging open each bedroom door, Caroline found no one to help her deal with this woman who had completely lost control.

She heard Penelope blundering about the lower rooms, crashing china, screaming hideously. The frightened girl could not conceive of struggling with her aging cousin. Penelope was far larger and strengthened by a maddened frenzy.

Tiptoeing to the plunder room, Caroline reached up, slid back the heavy bolt, slipped in quietly, and eased the door shut. There was no lock on the inside. Frantically, Caroline scanned the clutter of trunks and quilt chests. There were clothes hanging in the armoire, she remembered, but many of the trunks were empty. She must hide until someone heard Penelope's screaming and came to help. The shortness she had always regretted would allow her concealment in a trunk. She gritted her teeth and climbed in.

Shuddering at the similarity to Berry's coffin, Caroline felt as if she were smothering the minute she lowered the lid. It smelled of cedar, not cypress; there was air to breathe; but the chest-tightening, closed-in feeling made her fight for consciousness.

Straining to listen, to keep alert, Caroline heard the clump, clump of Penelope's heavy outdoor shoes pounding through each bedroom. Alternately laughing and crying, Penelope repeated Rufus's and Mary Lillian's names over and over in a harangue Caroline did not understand. One thing was clear to Caroline; because of her parents, Penelope hated her.

The thudding footsteps approached the door of the plunder room, stopped. She was quiet now, stalking. Caroline visualized her pursuer, standing, looking at the unlatched bolt. The door creaked open. Sound ceased. Silence stifled her. A trunk lid banged open. Caroline stopped breathing.

Moments hung suspended. Caroline feared Penelope would hear the beating of her heart. Suddenly, the footsteps left the room. Rather than searching each trunk, she must be waiting outside the door. Caroline's cramped muscles screamed with pain, but she was afraid to stir. Then she realized that her palms were prickling with sweat. Even though her whole body was drenched with perspiration, the tingling wetness of her hands was different.

Spreading her palms, drying them, she searched her air-starved brain for this new source of fear. Smoke! Her subconscious sensed it, warned her before she recognized the smell.

Throwing back the trunk lid, Caroline leaped out, ripping her skirt. Far worse than her dread of an enclosed place was the panic that seized her whenever smoke brought back her childhood experience with fire. Tugging to release her torn skirt, Caroline saw that a piece of yellow plaid had been left hanging out when she thought she was concealed. The very volume of material that had saved her at the cotton press had revealed her now.

Crackling, blazing fire blocked the doorway of the plunder room. Papers, chairs, and curtains fueled the entrapping flames. Horrified, she stared at the open trunk by the door and the trail of clothing. Penelope's mind was completely unbalanced. She had started the fire with Berry's clothes.

"Caroline, Caroline, where are you?"

Transfixed by the fire, she heard Jeremy's voice floating as in a dream and did not answer. He called again. Slowly, life stirred.

"I'm here, Jeremy. I'm here." Was that her voice answering? She could not recognize it through the ringing in her ears. "I can't get through the fire."

"Can you get to the window?" Jeremy yelled from behind the roaring wall of flames separating them.

"Yes, yes, I can."

"Get it open. Get ready to jump."

Tugging, pounding, pushing, she struggled with the heavy window. Her nose burned from the smoke that filled her brain and blocked thought. With muscles like jelly, her arms dropped weakly. Giving up, she turned away. She cried out to God. With one last try, she slid the wavery glass upward. She fumbled for the stick of wood that would hold it open, leaned out, and gulped for air. Boiling, swirling, the black smoke seemed worse outside the window. Caroline drew back inside.

Chaddy's voice bellowed her name. Forcing her head back through the swirl, Caroline looked down with watering eyes. The towering house, built high off the ground, elongated with lofty ceilings, presented a death-defying jump from this second-story window.

"Jeremy," she screamed. "Jeremy, help!"

The smoke drifted. Far below Caroline could see Jeremy, hobbling on his lame leg, running across the yard. Running away.

Chapter 19

Floundering, flailing her arms, Caroline fought the fluffy clouds of smoke. Thick, cottony, the billows did not give way to her beating hands. Strength waning, hope gone, she fell limp, but her fingers clutched involuntarily, closing on greasy cotton seeds. All of the nightmares of the summer swirled together, smothered down upon her.

The buzzing in her ears became the clanging, pealing of a deep-toned bell. Caroline exerted one last, feeble struggle. "Jeremy," she whimpered. "Oh, Jeremy, Jeremy."

"Caroline. My dearest darling." His deep voice tickled against her ear. Kissing softly, he whispered as though to soothe an infant. "Hush now. Everything's all right. Hush." His life-stirring lips pressed her eyelids, her lips, her clutching fingertips.

Fluttering her lashes, she looked up into his concerned face. Sustained, she lay quietly. Slowly, her senses returned. She was lying on a white mountain of cotton. "What?"

"Don't you remember?" Jeremy slipped his arm under her shoulders and helped her sit up in the submerging cotton. "I drove the wagon under the window. You jumped into it."

Clanging in her ears claimed her attention again. The farm bell summoned loudly. Looking down from her high perch, Caroline saw dark figures running, sloshing water from oak buckets, beating flames with pine boughs. She gasped, and her breath stayed in her throat. Stunned by the sight of the flames, she could not close her eyes. The house, the beautiful house they loved, wavered like a gigantic fireplace framed by the tall columns. Flames roared rapidly across the expanse in a blinding display. Caroline's throat ached. Searing pain seemed to make her once more a child, a little girl watching her home and all of her dolls burn. Now, all of her life seemed to be burning. Nothing would be left. Overwhelmed by weakness, Caroline, nevertheless, determined not to cry. She forced calmness that congealed to numbness.

Clinging to Jeremy, she huddled in the circle of his arms as they sat atop the high wagon and stared at the flames in a dreadful fascination that would not let them look away. When at last the fire began to burn itself out, he helped her slide down from the cotton. Her legs, a quivering, useless mass, gave way. Jeremy's arm came around her waist and she tottered like a two-year-old toward Cousin Sophronia.

Murmuring soothing endearments, Sophronia enfolded her in a loving embrace. "Oh, my dear," she said without her usual gasping. "I'm so sorry Chaddy and I had gone to the gazebo to cool just when you needed us most!" She pushed back wisps of hair, and her crinkled cheeks trembled in a smile. "We're here now. We'll look after you!" Her eyes looked into Caroline's with a clearness that indicated she was in complete possession of her faculties.

Caroline hugged her gratefully, thinking how wonderful it was that her mind and body seemed strong at the same time.

They helped Caroline to a bench in the gazebo. Bustling about, muttering, talking to herself about everything she was doing, Chaddy brought a basin and bathed Caroline's dirty face and hands. Then she hurried to the kitchen. It was a separate building to avoid the danger of fire spreading from the kitchen to the house and thus had been saved. She returned with milk and bread and commanded Caroline to eat.

Jeremy turned to speak gently to the old woman who was hovering around, ready to wait on the bedraggled girl. "I'm sorry we couldn't save the house, Miss Sophronia."

"You saved my most valued possession." Cousin Sophronia's sagging cheeks lifted in a sweet smile, and she patted Caroline's hand.

"I saved one other thing." Jeremy grinned and his eyes twinkled as he waggled his finger. He disappeared a moment and returned to place a bundle of dirty, wet fur in Caroline's arms.

"Shadow!" Caroline buried her face against the silky ears. Stroking and cooing, she nuzzled this one shred of her past and hugged the little dog tightly to her breast.

"When I pulled the wagon safely away from the fire," explained Jeremy, "Shadow must've come from the kitchen and caught your scent. I heard her yelping and screaming, and then the fire seemed to throw her into an absolute panic. She began circling in that endless arc and was whirling under the house. I had to run her down."

"Thank you," Caroline whispered fervently. Her eyes filled with tears because she knew what pain it must have caused him. His limp was most pronounced when he tried to move quickly. "I'm surprised," she murmured, "that she actually let you touch her." She blinked back the tears, feeling that she must not let them spill over, fearing that if she cried, she might collapse completely.

Jeremy laughed. "We're friends now. She's accepted the fact that you can love us both." He cocked his head to one side, and the deep, sad lines of his face lifted. Joy spread slowly upward, crinkling his eyes. The glow of his face warmed.

Caroline blushed, but Cousin Sophronia smiled approvingly. Contentedly, Caroline relaxed. With a sudden jerk, she sat up, remembering.

"Cousin Penelope? She—" Caroline clapped her hand over her mouth. Wide-eyed, she could not tell this sweet old lady what her sister had done.

"Penelope perished in the fire, dear," Sophronia replied sadly. Pushing back wisps of gray hair that straggled on her damp forehead, she added, "I believe that she intended to."

"Then you know . . ."

"Yes, dear. It's unfortunate that I did not suspect sooner. I've always had a niggling doubt about Adeline's death. I knew of Penelope's crippling jealousies, but I did not realize she had turned her rage on you until Berry's death. Umh—" She heaved a sigh and her shoulders shook shudderingly, but she continued firmly. "In her hysteria over his body, she said things that alerted

Aunt Chaddy's suspicions. She told me, and we began to guard you very closely."

Chaddy nodded vigorously, jingling her gold earrings. She shook a finger in Caroline's face. "That girl, Ret, was supposed to be watching you. When she absconded and you didn't mind me by staying safe by Miss Frony," she said, her fat cheeks jiggling, "I sent St. John to follow you and Miss Nell to the pond, and Will to fetch yo' sweetheart."

Caroline had felt so alone, so afraid of their watching eyes. Wonderingly, she looked from one to the other. All along they had been caring for her. Swallowing the emotion surging into her throat, she spoke haltingly, "But why did Cousin Penelope hate me so? I thought she respected my ability—wanted me to marry Berry."

"She did." Sophronia nodded consolingly. "Evidently she stopped trying to harm you when she thought you and Berry were to marry. Although she idolized him, she realized that he lacked the initiative to hold onto the land. She recognized your ability to set a goal and keep striving to reach it."

"She'd 'a' still been jealous if you'd married him," Chaddy said darkly. "She'd 'a' spoiled your life."

Caroline nodded in agreement with her and turned back to Cousin Sophronia. "Then you believe my life was in danger when I refused to marry Berry?"

"Yes, and I'm afraid you were in jeopardy before he asked you, too. I suspect now that Robert Abernathy told her as soon as I changed my will in your favor. Umh." She took a long, painful breath. "She was very angry that Berry would not own the land. I did what I thought was best." She stared into space reflectively. "Of course, I left him well fixed with other investments . . ."

"I'd wondered about Mr. Abernathy." Caroline pressed her hands to her temples. All of the strange events came popping back into her aching head. Weak as she was, she had to know, to understand. "Why was he around when I was pushed into the cotton press? There seemed no reason for him to be there."

"I didn't think about it at the time," said Jeremy, "but, later, the way he acted . . ."

"No." Sophronia shook her head. "I'm sure he had no part in her violence. His reason for being there is sad." Sophronia clucked her cheek. "He was in love with Penelope. Yes," she said, nodding at their surprised look. "He remained a bachelor because of her. The shy fellow hung around at every opportunity through all these years. But . . . she had shut up her heart—it all goes so far back—to when he was seeing Adeline, and Penelope was in love with Rufus."

"My father?"

"Yes, Rufus was never in love with her, but she fancied him her beau. Then your mother came to visit. Mary Lillian was so sweet and beautiful." Sophronia smiled and patted Caroline again. "Just like you, dear."

"Rufus was dazzled. They married as quickly as a proper wedding could be arranged. Penelope became dissolute." She pursed her lips and shook her head disapprovingly. "She wasted herself in a shocking affair!"

Sophronia paused in her story, saddened at the memory. "Many people have shattered dreams and recover, but Penelope, ah . . . ," she sighed. "She became embittered for the rest of her life. She set herself a terrible rule for living. If people did not show her awed respect and full attention when she first asked for it, they were then treated as though they did not exist—except that she would say harsh things about them. The only exception was Berry. She loved him fiercely, but he was never sure of it. He never knew what to expect from her. She would spoil him shamefully; but if he inadvertently displeased her, said some little thoughtless word to offend her, she would virtually stop speaking to him, completely ignore him until she finally considered he'd redeemed himself."

"How tragic," said Jeremy.

"More than you know." She wiped the tears that trickled down her wrinkled cheeks. "I tried so hard to show her that love given begets love, but love withheld begets hate."

"But why did she invite me here?" Caroline remembered the day of her arrival when Penelope wanted her and Sophronia did not.

"Rufus wrote us that he feared Wesleyan might close with the onslaught of war—I also suspect his funds were gone—Penelope became excited that your father would come here for you, and she could have him at last. I knew that would not be the case. I knew there would be more heartache and bitterness. I thought it would be better to send you to a friend."

"Then the letter came that Papa was dead. She had no more use for me," Caroline said, nodding at her in understanding.

"To make matters worse, you had grown up to look exactly like your mother did when Rufus fell in love with her . . ."

"Did she harm my mother?" Caroline was horrified.

"Oh, no. Your parents moved away from here. Mary Lillian died of complications after childbirth. But the fact that you looked like her made her hate you the moment she saw you."

"So she tried to frighten me away, but I had no way to leave."

"I'm sorry that I didn't realize. Aunt Chaddy tried to tell me." The trusted servant began to mutter, but Sophronia continued quickly. "I was ill at the time. I didn't understand that I should send you away—except perhaps in my subconscious." She smiled and shook her head. "I'm afraid, dear, that I was also selfish. After I got to know you, I wanted you to stay. You brought sunshine into my life each time you walked into the room."

"Speaking of sunshine," interrupted Jeremy, "I should have been watching the clouds." Rain spattered through the latticed gazebo. "We must get you to shelter."

"There's a potting shed right at the back of the garden." Sophronia gestured. "Hidden behind that Lady Banksia rose vine. I haven't been in there for ages, but maybe the roof won't leak."

Leaning on each other, they hurried to the shed. As Jeremy pushed open the lopsided door, Chaddy muttered about dust and cobwebs. Amazed, they stepped into a clean room. Two

Empire sofas were arranged with one of the finest heirloom tables and the Argand lamp.

"Penelope must have prepared this place at the first rumor of Sherman's coming," declared Sophronia.

"After all that's happened today, the threat of enemy conquest pales."

They settled on the sofas and fell into exhausted sleep. Time and again throughout the night, Caroline awakened sitting bolt upright with her palms sweating and her blistered nose sniffing smoke. Always, Cousin Sophronia was near, comforting, consoling.

Daylight came at last. With it came cold, gray despair. Wakening weak and sick, Caroline felt she could not face the world and begin life over with nothing to show that she had ever lived before this day except one torn and dirty dress.

While Caroline slept, Sophronia had been out inspecting the devastation. For a moment her great courage faltered. She sobbed because Josiah's portrait had burned. "All of our family records and pictures are gone." She wiped her eyes and dried her tissue-paper cheeks. Pulling herself together with great effort, she said, "That reminds me of the ambrotype. While we're alone, I'll tell you. I thought you guessed when you noticed that Berry resembled Penelope—but you didn't. He was *her* son."

"What?" Caroline asked, astounded.

"Yes." She blew her nose and began to speak. "I told you she became dissolute when Rufus married Mary Lillian. She threw away all her moral training and had a shocking affair with a German carpenter who was traveling through the countryside building houses. Of course, he moved on." She puckered her mouth. "He left her to bear an unnamed child."

Caroline stifled an amazed gasp with an upflung hand. "How did you conceal it?"

"It was simple enough to tell everyone that Josiah and I were expecting a child. When the time of confinement drew near, we cancelled all social engagements for Penelope as well as for me by saying Penelope did not want to leave me alone. No one ever knew except Chaddy and Dr. Head."

At that moment a knock announced the doctor and his wife. Bending to enter the low door of the shed, they came in with a great deal of false cheeriness and tongue clucking. Laden with bundles, Anne laughed at her scavenger ability. Bringing clothing and necessities of daily life, these dear friends lifted the forlorn women from the paralysis of despair.

After they had dispensed with the amenities, Sophronia explained, "Penelope had evidently been using this shed as a hideaway. There's something I want to show you, Doctor."

They followed her to a potting table in the back of the long rough building. Caroline's eyes fell immediately on Josiah's brooch, but Sophronia was indicating some long, narrow leaves and an old book, written by William Withering in 1785, entitled *An Account of the Foxglove and Some of Its Medical Uses: with Practical Remarks on Dropsy and Other Diseases.*

"Why would she have a medical book in a place for potting flowers?" asked Anne.

"I'm afraid I understand," replied Dr. Head, fingering the dry, crumbling leaves lying by the book. "These are foxglove, the common name for digitalis. It's an old drug, mentioned by Welsh physicians in 1250, and official by the time of the London Pharmacopoeia of 1650. Foxglove's frequently used for heart dropsy, but we recognize the low margin of safety. An overdose will cause digitalis intoxication. In these modern times, the dried leaves are made into the little gray pellets, such as I've given you, Miss Sophronia, and dispensed carefully from a glass vial."

"But Doctor," protested Anne, "I know we're about out of medicine, but weren't you giving Miss Sophronia enough tablets without Penelope producing her own risky supply?"

Anne was too innocent to comprehend, just as she had never realized Caroline's desperate reaching out to her; but Caroline understood Dr. Head's point. She picked up the book and scanned passages that Penelope had underlined. Quickly she read how Withering had recognized the toxicity of large, acute doses. He described how an overdose caused vomiting, dizziness, confused vision where objects appear yellow or sometimes green, and even delirium and hallucinations. She gasped. This was what Cousin Sophronia had been experiencing. Caroline turned a questioning gaze at Dr. Head.

"I can see, young lady, that you are wondering why I did not recognize those symptoms," the doctor said. "I hardly expected anyone to deliberately overdose and try to kill Miss Sophronia. The toxic effects of the drug are difficult to distinguish from the cardiac disease itself."

"The wonder is that I did not die," reflected Sophronia. "Perhaps one thing that helped was that I sometimes left off my dose. I hated to be taking medicine since drugs are scarce and many are doing without."

"Somehow you didn't take enough of what Penelope was trying to give you either." Dr. Head's furrowed brow showed his distress. "You surely would have died without Chaddy's constant care. She kept you from suffering malnutrition that would have brought on your death."

"I believed I did the right thing to prevent a scandal and give Penelope's child a name." Sophronia sighed. "I thought she loved me and appreciated what I'd done, but it's evident, now, that she hated me because Berry looked to me as his mother."

"I wonder about Adeline's death." Dr. Head rubbed his balding pate. "She was very young to have experienced congestive heart failure. There's no way to know now."

Caroline looked at them and knew their doubts were causing them grief. "There's one thing I'm sure about because of what she screamed when she was chasing me. She put a large dose of the foxglove in the opossum to kill me. Berry ate it instead and died two hours later." She fell silent, then spoke slowly, reflectively, "I barely tasted the opossum, but I ate lots of the sugar cookies Penelope made when we celebrated the last of the tea and sugar. I was very ill. Dr. Head, why didn't the foxglove kill me?"

"Because you have a strong, healthy heart," the doctor replied soberly.

"It's a good thing I saved most of the cookies for you." Sophronia smiled sadly.

Dr. Head nodded. "Berry evidently inherited the family tendency toward irregular heartbeat. The quinine he was probably taking would have increased his chance of death. Miss Sophronia, I can't tell you how sorry—"

"There's no way you could have known that our deception in concealing Berry's parentage could have grown to such hatred," she replied, patting his hand. "The grudges Penelope held grew, and festered, and poisoned her soul—just as surely as she tried to poison us."

For a long while after their friends had gone, Sophronia sat quietly weeping. Caroline remained beside her stonily, not knowing how to comfort her. She knew that she grieved for a few meager belongings while Sophronia had lost her beautiful home; she had lamented no one loving her, all the while Sophronia suffered vengeful hatred at the hands of one she loved. Hurt by Penelope's betrayal, Caroline wanted to lash out vindictively. When Sophronia began to speak softly, forgivingly, she could not believe it.

"Poor Penelope, I'm sorry I failed her. It's so very sad that she knew God's compassion but didn't feel that if we acknowledge our sin and repent, he frees us from that debt forever." She wiped her eyes and looked over her spectacles at Caroline. "She had that head knowledge, but she could never grasp the fact that we must not base the forgiveness we give other people on what they deserve either. We must live in an attitude of forgiveness to be able to receive the forgiveness offered by God."

Caroline swallowed bitterness. "Head knowledge and heart knowledge," she murmured.

Sophronia's wan face brightened. "That's why I scolded you about letting life be self-centered instead of Christ-centered."

"I'm so glad I didn't lose you," Caroline said fervently, kissing her soft cheek. The difference in their ages did not matter. This was the dearest friend she would ever have.

Sophronia understood the depths of her feelings and concerns. There was much yet of life's meaning she wanted to learn from her. "I just thought! Without the doses of foxglove, you won't have any more of those frightening spells! Your health will improve!" She flung her arms around Sophronia in a huge hug, blue eyes shining. "Oh, I'm glad I didn't lose you!"

The lines of deep sorrow lifted as Sophronia nodded at the vibrant young girl. "I would rather have died in the fire than bear all of this, if it didn't mean I have to leave you."

For the next few days, they merely existed. Jeremy came as often as he could slip away from his duty. He spoke no words of love, gave no promises. He merely looked anxiously from one face to the other in search of a sign that they were recovering from their mental and physical exhaustion.

Suspended in a state of numbness, feeling she had born all there was to bear, Caroline gradually realized that Jeremy's eyes were hollow with the tension of terrible strain.

Feeling stronger now, she followed him and stood with her hand on the neck of his black horse. "What is it, Jeremy?" she asked, trying to pull herself from her own concerns to share his.

For a long moment he looked down at her without answering. Then in a desperate voice he replied, "The final blow's descending. On September 2, Sherman captured Atlanta!"

"Oh!" she gasped in horror. Then she brightened. "That means he's not as near as we'd thought." Seeing the hopelessness in his eyes, she faltered but then said, "But it took him four months to fight the hundred thirty or forty miles between Chattanooga and Atlanta . . ."

"With Atlanta fallen," he replied gravely, "there's nothing to protect us from the advance of the enemy!"

Chapter 20

Eerily floating through the darkness of midnight, the mournful whistle of a train alerted them that something was happening in Andersonville. Huddling in the lopsided shed, Caroline and Sophronia prayed that the huge, old rose vine sufficiently concealed their hideaway.

Jeremy came early the next morning, September 8. "The prison's surely a magnet drawing Sherman," he said, walking nervously about as he talked. "We'd been trying for months to relocate some prisoners. Transportation finally came during the night." The lines of his face still sagged tiredly, but he smiled as if greatly relieved. "Eighteen detachments of prisoners left by train bound for Savannah and Charleston." He sighed heavily. "The poor wretches will finally receive better care."

"Will Sherman come?" Caroline searched his face, longing to put her arms around his hunched shoulders. He remained stiffly withdrawn from her as though his former tenderness had merely been concern.

"Who knows?" Jeremy threw up both hands in a wildly helpless gesture. "Rumor has it, he's cleared Atlanta of its civilian population. Is he resting his men there? Or will he head directly here? We can only wonder and wait."

Jeremy hurried back to his duty. With events swirling swiftly around them, they snatched only brief moments together during the ensuing days. Caroline's every nerve screamed as stifling September days passed with the ponderous slowness of dripping water. Although Jeremy still did not speak the words of love Caroline longed to hear, she dammed up her tears, waiting, waiting. She ached to know he would always be there when she needed him. Deep within her hope stirred.

Gradually Caroline grasped that she had called upon God only when she thought she was dying. Now in these desperate days, she learned that He supplied strength for the living. Sophronia had been reading her Bible in the gazebo when the fire occurred. Prayerfully, they read together now for sustenance.

Everyone on Looking Glass Plantation turned to Caroline as director and protector. Rumors that a Federal Calvary unit was approaching Andersonville from the west were whispered in town. Hoping no one on the farm would hear the rumors, Caroline issued confident-sounding orders and set the hands to cleaning up the fire damage. Everyone would be less afraid if kept busy.

Food supplies were nearly gone. The whole South was hungry. Chaddy happily supplemented their meager meals with fruits and berries from the woods.

She missed the help of Ret, who never reappeared. All of Ret's belongings were gone. They surmised that Penelope had realized the girl was Caroline's watchguard and had somehow frightened her away.

In spite of the tension and discomforts, which she bore valiantly, Cousin Sophronia's health gradually improved. Caroline left her one afternoon to go into the village in hopes of buying supplies. She stopped to listen to a group in front of Dykes' Store talking in shocked tones of General Winder's fatal heart attack.

"The entire Confederacy's in chaos," the storekeeper told Caroline. "Communications are cut between Richmond and Anderson. Those left in command here are acting without official orders." He wiped his hands on his apron. "I've nothing to sell you. Supplies to feed the prisoners are completely cut off. There's nothing even to feed the guards."

Caroline turned back into the glare of the sun with the basket upon her arm, empty. Her rocking skirt sent up swirls of red dust as she started down the street, hoping to see Jeremy.

Tension quivered on the sultry air. Her eyes darted about nervously as she noticed that clusters of soldiers waited.

Suddenly the village filled with the roar of a locomotive. With enveloping clouds of hissing steam and ear-piercing screeching of brakes, it ground to a halt. The crowd surged forward. Jeremy's friend, Lt. J. J. Easterlin, stepped down from the train.

"He was sent to deliver 6,000 prisoners to the Federals stationed in St. Augustine, Florida, without asking exchange," a raw-boned woman told Caroline.

Easterlin signaled to the crowd. "The Federal commander refused to receive them," Easterlin said. "As ragged and diseased as they were, he commanded me to return them to the prison," Easterlin reported incredulously. "We started back, but we just closed our eyes in that wilderness around Jacksonville, Florida. We let the Yankees loose with a wagonload of corn."

The townsfolk moved away murmuring in relief.

The woman looked down at Caroline and warned her seriously. "There's still 5,000 men imprisoned here. The guard's depleted. There are nightly escapes. Be careful!"

Jeremy was nowhere to be seen. Sighing, Caroline started for home. Driving down the narrow road snaking its way through thick undergrowth, Caroline jumped at every flickering of sunlight and shadow.

Reaching Looking Glass Plantation at last, she forgot her empty basket and wandered unseeingly down the paths through the withering flowers, seeking the seclusion of the gazebo. Sinking to the cool marble floor, she knelt with her head on her clasped hands with the bench for her altar.

"Dear Heavenly Father," she prayed aloud. "Forgive me for taking my Christianity for granted. Oh, Lord, I thank you that you didn't wait until I loved you fully. You reached down for me in my sin. Thank you for giving me Cousin Sophronia to guide me and help me grow from head knowledge to the heart knowledge of living for Thee. Thank you for bringing us through these hard times. Strengthen me to help Cousin Sophronia and Jeremy . . ."

She sensed a presence and turned. "Oh!"

Jeremy smiled. He shook his head slightly as she started to move and dropped to one knee beside her. One hand covered hers while the other clasped her waist. His brown head bowed against her golden one and moments suspended as they prayed silently together.

Tightening his grip, pulling her against him until their beating hearts matched rhythm, Jeremy prayed with his lips moving against the ringlets on her forehead. "Oh, God, our world is falling around our ears. We are helpless. But we know we are safe in Thy hands. We claim Thy promise to be with us always and see us through to the end. In Jesus' name, we pray. Amen."

Caroline's breath held, and she could not move as he gently released her. Overwhelmed by emotions flooding through her small body, she gazed up at him in wonder.

Caressing her face between his hands, Jeremy laughed huskily at her expression. "Oh, my darling little one, only the sunshine of your smile over this awful sea of misery has kept me knowing that God's love would see us through."

He kissed her forehead, her cheeks, her waiting lips. Laughing at her awakening response, his smile lifting his whole face and shining in his blue eyes that spoke clearly of his love, he lifted her to the bench. Seated close beside her, hugging her as if he could never let go, he spoke urgently. "Caroline, dearest Caroline, I know I should wait until times are better to ask for you, but I've waited far too long now." He kissed her knuckles and his eyes shadowed again. "I failed you when you were in danger. If I'd lost you in that fire . . ."

"Jeremy?" Caroline's round cheeks quivered in surprise. "You've never failed me. You've always been here when I really needed you!"

"No, I should have been stronger." Jeremy shook his head and grinned like a small boy. "I felt unworthy to speak to you . . ."

Around them the garden lay quiet, still. Suddenly a breeze whispered through the lattice of the gazebo, rustled the flowers, lifted drooping blossoms. Jeremy's smile lifted the drooping corners of his mustache, spread over his lean cheeks, and danced in his blue eyes.

His voice throbbed on a rising note. "But I've loved you from the first moment I saw you." He laughed uncertainly. "You and that silly dog."

Music seemed to flow around them in the buzzing bees, the singing pines. Caroline's laughter rippled in the breeze. "Oh, my darling Jeremy, I've loved you from that first moment, too! I'll never forget that day when you scared us to death."

As she chuckled heartily, Shadow snuggled against their feet. Shaggy black hair concealed her eyes, but there was no doubt that she accepted Jeremy. Above her gray goatee, Shadow's little mouth kept opening as if to add a word to the conversation. Laughing, they reached down together and patted the dog.

Jeremy turned to Caroline, rough palms extended. His painful tension floated away as the young woman snuggled into the shelter of his arms.

Yellow butterflies fluttered along the path, kissing the flowers. Caroline and Jeremy sat quietly drinking in the beauty, savoring their love. Suddenly Caroline frowned and stirred in his arms. She twisted to turn an inquiring gaze into his peaceful face.

"Jeremy, I've loved you from the beginning." Her voice shrilled. "But I was afraid to show it, embarrassed when I did." She dropped her head and whispered, "I held back because you didn't show you loved me. Just as I would think you did—hope you did—you'd draw away from me, shut me out of your inner self." Her innocent blue eyes beseeched him to make her understand.

"I'm sorry," he muttered hoarsely. "I thought I couldn't ask you to love me . . ." His arms fell from around her. Getting up, he paced the gazebo.

The obvious pain in his lagging leg stabbed Caroline's heart. She leaned forward, and her ears ached as she strained to distinguish his words as he stopped and leaned his forehead against the green shutter.

"I have nothing to offer you," he mumbled miserably, "not even a good name, thanks to the Northern newspapers." He turned to face her. With every muscle in his tall lean body taut, he flung out bitterly, "You know that all of my property was destroyed in the war."

"I know that." She rushed across the small summerhouse and stroked his quivering arms. "It doesn't matter to me."

"But you are used to gracious living," he said in a voice that still held concern.

Caroline tossed her golden hair and laughed. "Oh, yes, I'm very rich." She shook her ill-fitting, hand-me-down skirt.

Jeremy grinned crookedly. "That wasn't quite all." His cheeks reddened beneath the tan, and he avoided her eyes. "You had Berry. He had so much more to offer. And . . . he was a whole man. My leg slows me down, keeps me from . . . working hard. I'll never accomplish as much as you deserve—"

"Oh, Jeremy," she interrupted. "I've failed you, thinking only of myself when you needed to know how I cared. Darling Jeremy, your limp only endeared you to me from the beginning. What work you're able to do doesn't matter. As for Berry," she laughed shortly, embarrassed, "he didn't love me. I'm sure Penelope insisted he propose. I know he was in on at least part of her devilment."

"That's what hurt me so," he replied earnestly. "My foolish pride almost got you killed. I let you stay here rather than ask you to share a shanty with me. I let you go through so much alone when I was in agony to be with you." Jeremy's whole body strained as he tried to explain the thing that had lain between them, keeping them apart.

Tracing her fingertips over the hollows of his cheeks, Caroline pressed her hand over his mouth. "Hush, hush," she murmured tenderly. "We'll forget it. Forget it all."

Jeremy pulled her hand aside. Wanting to be certain she understood, he continued talking feverishly. "All this time I kept telling myself if I really loved you, I would do what was best for you. Stay away. I told myself I had lofty intentions." He shook his head. "When it was really selfish pride." He caught her hand, kissed her palms, her fingertips. "Can you forgive me?"

"Oh, Jeremy, forgive *me!* I was foolish, too, afraid to let myself love you—'til you first declared your love for me. You couldn't know how I loved you, needed you."

Jeremy's arms came around her, crushing her against him. The ardor of his kisses sent her spirits trilling. The tempo of the music might change, but the melody would never cease.

"Will you marry me?" His voice was a mellow throb against her ear.

"Yes! Oh, Jeremy, of course I will!" Caroline clasped his cheek to turn his face to her seeking lips.

"No, wait." Jeremy held her away and searched her face. "I mean now. Right now with our world collapsing around us. Sherman . . ." He bristled as he spat the name, and Shadow growled. ". . . won't rest his men much longer. We don't know at what moment the enemy will swoop down upon us. There are less prisoners now. I'll be with you all I can." Caroline was smiling, nodding, lifting her lips for his kiss, but still he held her back. "I have nothing to offer you, just love. But I must be where I can take care of you. If you're my wife—whatever happens—I can have you in my arms."

"That's all I need."

As they kissed in a commitment that whatever lay ahead they would meet together, the gazebo floated apart from the garden like a golden island. Encircled with a peace that kept their little world beautiful, they made their wedding plans.

Even when they walked back through the garden where the last flowers of summer were fading, dying, and stepped into a world which was not so sweet, their joy remained. No mere distance could ever part them again.

Rain washed away September's dust. October's laundered skies shone as brilliantly blue and sparkling as Caroline's eyes as she ran into the garden for one last check of the table Anne Head and Chaddy had set in the gazebo. Reborn by the life-giving water and the crisp, cool nights of autumn, the garden twinkled with reds and yellows of chrysanthemums. Their faint perfume swirled around the fluttering flounces of her tiered skirt. Stroking the lustrous white satin and smilingly fingering the scallops of embroidered pearls, Caroline thanked Anne for lending her own wedding gown so that in spite of everything, Jeremy would behold a beautiful bride.

Miraculously, Anne and Chaddy had produced reception refreshments. Beaming, Chaddy dipped into the crystal bowl and offered Caroline a glowing golden punch. She sipped, savoring the delicate flavor of scuppernongs. "Delicious!"

"Hurry now, it's time to go to the church." Anne adjusted the filmy veil floating like a cloud around Caroline's golden curls.

At the altar of the little church in Andersonville, Caroline Hannah and Jeremy Medlock committed their love to God and their lives to each other.

Laughing, they ran up the aisle to the exhilarating trills of Mendelssohn and out under an "arch of steel," the sabers raised by Jeremy's men. They jumped into a buggy bearing a "Just Married" sign and dragging old shoes. Gaily they rode back to the party in the waiting garden.

Caroline and Jeremy moved into a small cabin in the quarters on the plantation, a snug haven in a world gone mad around them.

Sherman was on the march! Leaving Atlanta ablaze on November 15, the Yankees terrorized Georgia, ruthlessly burning everything in their path.

Daily, they anguished, expecting the Yankees to sweep into Andersonville to release the 5,000 sick men dying there.

Nightly, they lay with the winter wind whistling through the cabin, wondering, wondering. Many midnights, Caroline awakened sitting bolt upright, imagining smoke. Jeremy's tender voice soothed. The circle of his secure embrace comforted. Nearly as often, Jeremy's moans roused her as he tossed, sweating, clutching, haunted by the living nightmare of Andersonville Prison.

Sherman did not come. He did nothing to rescue his wretched fellow soldiers. Even though his thirty-two-day march was a swath of waste and destruction sixty miles wide, four hundred miles long from Atlanta to Savannah on the sea, his smoldering path veered to the east.

Sherman said, "War is hell," and a blazing, burning Georgia believed him to be the devil.

The prisoners had expected their army to release them. The Yankees did not bother to come. The prisoners wept.

Caroline wept. Through all of the agonizing months of waiting for the end to come, through all of the terror of Penelope's fury and the fire, she had not cried. It was bitter irony that, even though Sherman had not set the blaze, their home was ashes. With the sudden relief of his passing, her tears melted in an unstoppable flood.

Fleeing into the garden, she walked and sobbed for her lost past. She cried for Papa, for Samuel, and for others from her childhood. Letting her mind move slowly over the image of each small and silly thing she had lost to the war and to the fire, she wept afresh for each in turn. When all of her tears were spent, she regained control, felt better, was ready to begin life anew.

Lee surrendered to Grant on April 1, 1865. After a few futile skirmishes, the war was over.

The Bluecoats were suddenly everywhere, as the Federal Army of Occupation ground the South beneath its heel with Reconstruction laws made harsher by the fact of Lincoln's assassination. Wirz was arrested, taken to Washington for a sensational trial for conspiring to injure the health of the soldiers and committing vicious personal murders.

Jeremy grasped Caroline's shoulders and shook her beseechingly. "He's just a scapegoat. You know he couldn't physically commit those murders." He implored her understanding. "We did the very best we could in an utterly hopeless situation."

"I know, my love," she said soothingly and hugged him. "I do understand."

Wirz was hanged on November 10, 1865, the only prison commandant to be executed. Jeremy buried his face against Caroline's neck and wept.

Friends were moving to Texas. Others were escaping the harsh rule, the poverty, and devastation by starting a new community in Brazil. Caroline and Jeremy chose to remain. Clearing away the shattered pieces in the ashes of Looking Glass Plantation, they dug up long buried treasures and began to repair, to rebuild. Cousin Sophronia, Chaddy, Will, and the others were looking to them for direction, needing them to give love and care.

Caroline's and Jeremy's days filled with purpose, peace, joy. With time, their nightmares ceased. When spring came again and the garden blossomed as beautifully as their love, Caroline could scarcely contain her excitement as she led Jeremy along the garden path past fragrant roses to the gazebo. Seated on the bench in the circle of his arms, she whispered the news that within her new life stirred.

Never again would they fearfully hold back, waiting to be loved. They knew now that days are filled with happiness when love is poured out freely.

Jacquelyn Cook

Acknowledgments

The events in this book are accurate to the smallest detail, down to the time of day it rained that fateful afternoon in 1864. The officers at Camp Sumter, the drummer boy, and Dr. and Mrs. B.J. Head are true to their actual characters. Shadow's real name is "Baby Dog," which is too unbelievable for fiction. Lieutenant Medlock, the people of Looking Glass Plantation, and the plantation itself exist only in my imagination.

Anecdotes and details are true. I am deeply indebted to John Grover Cleveland Pace, who is 101 years of age at this writing. His step-grandfather, Alfred Dorman, was a guard, and his father, Robert Gilford Pace, was a boy there at the time of this story. With total recall, Pace has shared eyewitness accounts. His story of the horses hidden from Sherman actually happened. Endless small details of life at the time were supplied by him.

John Clark Burton, my great-grandfather, was a guard at age 15.

Mrs. Robert J. Hodges, who still occupies Tudor Hall at the plantation near Andersonville, which was owned by the Hodges family during the Civil War, graciously shared personal letters, mementos such as the brooch, descriptions of furnishings, and memories of her family's entertaining of Captain Wirz and the other officers.

My thanks also go to Andersonville mayor Lewis B. Easterlin, who allowed me to research his records. The village has been restored to look much as it did in 1864, and is open to tourists the year around with costumed recreations at the historic fair the first weekend of each October. The Cemetery-Prison Park is a National Historic Site.

Although the events depicted are seen through the eyes of those who lived there, they reflect the view of today's historians who have all facts at hand. Much of the material came from a book by my friend, Peggy Sheppard, *Andersonville, Georgia, U.S.A.* (Leslie, Georgia: Sheppard Publications, 1973). From Yonkers, New York, she endeavored to give an unbiased account.

The horrors of Andersonville and the assassination of Lincoln were the two main reasons for the harsh Reconstruction laws imposed upon the South. Historian Bruce Catton in his introduction to *John Ransom's Diary* (New York: Paul S. Erikson Inc., 1963), states that, "the horrors endured by the POW's were not created willfully and malevolently in order to kill them—as many good people believed at the time—but by the combination of . . . the horrors that make up war itself." He further states that in prison camps North and South "two and one-half times as many soldiers were subjected to the hunger, pestilence, and soul-sickness of the prison camps as were exposed to the deadly fire and crossfire of the guns of Gettysburg—and the camps killed nearly ten times as many as died on that battlefield. The Confederacy imprisoned 194,000 Union soldiers, of whom 36,400 died, and the Union held 220,000 Confederates, of whom 30,150 died."

William B. Hesseltine in *Civil War Prisoners: A Study in War Psychology* (New York: Frederick Ungar Publishing Co., 1930) states that "statistics show no reason why the North should reproach the South. If we add to one side the account of the North's refusal to exchange the prisoners and their greater resources, and to the other the distress of the Confederacy, the balance will not be far from even."

My research was done in an endless number of books. One of the most helpful was Clarence Poe, *True Tales of the South at War* (Chapel Hill: The University of North Carolina Press, 1961).

Many firsthand details were gleaned from Edwin C. Bearss, *Andersonville National Historic Site Historic Resource Study and Historical Base Map* (Washington, D.C.: U.S. Department Interior, National Park Service).

Firsthand visual knowledge was gained at the antebellum plantation in Stone Mountain Park, near Atlanta. Other details were culled from the 1850 village of Westville, near Lumpkin. It was there that I saw cotton ginned at the Bagley Gin House. Built in 1840, it is the only such operating gin in the United States.

My appreciation also goes to Mrs. T. Schley Gatewood, Sr., for details of Wesleyan College, to Dr. Robert A. Collins, Jr., and Robert Jones for medical and pharmacological information, to Jane Hendrix and the staff at Lake Blackshear Regional Library, and to Betty Pace Clay, who showed me the image in the looking glass.

My special love is dedicated to the memory of Mrs. W. H. Sumerford, Miss Sidney, who undergirded me, knew Goethe, and especially knew her Lord.

About Jacquelyn Cook

Although Jacquelyn Cook has been a nationally published writer since 1963, selling over 500,000 copies of her first thirteen books, she considers herself first and foremost a Southern author.

"My goal has been to write timeless stories of lasting values," says Cook. "I want to preserve our culture and history and the beauty of our landscape, but most of all I like to reflect the Southerner's love of God, country, family and fellowman."

After gaining experience in journalism, Cook started writing the five-book *River* series that began with *The River Between*, published in 1985. After twenty-five years, these books are still in demand. In 2002, Barbour Books combined four of the popular stories in one volume called *Magnolias*, making it the complete novel Jacquelyn desired. Now, in 2010, Bell BridgeBooks is publishing beautiful new editions of the River series.

Wanting to write a longer, more fully developed novel, Cook began a new phase of her career with *Sunrise*, which was released in February 2008 by BelleBooks. Set in Macon, it is the fictionalized account of the true story of Anne Tracy and William Butler Johnston, who built the fabulous Johnston-Felton-Hay house in Macon, Georgia. Cook's extensive research was enhanced by family reminiscence of the Johnston's great-grandson George Felton. These personal materials made the story come alive.

Jacquelyn Cook has early ties to Macon because she majored in voice at Wesleyan Conservatory in the original building on College Street. "Memories of my days there have colored several of my books," she says.

An epic novel of the Civil War, *The Gates of Trevalyan*,

followed in September 2008. The story of the King family on Trevalyan Plantation weaves into the tapestry of the most compelling historical figures of the time. Three love stories and exciting action keep pages turning.

The Greenwood Legacy, the true story of an amazing family who began the plantation culture that still exists in Thomasville, Georgia, was released in 2009. It has delighted all who have read this novel of faith, family, love, and courage.

Mrs. Cook's family enjoys life on the ancestral farm near Lake Blackshear in Southwest Georgia. Jacquelyn's hobby is keeping flowers growing all year long. Three and a half dogs own her, two Shih Tzu lapdogs, a guardian Australian Shepherd, and the half a dog, a huge Labrador retriever who belongs to her son's family. The minute they leave home, the sociable lab visits grandmother. On holidays, the table swells with her daughter's family from the city. Everyone gathers for Jacquelyn Cook's Old South meals, especially Virginia-baked ham and devil's food cake with mocha frosting.

Made in the USA
Lexington, KY
14 December 2016